NEW YEAR

Library and Archives Canada Cataloguing in Publication

Smith, Caighlan, 1994-, author
New Year / Caighlan Smith.

(Surreality ; book 2)
ISBN 978-1-927099-47-6 (pbk.)

I. Title.

PS8637.M558N49 2014   jC813'.6   C2014-901634-4

Published by Boulder Publications
Portugal Cove-St. Philip's, Newfoundland and Labrador
www.boulderpublications.ca

Editor: Stephanie Porter
Copy editor: Iona Bulgin
Design and layout: Mona Atari

Printed in Canada

Newfoundland
Labrador

We acknowledge the financial support of the
Government of Newfoundland and Labrador
through the Department of Tourism, Culture and
Recreation.

We acknowledge the financial support for our publishing program by
the Government of Canada and the Department of Canadian Heritage
through the Canada Book Fund.

NEW YEAR

SURREALITY BOOK TWO

CAIGHLAN SMITH

BOULDER
PUBLICATIONS

Chapter I

Kanta woke up to knocking. Loud, insistent knocking.

There was a chorus of groans and complaints as people, who were sprawled on couches and curled into tatty blankets on the living room floor, tried to go back to sleep. The knocking persisted. A groggy voice begged for a volunteer to answer the door. With a heavy sigh, Kanta pulled his head from deep within the couch cushions and pushed himself up. He bumped into a side table on his way to the door, cursing when a picture frame fell off and onto someone, eliciting a curse from that person as well. A half-asleep person nearby laughed so hard it almost drowned out the angry knocking.

Kanta threw open the door, revealing a short, skinny girl with long black hair tied in two tails, one on either side of her head, and a pair of goggles around her neck. Her fist was still raised, poised to knock again.

"What's your problem?" Kanta demanded, stepping outside and closing the door behind him. "You wanna wake everyone up? What are you doing here, anyway?"

"What the hell do you think, Kanta? I'm here to bring your dumb ass back to camp. Apparently you don't know how to find it on your own."

"Oh, I can find it all right. In fact, I was on my way back earlier." Kanta leaned against the door, arms crossed, and smirked. "I just got sidetracked."

"Don't, Kanta. Just don't. This isn't funny. Do you know how pissed Thalus is with you?"

"C'mon, Mid, we both know the others covered for me. Speaking of Freid and the guys—they're the ones who told you where I was, right?"

"Duh! Now can we go? Before Thalus realizes we're both missing?" Mid whirled away and stomped down the road.

Bear was waiting for Mid just inside the village walls.

"Why'd you leave him here?" Kanta asked.

"It was faster. But, trust me, I was tempted to bring him with me. Bear could have helped me give you the wake-up call you deserve. Plus, I wouldn't have had to knock forever."

"You weren't knocking forever. What you were was knocking *loudly*. Seriously, you could have awakened everyone. They might just be villagers but, with the wild parties they throw, I wouldn't be surprised if they went all mob-riot on a little girl who causes sleep deprivation. If they had plasma, they could probably take on a dozen bosses."

"Huh. Maybe we should offer them your place on the unit, considering how little you care about it."

"C'mon, Mid. I go out sometimes, but I always get back and do my job. What's the big deal?"

"'What's the big deal?' he asks." Mid looked up at Bear, walking beside her. "Bear, would you care to explain to my dumb-ass brother why partying every night he can sneak out of camp—not to mention chasing girls when he should be prepping for a hunt—is as good an idea as getting soul-ripped by a boss during Hallow Hour?"

Bear was silent.

"No, I don't think it needs explanation, either." Mid turned her attention back to the road. She'd put her goggles back on when they had left the village. Yet another reason Kanta loved his ghost eyes: they gave him natural night vision, whereas Mid needed her goggles to see in the dark.

"Who caved and told you where I was? Was it Freid? I bet it was Freid. It's always Freid."

"It wasn't Freid."

"Fine. It couldn't have been Browen, so ... Yano?" Mid kept her gaze ahead.

"It was, wasn't it?" Kanta shook his head, grinning. "That jerk! What did it take for him to give me up?"

"I switched a cooking shift for a guard shift."

"Really? You actually took cooking over guarding? For me?"

"Don't act even dumber than you are. He took the cooking shift. I took his overnight guard shift."

Kanta was confused. Yano didn't like cooking, and wasn't any good at it either. Then again, guard shifts also bored him, and he liked his sleep.

"It was actually a pretty good trade," Mid went on. "I would have asked him to switch with me anyway, so everything worked out. But don't worry—if I hadn't had that leverage, I'm sure I could have gotten Freid to tell me."

Kanta was sure too. Even if they'd sort of become friends over the past two years—in a love/hate kind of way—Freid still couldn't resist getting Kanta into trouble. It was an uneasy friendship, Kanta admitted, but after Lira had switched units a year ago, most of the animosity Freid had felt toward Kanta dissipated. Fried was still competitive, and easily annoyed by Kanta, but that was fine, since Kanta liked annoying him—almost as much as he liked annoying his sister. And right now she looked extremely annoyed.

Feeling smug, Kanta settled into the rhythm of walking, enjoying the frustration that radiated from Mid.

Their unit had finished clearing the ghost town— a much smaller place than a ghost city, but still classified as a haunted area—near the village the night before. Kanta, Browen, Yano, and Freid had gone to the village tavern to celebrate, as had become their tradition. Browen and Yano were both 20, a year older than Kanta, and had joined the unit almost 12 months ago. Kanta had met them during classes at the Hunter Association Headquarters, after he had been advanced by a year in training. Browen was Mist's nephew, and Yano was Ike's stepson. Browen and Yano had field-trained in other units before officially joining Thalus's unit.

The dingy tavern had been crowded with villagers, all celebrating the recent clearing with the hunters. As always, when the guys left early and Kanta decided to stay for the after-party at a villager's house, they promised to cover for him at camp until he returned. And, as always, it had been Mid who showed up to collect Kanta before he had a chance to return on his own.

Kanta didn't mind—not really. It was easier having Mid drag him back than slinking back to camp at dawn by himself, still half asleep.

When they reached camp, Mid waved goodbye with her middle fingers as she slipped off to the women's tent, Bear following her to take guard outside. Since Mid had become an official field trainee, she'd stopped using her own tent and had conceded to sleep in the women's communal tent with the other female hunters. She kept her trinkets and collectibles in Wendy's tent, although she'd left a stash back at their house in Hunters City.

Sneaking into the men's tent, Kanta managed to slip to his cot between Browen's and Freid's without either of them noticing. But someone else did.

Just as Kanta closed his eyes to fall asleep for the second time that night, a shadow fell over him. Opening his eyes, Kanta had to keep himself from shouting out when he saw Yano's face inches from his own, thin black eyes peering at him curiously.

"So?" Yano whispered. "How was the after-party?"

"Gods, Yano!" Kanta shoved him away. Yano had personal-space issues. Yano's cot, on the other side of Browen's, was empty. He was standing, wedged between Kanta and Browen, leaning over Kanta.

"Oh, come on, we're buds, aren't we? Don't hold out on your bud." Yano poked Kanta's shoulder. Browen didn't stir.

"Come on ..." Yano wheedled, poking Kanta again.

"Would you two shut up?" Freid demanded, his back to both of them. "I'm trying to sleep."

"I'm trying to sleep too," Kanta hissed, batting away Yano's hand. "This guy is the problem."

Freid glared over his shoulder at Yano. "Don't you have a guard shift now or something?"

"I did, in an hour, but the Marvellous Midget took it off my hands."

"Great." Freid rolled away again. "Leave anyway."

"Aw, Freidrick's such a meanie. You've gotta be interested too, right, Freiddie? Don't you want to hear about Kanta's night? It's the least we deserve, after making sure he didn't get caught."

"Says the guy who sold me out to my sister."

"It was a fair trade. Besides, you took that girl at the tavern from me."

"Who?"

"You know! That girl! She was really into me too. Our eyes met over your shoulder after you cut in when she was dancing with Freid. I decided not to go for her, though, 'cause you're my bud. And you know what buds do ..."

"They go to sleep," Freid asserted.

"You're not my bud. You could be, if you were trained properly."

Freid tensed and Kanta felt another one of their arguments coming on—arguments Yano never took seriously. Kanta sighed, deciding to end it now so they could go to sleep. "I'll tell you tomorrow, okay Yano?"

"Not *okay Yano*. Tell me now, so I can dream about it with me in your place. I want to know what it's like to be a dashing, irresponsible rake of a hunter!"

"I'm sure you can dream something up on your own ... wait, did you say irresponsible?"

"Details? Please? For me? Your bud of buds?"

"Yano," Freid hissed. "Just shut up. I'm really tired, and you're giving me a headache. A bad one."

"Your complaining's giving *me* a headache. Sheesh, no wonder that girl was so relieved when Kanta cut in."

Just as Freid bolted up in bed, fury written in every feature, Browen's arm shot out, grabbed Yano, and directed him back to his own cot. Browen didn't say a word, but his action ended everything. Freid, now wide awake, lay down again, uncertainly. Yano sat up long enough to waggle his fingers at Kanta and Freid before Browen pushed him back down.

Lying on his back, Kanta closed his eyes and tried to get comfortable, which proved difficult as he felt a headache of his own coming on.

Chapter II

And then I had to get up for a bloody guard shift an hour after bringing him back to camp, and he got to sleep blissfully all bloody morning and now I'm tired and unhappy and life just isn't *fair*." Mid kicked her feet in the air before slamming them back onto the desk she was sitting on. "I hate my brother! I hate him! Hate, hate, hate!"

"I know, Mid." Wendy wore a pair of glasses that magnified everything but which helped him repair Freid's plasma rifle, which had malfunctioned several nights ago.

"He's so irresponsible!" Mid went on. "And completely ungrateful! I'm always cleaning up after him, dragging his ass back, making sure he doesn't get in trouble! And does he thank me? Does he change his ways? No, no, definitely no! I'm the younger sibling! Aren't I supposed to be the irresponsible one?"

"You're very mature, Mid."

"Yeah, I know! I'm, like, 25 compared to Kanta's eight-year-old mentality. But he still calls me a kid and gives me those condescending smiles—like this!" Mid did her best version of Kanta's smug grin for Wendy. The tech just blinked at her with his oversized eyes behind the specs. Mid's composure cracked and she covered a laugh.

"Yes, that's … I suppose that's condescending. Your laughter certainly is." Wendy adjusted the band that was keeping the glasses in place around his head.

"You do know these are incredibly helpful, despite how silly they might look."

"Yeah, yeah. Here, let me try them!"

"Mid, these are tools for my work bought by the Hunter Association—"

Mid, ignoring Wendy completely, tugged off his glasses. She pulled them over her own head and fixed them in place.

She grinned at Wendy, whose face was suddenly huge. She could see the start of a few pimples on his cheek, the scruff of hair around his chin, and the slight scar over his left eyebrow from the time he'd tripped while playing Plasma Tag.

"How do I look?" Mid asked. "Fantastic?"

Wendy gave up trying to be frustrated. "Fantastic times four."

Mid beamed, took off glasses, and handed them back. "By the way, Wend, you need to shave."

"I know. I've just been so busy lately."

"That, and you don't like shaving 'cause you suck at it and scratch yourself a bunch."

Wendy flushed. "I'm still learning—"

"You'll learn faster if you quit putting it off. Seriously, Wend, this is an order from the Old World Club President: shave. Your face looks dirty like that."

"Hold on—you're the President?"

"Let's not have this discussion again. It always takes so long and you always lose. Just accept the facts, Wendy. I'm President. Of *everything*. You can be Treasurer."

"Treasurer?"

"Yeah. You look after all the President's important stuff." Mid waved at the boxes on Wendy's shelf, at those marked *Mid's Important Stuff: Touch*

Not in her distinctive scrawl. Pushing herself off the desk, Mid brushed off her blue plaid skirt and black leggings. "I'm gonna go get us something to eat."

Still looking doubtful about his Old World Club position, Wendy returned to Freid's plasma rifle.

It was just past 2 p.m. and the camp was busy. Mid spotted clusters of new field trainees around the campfires, some eating, others cleaning their weapons and chatting. Technically, Mid was one of them now, an actual field trainee since last winter, in the eyes of the Hunter Association. For years before that she'd unofficially been a field trainee and officially Thalus's ward who just happened to be receiving beginner's training in the field.

Maybe that's why Mid felt separate from the new batch of trainees, who had joined less than a year ago. She'd been training in the field for about four years now, while this was the first season for all of them—they'd done their beginner training at the Hunter Association Headquarters. Or maybe she felt like that because most of them were older than her, having started training at a later age. Mid could have waited until she was older to start training and then she would have had to train for only a few years at the Association before entering the field. That would have meant staying in Hunters City while Kanta paraded around with Thalus's unit, stealing even more spotlight than he already had. No way would Mid have let that stand.

The cooking tent was empty except for the two on duty. Kanta's friend Yano was leaning against one of the tables, chatting as he washed a dish—a dish he'd probably mindlessly washed for the last 10 minutes, if Mid knew him at all. Yano wasn't quite as tall as Kanta, but, still, he was tall. He was slighter than Kanta, with narrower shoulders, although he still had the muscles most hunters developed. He was wearing his usual tiger-print bandana over his black hair, which he kept tied in a short ponytail. Yano was tanned, with almond-shaped black eyes. His mother was from the East, where she and her late husband had worked with the Eastern Hunter Association before being sent to the West to fill the liaison position on their Council. Yano's father had joined a hunting unit and had been killed in action when Yano was still a kid. Several years later, Yano's mother had met and married Ike. Yano didn't seem to bear any grudge against Ike for having replaced his father, and he was a good big brother to Jun and Kyo, the two children his mother and Ike had together. Yano had even requested to join Ike's unit.

Mid wondered if she'd have been able to act like Yano in the same situation. If one of her parents had remarried and had more children, could she accept it and love her new family? She didn't wonder about it much, though, because it would never happen to her. Both of her parents were dead.

Yano nattered away to Rudy, who looked amused, either by what he was saying or how much he was saying. After joining the unit, Yano had quickly estab-lished himself as a chatterbox. Or, as Freid had once called him, a never-shut-up-box.

"I see why he switched with you now." Kanta spoke from behind her, his voice gravelly. Mid glanced over her shoulder. Like Wendy, her brother needed to shave. Unlike Wendy, her brother had ugly bags under his red-rimmed eyes.

"Attractive face," Mid complimented him. "You

should go back to the village right now. Alanna would definitely want you sleeping on her couch with a face like that."

Kanta didn't even correct the name, which Mid knew was wrong. "She'd probably want more than that."

"Eew. Just go die now, please."

"At the next ghost town, gladly." Kanta yawned as he shuffled into the dining tent. Rudy was the first to notice him. Her brows rose under her bangs when she saw him.

"I take it ye two enjoyed that tavern last night."

"Ye four," Kanta corrected, grabbing a bowl. Mid came up beside him and took two. "Freid and Browen were with us. They're still asleep."

"You should have come, Rudy," Yano said eagerly. "You and me, we could have shown those villagers how to really dance."

"Could we now?"

"For sure! And man, the music! They had this band, and it was just as good as any at Hunters City!"

"I wish they'd been quieter than those at Hunters City." Kanta took his portions of stew and bread. "At least, my head's wishing."

"Shut it, Kanta. You've no right to complain, not when you had a line of waiting dance partners going out the back of the tavern."

"Whatever. Where the hell's your headache anyway?"

"Gave it to Freid. He'll be even more pleasant than usual when he wakes up, so you know."

"I'm looking forward to it." Kanta sat down, sliding his plate next to the stew pot and picking at his bread. Rudy turned back to the counter. As soon as she did,

Yano mouthed *Leave!* at Kanta, which Kanta didn't acknowledge. Despite being almost 10 years younger than Rudy, Yano had taken a liking to her and tried to get time alone with her whenever possible. Rudy was more amused by Yano than anything else, but that didn't deter him.

"These came in for ya last night." Rudy turned toward the young hunters with a wad of letters in her hand. She went to the table and laid the majority in front of Kanta, then held one out for Mid, who was busy picking as much meat out of the pot as she could for her own bowl of stew.

"It was odd, see. When Marsh came back with 'em, she couldn't find either of ya. I said I'd take the pleasure of deliverin' 'em for 'er."

Mid took the letter sheepishly, not meeting Rudy's eyes. "I was, uh, on guard shift last night. Switched last minute, so, um, she wouldn't have known. Kanta ..." Mid looked at her brother, waiting for him to come up with his own excuse. Instead, he ripped open one letter, seeming to have more energy than before.

"Who's it from?"

"Who do you think?" Kanta yanked out his letter.

"I didn't know you'd be so excited to hear from Kite. He'd be touched."

Kanta snorted and read his letter, a smile slowly inching onto his face. Yano—who was now cleaning another plate Rudy had managed to shove in his hands—peered over his shoulder. "Is it from that hot blonde at the City?"

Kanta ignored him and laughed at something in the letter. Unperturbed, Yano picked up Kanta's other letters. "Kite? Thalus's brat sent you one too, huh?

What is it, a science report on how the moon cycle affects hellcats or something?"

"Probably." Kanta continued reading.

"Isn't he apprenticed to a scientist at the H.A. or something?"

When Kanta didn't reply, Mid did. "He's training with one of the head scientists in plasma research."

"Isn't that the same department as your aunt?" When Mid nodded, Yano's eyes widened. "That kid designs plasma weapons?"

"He's training to."

Yano looked at the letter in his hand. "So this could contain info on the latest goodies in ghost extermination?"

"Nah, it's never anything cool like that." Mid stuffed her own letter away for later. "I ask him about it, but he always says it's classified. Apparently he can't tell anyone, even his favourite cousin."

"He doesn't have one, remember?" Kanta interjected. "He said between the two he has to choose from, he's neutral."

"That's 'cause he doesn't want to hurt your feelings," Mid replied, then gestured to Kanta's letter. "What did the Fire Demon say?"

Kanta frowned at the nickname. "She said training's going well. They're heading out for their field test next week."

"Okay, and? That's not exactly funny, and you were laughing."

"You don't tell me what Kite writes to you, do you really think I'm going to tell you what she writes to me?"

"I don't tell you what Kite writes because his letters sum up to 'I'm fine. How are you?' and absolutely nothing else. Besides, he probably sends you a copy of the same letter. I barely ever hear from anyone else. You should indulge me."

"You *could* hear from other people. Paige would probably write to you, if you were ever nice to her."

"I'm nice enough."

Kanta gave her a skeptical look. Even Rudy, who'd continued to tidy during this, raised an eyebrow at Mid.

"What? I am!"

"Paige? Is that the blonde's sister?" Yano asked, looking at another of Kanta's letters. "You dog, Kanta! Both sisters writing to you! Do they know about this?"

Kanta snatched the letters from Yano. "Can you not look at my mail? That's private."

"Clearly, you two-timing bastard!" Yano clapped Kanta on the shoulder, beaming.

"Paige wrote you?" Mid demanded. "Since when does she do that?"

"Does it really matter?" Kanta stood, leaving his barely touched meal as he put his letters in his jacket pocket. "Thanks for the food, Rudy."

"What about me?" Yano asked. "I helped too, and you didn't even finish it! Blood, sweat, and tears, Kanta. Blood, sweat, and tears!"

Confused, Mid watched her brother leave. For almost two years, Kanta and Tai had written to each other, which Mid had known about. This was the first she'd heard that Paige was writing to him, and Kanta hadn't seemed surprised, which meant it probably wasn't the first time. What would he and Paige possibly have to talk about?

Kanta stuffed his hands deep into his pockets and marched through camp. It was sunny and the sky was clear, making it warm despite being only weeks before winter. Winter weather always started later than winter itself—it didn't really get unbearably cold until the end of December, and snow rarely fell before January. They'd be back at Hunters City then, for the two months that the weather was too rough for them to travel and hunt. Special groups were sent out during that time to keep high-risk haunted areas under control until regular hunting season started up again.

Kanta's hand curled around the crumpled letters in his pocket. He passed Freid and Browen on his way through camp. Freid did indeed look like he was fighting two vicious headaches; he didn't even notice Kanta. Browen did, and offered a curt nod.

Browen looked like his aunt, both in his height and dark colouring. He was taller and broader than Kanta and kept his dark hair shaved close to his head. He was wearing a sleeveless green tunic that showed off his arm muscles—muscles of which even Kanta was jealous. Not that he'd ever say so.

As Freid and Browen continued toward the dining tent, Kanta slipped behind the men's tent, where he was hidden from the rest of the camp. He should have done this earlier: found somewhere private to read his letters. He usually did, but he'd been so out of it from the night before that it hadn't occurred to him.

Sitting cross-legged on the ground, too tired to care about getting dirt on his pants, Kanta took out Paige's letter.

He always anticipated Tai's letters. Paige's letters, although he appreciated them, he always dreaded. Scanning the text Paige had written in her gentle, curving hand, Kanta relaxed. Tai was doing fine. She was still herself. There were no signs of anything wrong.

Kanta folded the letter and put it away to burn

later, turning his attention to Tai's letter.

After Brighton had disappeared two years ago, Kanta, as promised, had helped Tai search for her brother, wherever and whenever he could. But he'd done so half-heartedly, always worrying they'd find evidence of the creature that had her brother's likeness and that Tai would follow that trail and find him and the truth.

Not long after Brighton had run away, Kanta took Paige aside and told her he knew everything. As it turned out, he didn't.

At first, Paige had been horrified that Kanta knew— she'd thought that he'd tell Tai, Thalus, and the Hunter Association, that she'd be tried as a witch and her family would fall apart—but Kanta had reassured her that all he wanted to do was help. And understand. He told her what Brighton had told him and that he had sworn he wouldn't let Tai find out—a promise he intended to keep.

Paige had been relieved but was still jumpy. Slowly, awkwardly, she'd told him the truth. All of it.

About a year before Paige, Tai, and the other siblings had encountered the hunters, their family's shack had caught fire. Tai had been in the city at the time, killing ghosts. Although the fire had been extinguished before the house was completely destroyed, the flames spread quickly, burning up almost the whole interior and catching Brighton. Paige remembered it in horrifyingly clear detail and had recounted it to Kanta. The siblings had been trapped in the bedroom they all shared. The fire entered the room just as Brighton hoisted Paige through the window. He passed Grippa and Alton to her, but, when it was his turn to come out, it was too late. Paige didn't know if the fire had caught up with him first or the smoke, but, when the body was recovered, it was burned to a crisp.

Paige had cried as she told the story. But she had collected herself and told the rest of the tale.

"There was a w-w-witch going through our village. They w-w-wouldn't let her inside the walls so she c-c-camped just outside. We could see her c-c-caravan from our house. T-T-Tai and Brighton both t-t-told us not to go near it, or speak to her. If she c-c-came to the door, we were to ignore her. That n-n-night, while the villagers were putting out the fire, she c-c-came up to me. She said it was about my brother, and that it was urgent. I already knew he was d-d-dead—I'd already seen them pull out the b-b-body—but I c-c-couldn't help it. One of the shopkeepers from the village who had always been nice to us was looking after the little t-t-twins, so I went with the w-w-witch. No one saw her, and no one saw us leave. She t-t-took me to her c-c-caravan and … and inside there was … there was Brighton. It was him, his body p-p-perfect and unburned. I tried to run to him, to w-w-wake him up, because he looked like he was sleeping, but the w-w-witch grabbed my arm and said, 'That isn't your brother, but it c-c-can be.'"

The witch had seen the fire and had heard whispers of Brighton's death from the crowd outside Paige's house. She'd explained to Paige that she specialized in golems, which were made of the elements to take the appearance of whatever human their master chose and were given whatever memories their master wanted. She'd told Paige that, although her brother was gone, it was possible to give the golem his memories and to make him a copy of her brother.

"I refused. At first I refused. B-B-Brighton had only just d-d-died, and I was still in shock. I c-c-couldn't think straight, and I didn't know what to d-d-do, and T-T-Tai was still gone. But then the w-w-witch said, 'I know about the c-c-curse.'"

The witch explained that, if she were to use the golem, Tai would keep her sanity. If she believed wholeheartedly that Brighton was still alive, and had physical proof, then the curse wouldn't take effect.

"In the end, what else c-c-could I do?" Paige had sobbed. "She showed me how to c-c-cast the spell, how to give the golem every memory I c-c-could muster of my brother. She showed me what materials I'd need and explained to me that I had to recast the spell every year, on Samhain—H-H-Halloween, the most important festival of the w-w-witches—if I w-w-wanted the golem to k-k-keep his memories and form, to k-k-keep being Brighton …

"It was horrible. Wh-Wh-When Brighton … when the golem w-w-woke up, he actually thought he was Brighton. The w-w-witch told me that that was good and that I'd perfectly transferred my image and memories of my brother for it to think it actually was my brother, but then I had to explain to it that it wasn't. I had to t-t-tell B-B-Brighton he was d-d-dead, and what he really was, otherwise he wouldn't be able to help me perform the yearly ritual. It … it was like I k-k-killed my brother all over again. At first he didn't believe me, but with the w-w-witch's help …" Paige had pressed a palm to her eyes. "The look on his face. I'd never seen a look like that on Brighton's face before, but it was his face, to the finest d-d-detail. He was shocked and c-c-crushed and horrified all at once. I'd never seen him like that before, and it was horrible. And … and he had B-B-Brighton's voice. It was his v-v-voice exactly."

Kanta had waited awhile before gently asking,

"The witch … she showed you how to cast the spell? So you're able to cast spells yourself? Does that mean …"

Paige had nodded, hiding her face behind her hair. "I'm a w-w-witch. I—she said I had p-p-potential to become one and that she'd noticed it right away and that it was the r-r-reason she'd stayed in town as long as she had, hoping to c-c-convince me to become her apprentice. But I'd always been with either T-T-Tai or Brighton, so she didn't dare approach me. She said … after what happened that night, after she helped me, she said she'd c-c-come back again one d-d-day and ask me to become her apprentice. I … I d-d-didn't want to. I d-d-don't want to. I'm a w-w-witch now, but I never w-w-wanted to be." Paige had turned her tear-streaked face to Kanta. "You've g-g-got to under-stand: I just wanted my family to stay t-t-together. We k-k-keep getting ripped apart, and I just wanted to t-t-try. I just wanted us to t-t-try and b-b-be happy."

Kanta had hugged her. Paige had been surprised at first, but then she'd cried into his shoulder. It was probably the first time, Kanta realized, that Paige had been able to share her grief. The first time she'd had a shoulder to cry on after her older brother's death.

"We can do this," Kanta had said, pulling back when Paige was done crying. "I'll help you. We'll make sure Tai never finds out. You guys can still be happy. It might take some time, but it can happen. Between the two of us, we'll make it happen."

Paige had been shocked by Kanta's willingness to help, but then she'd smiled, looking more relieved than Kanta had ever seen her.

Kanta had kept his word, to Paige, the golem, and Tai. He'd helped Tai search for Brighton, and as their search turned up no results over the first month, he'd helped her cope. Then, one day, Tai had stopped wanting to search. It had been abrupt and unexpected. Every time after that when Kanta asked if she wanted to question villagers, or look for Brighton in a town, Tai had snapped at him. Since then, in letters or in person, Brighton's name was taboo.

Tai showed no signs of the curse. Paige had promised to report to Kanta on Tai's demeanour every few weeks when their mail reached camp. Kanta tried to ensure that their letters weren't just about Tai. Paige still had her older sister and younger siblings but none of them knew the truth about Brighton—only Kanta. It had to make her lonely, carrying that secret on her own. Now that Kanta carried the secret with her, he did his best to show an interest in how Paige's life was going, as well as Tai's, so that she didn't feel completely isolated. Just as Tai was moving on from Brighton's disappearance, he wanted to help Paige move on from his death.

If anyone had asked him why he was putting in so much effort, Kanta wasn't sure what he would say. Maybe Freid had been right that first time he'd spoken to Kanta about bringing Tai's family to camp two years ago. Maybe Kanta really was being sentimental. One orphan to another.

Chapter III

As usual, Tai was the last to leave the locker room. Although most trainees went straight to the mess hall for lunch after changing out of their practice gear, Tai liked to stay behind and shower. The two hours after lunch were used for classroom instruction—all their physical training was done in the four hours before lunch. Most waited until the day's lessons were completely finished before showering, but Tai didn't like being sweaty throughout the afternoon. She preferred showering when there weren't loud, chatty female trainees in the stalls next to her.

Tai dried her hair and pulled it into a high ponytail, the end slapping between her shoulder blades. She ran a hand through her bangs, attempting to push them behind her ear. It didn't really matter now, anyway. The only time she really needed to keep her hair out of her eyes was during morning practice.

Tai took her practice clothes—a sleeveless black tunic, black capris, and sleek black sneakers—and shoved them into her locker to pick up later. She switched to her white sneakers, resting in the bottom of her locker, and pulled her black trainee jacket on over the white T-shirt and black pants she'd changed into. Tai generally wore a medium, but the jacket, a large, hung down past her T-shirt and bunched in the sleeves. It was comfortable and, despite the fact she was not a fan of the neon green insignia over the breast and in stripes around the wrists and hem, Tai liked it. She'd gotten it after enrolling at the Association, as all trainees did.

Tai closed her locker and left the room. As she walked down the now-familiar halls, passing the doors to one of the training gymnasiums, Tai stuffed her hands deep in her jacket pockets. She passed her marksmen instructor, who was talking to a fellow instructor Tai remembered from her summer training. They both smiled at Tai, not breaking from their conversation, and she inclined her head in reply, not breaking her stride.

The mess hall was full. There was barely any room at the long wooden tables and benches, which were occupied by trainees, instructors, and visiting hunters. The food line was long. Tai took her spot at the end, hands still shoved in her pockets.

When Tai and her family had accompanied the hunters on their return to Hunters City for the winter two years before, Tai had expected to hate it. A city—a new city, built after the End of the World and never haunted—filled with hunters, where hunters lived and trained. If it had been three, even two, months earlier, Tai would have refused to go. But they'd arrived a few weeks after she'd given up on Brighton, and Tai was caught off guard.

Hunters City was full of hunters—she hadn't been wrong about that. But it was safe, one of the safest settlements in the New World. It was also the largest, with a steep wall around the perimeter that would have circled the city by her old village twice, lined with more plasma lanterns than she had ever seen. Not only that, but there was a place for Tai and her siblings to stay in the City, with Kanta and Mid's aunt. Tai had been uncomfortable about that at first, and still was to a degree, but their aunt had welcomed them, and the house was huge—a manor, with more than enough room for both her family and Kanta's. It was one of the first houses built in Hunters City and originally had been an inn, which explained all the rooms. Even then the manor was in Kanta's family, or so he claimed.

Tai didn't hate the City, and she noticed that her younger siblings really liked it. There was a school for Grippa and Alton, and plenty of opportunities for a trade apprenticeship for Paige, if she wanted that. And it was far away. Far from their village. Far from where Brighton had left them. But Tai didn't think about him anymore.

It was then that Tai had decided to join the hunters, to become one of them. When she had told her plans to Paige and Kanta—separately—both were shocked. Why would anti-hunter, anti-plasma Tai want to become a hunter trainee?

She'd resented their surprise, even though she knew it was justified. But becoming a trainee was logical at that point. Kanta had told her that hunters were secure financially. If Tai became a hunter, she could take care of her family, and they would be able to stay in Hunters City, where they'd be safe. They could start over. As long as they forgot everything that had come before.

Tai was surprised when Kanta had tried to dissuade her. He tried to convince her to take her ghost-killing methods to the Council, but she'd held her ground. Even if the Council believed her, why bother? She was no longer worried about being written off as crazy—at least, not so much—but she honestly didn't see a point in it anymore.

After they'd stopped looking for Brighton, she tried to teach Kanta her methods, but it hadn't worked. He just couldn't sense ghosts like she could—couldn't sense their heartbeats. That had taken them both aback, so Tai had even tried to teach Mid the same methods, with no results. It had been the same with Rudy, who volunteered to be a student. None of them could feel the heartbeat, and Tai didn't know how to make them feel it.

That wouldn't change, no matter how many hunters she tried to train, and she sensed it would be the same with all of them. So, really, what was the point? Even if she could kill ghosts, no one else could. Ridding the world of ghosts wasn't something she could accomplish on her own. Better that she forget those foolish dreams and focus on her younger siblings, on making and keeping them happy and safe. So they wouldn't want to leave her too.

Tai shook her head as she reached the buffet of typical hunter food. She'd vetoed those thoughts two years ago. Still, sometimes they resurfaced and, when they did, she pushed them away as quickly as possible. Dwelling on the past wasted time and effort she could dedicate to training.

She *had* become a dedicated trainee, even if she was behind the other trainees in her class, simply because of her age. Although she was two years older than most in her group, she still managed to join them in regular training after taking the rigorous summer catch-up classes offered for new recruits. Now, after two years of training the group's field test was approaching. After passing that, Tai would be assigned to a unit to do field training before being permanently assigned as an official hunter.

Kanta had assured her she'd be assigned to Thalus's unit for training and then as an actual member after her two years of field training. He'd seemed sure of himself, as usual. Tai was anything but sure that Kanta had that kind of sway over who his uncle admitted to his unit.

When Brighton first disappeared, Kanta had helped her search every village and town, question every citizen, follow leads that always led nowhere … Kanta had kept his promise. She'd been the one to give up. But what choice did she have? Not knowing where Brighton could be, why he had left—it was exhausting. Both looking for him and wondering. Exhausting and confusing. Finally Tai had to stop.

"Tai! Tai, over here!" A dark-skinned girl waved at Tai. Her black hair was pulled taut in a bun on the top of her head, and she was wearing the same clothing as Tai, as were all the trainees, except she didn't have her jacket on. She was also wearing a much smaller size than Tai.

Tai carried her tray toward the girl, who returned to her conversation with the people at her table. Tai didn't need to be waved over—the same group sat in the same place every lunch hour, after all, and Tai's seat was always saved—but Silsa persisted. Tai had learned that early on about Silsa. She was persistent.

Before Tai had decided to become a trainee, Kanta and Mid introduced her to Silsa, who had become a trainee at 15 and never had to take summer classes. She was Mist's niece and the younger sister of Kanta's friend Browen. When Silsa found out Tai was becoming a trainee and, pending her summer training, would join in the same year, the younger girl was excited and insisted on showing Tai the ropes and making her comfortable. Tai hadn't exactly been comfortable, but Silsa had certainly put in the effort, making sure she sat with the other trainees and sticking by her during training. It hadn't been necessary—Tai had always managed on her own—but she appreciated the sentiment.

Tai slid onto the bench next to Silsa, who was enraptured by the words of another trainee sitting across from her. He was tall but had a tiny, turned-up nose, which proved perfect for perching his wiry spectacles. His brown hair was kept shaven, so only a little stubble covered his head, contrasting with his thick eyebrows. A year and a half after meeting him, Tai thought Gareth still looked the same.

"As I was saying," Gareth went on, "it has to be fake. A boss with claws as long as someone's arm that can paralyze anyone who sees its third eye? If there really was such a ghost, everyone would know about it, and every hunter would be lining up to take it out."

The Splicer, Silsa mouthed before returning her attention to Gareth.

Tai felt her shoulders slump. The Splicer was a legendary ghost, one she'd heard of for the first time at Hunters City. Gareth had recently taken an interest in ghost legends and had decided to share them with his group—legends which sometimes involved ghost gods.

"Why would hunters line up to get their minds sliced open with claws like that?" Korel demanded, pointing her fork at Gareth in challenge from her seat on Silsa's other side. It wasn't Gareth who replied, but Damian, who sat next to him. Damian was the same age as Tai and had also started training late. He had cropped brown hair that spiked up a little, reminding Tai of Kanta. But the physical similarities ended there. His handsomeness was in his chiselled jaw and hazel eyes, whereas Kanta's charm came from his overall demeanour and annoyingly enchanting grin.

"Don't be stupid, Kor," Damian admonished. "A hunter who vanquishes a ghost like that? They'd go down in hunting history. Instant fame."

"Yeah, but all the others before that would die."

"Isn't that the point? If people don't get killed trying to destroy the famous evil ghost, then it doesn't get famous, and neither does its destroyer."

"That's my point, guys!" Gareth interjected. "It isn't famous. Not anymore. None of you would know about the Splicer if not for me!"

"I would," Damian put in. "You know my mother runs the library and archives. Tons of ghost stories in there."

"Oh yeah?" Korel demanded. "And when exactly was the last time you took a book from the library? I bet I've been in there more than you."

"Guys, guys, guys, just listen, okay?" Gareth spread his arms out, demanding silence. "As I was saying before, the Splicer can't be real, since nobody really knows about it. But, where did all these stories come from? 'Cause I found this one source that mentioned the Splicer being connected to one of the ghost gods."

Tai dropped her fork. Only Silsa noticed, and whispered, "You okay?"

Tai nodded but didn't pick up her fork right away. Instead she curled her hands in her lap, waiting for them to stop shaking. Even after so much time, the mention of the ghost gods set her on edge.

"Which god?" Damian asked.

"Hm? Oh, it was Spectora, I think. Or Phantasma. It wasn't that specific."

"So in other words you don't know," Damian asserted. "You're just bull-shitting as usual. There probably isn't even a legend about this Splicer ghost. Definitely sounds like one of your made-up names."

"It's true!" Gareth turned to the boy sitting beside him. "You've heard about the Splicer, right, Mao? I'm not lying. It's a real legend!"

Tai's gaze skipped to the trainee next to Gareth. There was a noticeable space between them, as usual. Tai often thought that, if the mess wasn't so crowded, Mao would sit by himself.

Mao was 17, like most of the trainees in Tai's class. The smallest male trainee, he had fine features and was only a few inches taller than Tai herself. He kept his black hair so long in front that it covered his eyes in curtains. Silsa had commented once to Tai, privately, that Mao let his hair grow out like that to hide his right eye, because his eyelid drooped slightly. His eyes were grey, and very pale, although Mao was darkly tanned.

Mao didn't reply right away—didn't give any indication of having heard Gareth. He picked at his small serving of meatloaf and rice, head tilted forward to optimize the hiding of his face with his bangs.

"It's true," Mao said finally, his voice soft, with traces of a lisp he might have had as a child. "There's a legend about a ghost called the Splicer, and it was associated with a ghost god, but not Spectora or Phantasma. Spectora is the ghost of children and Phantasma the ghost of revenge. The ghost god in the Splicer legend is Absoulute."

"I've heard of that one!" Silsa exclaimed. "He's, like, the main ghost god, isn't he?"

"Yeah, I've heard of him too," Damian inserted. "Doesn't he have some sort of cult? You know, with witches?"

Korel scrunched up her nose. "*Creepy.* Do they make sacrifices to him and stuff?"

"Probably."

"What's he the god of again?" Silsa asked Mao. "Or is he just the ruler of all the ghost gods?"

Mao averted his gaze, and Gareth answered. "Yeah, he's like the ruler. The god of ghosts, in general."

Mao pressed his lips into a thin line but didn't say anything else. Catching Tai looking at him, he met her eyes through his bangs just long enough to glare.

"Have you ever heard of Absoulute, Tai?" Silsa tried, as she always did, to drag Tai into the conversation.

Tai shook her head.

"Personally, I don't believe in the ghost gods," Gareth announced. "Just like I don't believe in the Splicer. If ghosts that powerful exist, everyone would know about them."

"If ghosts that powerful existed, no one would know about them," Damian corrected. "We'd all be dead."

"I'm not so sure," Silsa mused. "Maybe they're like the gods from the Old World, who never intervened in anything even though they were really powerful."

"Yeah, but the gods in the Old World weren't real either," Damian stated emphatically. "What about you, Mao? Do you believe in the ghost gods? You seem to know a lot about that shit."

"I don't see why they can't be real. Ghosts are."

"Whatever. I'm with Gareth. If they were real, we'd know."

"Yeah, I think so too." Korel twisted a knot of her auburn hair in her fist. "All this crap about ghost gods and legendary ghosts is made up."

"What about you, Tai?" Damian asked. "Do you believe in the ghost gods?"

Tai knew the others were looking at her. Even though it was a yes or no question and she could just nod or shake her head as she usually did, Tai spoke without hesitation. "No. I don't."

Chapter IV

"Can we go home?" Alton whined, scuffing his shoes on the cobblestones. "I'm bored."

"I'm sorry, Altie. We'll go home soon." Paige checked her list. "I just need to make this last stop. Why don't you come inside and pick out a sweet?"

Alton brightened and rushed into the shop ahead of his sister. Smiling to herself, Paige followed, catching the door in time to keep the bell from ringing again.

This general shop was at the edge of the westernmost outdoor market. There were four large outdoor markets in Hunters City, each set up around squares that were always filled with crowds, merchants shouting their wares, and heralds announcing the latest news from the Hunter Association. The Western Market was closest to Regailia's manor, and offered, more or less, the same selection as the others. Paige always did her shopping there. It was her way of helping to keep the house running, since Regailia let them stay free of charge. Paige helped the housekeeper with cooking and cleaning and did all the runs to the market. Over the past two years, Paige had gotten to know the denizens of the market quite well.

This was one of her favourite shops. It was small but cozy, with a variety of goods in the wooden bins. Behind the counter was a set of shelves with jars and boxes filled with assorted wares. Next to the shelves was a set of stairs that led to the top flat, where the shopowner and her family lived. Today, her son was at the counter, leaning back on his stool at the cash. Spotting Paige, he got to his feet, a smile lighting his face.

"Hi." Paige handed him the list while Alton poked in the sweet section.

"Hi." Harven, a few years older than Paige, had a head of sandy hair and dark brown eyes. His broad shoulders had filled out in the past year. "I didn't think I'd see you today."

"Oh?"

He turned to fill Paige's order from the bins of cooking supplies behind the counter, without looking at the list. "It's a nice surprise."

Even though he wasn't looking at her, Paige ducked her head to hide her blush.

She'd met Harven when she first visited the market, not long after Tai had become a hunter trainee and they'd taken up residence at Regailia's house. Harven had always been nice to her, and several months ago he'd taken her to a summer fair at the market, which no one else from her household had been interested in attending, except the little twins. They'd taken Grippa and Alton from booth to booth all afternoon, which hadn't been Paige's vision for the day, but Harven hadn't seemed to mind. He was good with them.

"Where's the other half?" Harven asked, nodding to Alton, as he set the sacks of flour and oats in front of Paige.

"Grippa went to a friend's house after school. She ran off without telling me, expecting Alton to deliver the message."

Harven rested his arms on the counter. "At least she's made friends."

"I guess so, but sometimes I think she's made too

many friends. She's visited the house of every child in her class by now, and she only ever repeats a visit when she liked the dinner they had."

"Befriending for the food. Smart girl. Though I don't know why she's looking for delicacies elsewhere when she has a big sister like you to cook for her."

Paige blushed again. "Henna does most of the cooking. I'm not really that good at it. It was my brother who could really—" Paige clamped her mouth shut.

"C'mon, Paige. You can talk about him to me, if you want."

"No, it's just … I didn't mean to …"

"Really, it's okay. I know your sister doesn't like your talking about him, but she's not here. I am. If you want to talk about him, talk. If you want to say his name …"

"I … I should get going. Tai's coming back tonight, for the weekend. It's her last weekend with us before field training."

As a hunter trainee, Tai was given room and board in the Hunter Association Headquarters. During weekends and holidays she returned to the manor to spend time with her siblings.

"Right, I forgot about that. She's really leaving this weekend?"

Paige nodded.

"She'll be okay, you know. Your big sis is tough; those ghosts won't dare touch her. Cheer up. While she's gone, I promise to keep you company."

Paige returned Harven's smile. "Thank you."

"No problem. And don't worry, I'll keep good on my word."

Alton ran up to the counter then, plopping a bag

of candies on the counter. "I want these!" Then, at a nudge from Paige. "*Please*! I want these, please!"

Harven laughed and rang up their order. Paige paid him with the money the housekeeper had given her and held out her own coins for the candy. Harven waved her off, as he usually did.

He tossed the bag of candy to Alton. "Just enjoy them. That's all the payment I need."

"Are you sure your mother won't be mad?" Paige asked, while Alton ran outside, already digging into his candy bag.

"Are you kidding? She'd tell me to give him a bag for his sister. She loves your little siblings. Says they're the kind of kids she always wanted—perfect little angels."

"Angels?"

"Yeah, she's only really seen them for short periods of time. But I can't blame her for thinking like that. I mean, with their hair and eyes, they do look angelic. Just like their sister … Tai, I mean."

Paige gave him a light swat. "Harven!"

Harven laughed and tugged at her short hair. "I'm only joking. If anyone's a real angel, Paige, it's you."

This time Paige definitely couldn't hide her blush, and she was sure Harven could hear her heart hammering. Quickly collecting her purchases, Paige mumbled. "I … I'll see you l-l-later. Th-Thanks."

Harven looked amused. By now, Paige had almost outgrown her stutter. It was only when she felt intimidated or stressed that it came out. Or profoundly embarrassed.

Alton had already finished his sweets by the time Paige went back outside. His mouth was sticky with sugar.

"Shouldn't you have saved some for Grip?" Paige

asked as they walked down the road, passing throngs of other citizens going to or coming from the market.

"Why? She didn't ask me over to her friend's house with her."

"Which friend was it?"

"Dunno. Some girl."

Paige couldn't help smiling at that. Alton had gotten to the age where he defiantly hated all members of the other gender to whom he wasn't related. Whether Grippa had actually asked her brother along or not, Paige knew he wouldn't have wanted to go.

They entered the manor through the back kitchen door. Henna, the housekeeper who'd worked there since Regailia was a child, was at the kitchen counter preparing tea. Paige had discovered that tea was routine in the manor. They had it at noon every day, and Henna always served it when there was a guest, which happened rarely, and when Tai came home, which happened weekly. Paige had always liked tea and quickly adjusted to the tradition. The little twins, however, developed an aversion to the beverage after their first sips. Henna continued to pour it down their throats, though, promising to do so until they properly appreciated the value of tea. So far, it wasn't working.

Henna went through Paige's packages as she stuffed the change in her apron pocket. "That boy at the general shop was working today, I take it?"

"Why d-d-do you say that?"

"He gave you extra. He always gives you extra. When I was young, men gave me flowers, not *flour*. Though I must say, this is far more useful."

Paige wanted to protest, to tell Henna it wasn't what she thought, but Paige wasn't sure if it was or not. So she kept quiet and helped Henna prepare the tea.

"Go wash up," Henna told Alton. "Dress in something nice for your sister."

"Tai doesn't like it when we dress up." Alton swirled around the water that remained in his glass.

"Tai might not, but I do, and I'm the one feeding you, child."

"But I don't even want tea—"

Henna jutted her chin toward the door. "Up and cleaned, little sir. Right now."

Alton pushed away from the kitchen table, where he'd been sitting, and shuffled into the hall, grumbling about Grippa's being lucky to have gone to a friend's house. Henna picked up Alton's glass, tut-tutting at the circle of water it had left on the table.

"Should I change too?" Paige asked, suddenly unsure about her appearance, as she handed Henna a dishcloth to wipe up the water. Paige wore a dress she'd bought a year ago from one of the cheaper tailors: blue cotton with a frilly white hem which cut off at her calves and a scoop neck. It was one of Paige's favourites, and she wore it often.

"You look perfectly fine." Henna didn't bother to assess Paige's outfit. "It was that brother of yours who needed changing. He had sugar powder all over his clothes, which in itself is quite curious. Who would give him candy right before tea?"

"I didn't mean for him to eat them right away."

"I'm sure you didn't." Henna hung up the dishcloth and gestured to a cupboard. "Can you get the biscuits down? The ones in the blue tin? Let's give your sister something sweet as well."

Kite glared at the papers strewn on his desk, at the formulas and designs and notes they contained. Groaning in frustration, he viciously pushed his chair back and got up. He couldn't stand it anymore—couldn't stand his estimations not working, couldn't stand the flaws in the design he couldn't solve, couldn't stand the project.

Leaving his room, Kite slammed the door behind him. He was starting down the hall when Alton came running up. The boy was full of sugar.

That meant he'd been to the general shop, and that commoner boy had dished out more freebies in a pitiful attempt to impress Paige. A pitiful attempt that was working.

"Why are you running?" Kite asked.

"Henna said I gotta change and clean up, for Tai. Are you cleaning up too, Kite?"

"I'm already clean." Kite didn't add that there was no reason for him to make an effort for Alton's eldest sister.

"Oh." Alton dug through his pockets. He pulled out a little plastic bag containing an orange sour candy. He held it out to Kite. "Here you go. I saved it for you, 'cause I don't like the orange flavour that much, but it's your favourite."

Kite gingerly accepted the bag, which was sticky to the touch. "Thank you."

"S'okay. Harven gave them to me. Next time want me to get you a bag? I got one for Grips, see?" Alton produced a full bag from his other pocket. "I'm gonna give it to her later, if she's nice to me."

"Harven gave you two?"

"Eer … kinda. He was talking to Paige, but I'm pretty sure he saw me take it. That makes it okay, right?"

If he was busy talking to Paige, Kite doubted the commoner boy noticed what else was happening in the shop, so it was his own fault. "Yes, Alton. That's perfectly fine."

"Great! I'll get you one next time, too!"

Before Kite could tell him not to bother, Alton took off down the hall.

Stuffing the bag in his pocket, Kite went downstairs. He was on his way to the front hall when he crossed paths with Paige, who was taking a tray of biscuits, crackers, and cheese to the sitting room, where Henna liked taking guests.

"Oh!" Paige was evidently taken aback. "I d-d-didn't hear you come d-d-down."

Kite tried not to let his annoyance show. Paige rarely stuttered when she talked to other people, but she'd never shaken the habit with him. Maybe it was because they rarely spoke to each other, even though they'd lived in the same house for nearly two years. Kite had never been, and still was not, comfortable with the arrangement.

Maybe it was also because in the past two years Kite had actually grown and, even though he remained awkwardly gangly, towered over Paige.

"Tell Henna I'll be back for dinner," Kite said, stepping around her.

"You're n-n-not staying for t-t-tea?"

"No." Kite took his coat from the hook in the foyer. He probably didn't need it, but he always felt uncomfortable walking around in public without his coat on.

"But T-T-Tai's going to be g-g-gone in a couple of days—"

"I'll say goodbye later," Kite replied, shrugging on his coat. Before Paige could reply, he left, closing and locking the door behind him. He had his keys, and when

Tai arrived she could either use hers or get one of the others to let her in. Kite hated leaving the front door un-locked—as everyone else except his mother tended to do—even when there were people at home.

Taking the front steps, Kite glanced back at his house. It was two stories and made with dark grey stone, looking every bit the Gothic manor. A place ghosts would be expected to inhabit in Old World legends—in the days before ghosts took over most of the cities in the world. A fence around the manor's grounds separated it from the other houses that had been built in close proximity as the City grew. In stark contrast to the old manor, these newer houses were made of timber frames and plaster, with thatched roofs and wooden shutters to cover the glassless windows, like most buildings in Hunters City. In the sections closest to the Hunter Association Headquarters, including the Headquarters itself, glass windows and tiled roofs were more common. Those wealthier areas were also more private. Thanks to the City's expansion, the manor was hardly private, but with its fence, thick walls, and glassed windows it offered a degree of isolation—a quality Kite had always appreciated.

Closing the gate, Kite started down the street, debating taking a trip to the library and archives. There was always something to read there to take his mind off apprenticeship problems. Besides, it was quiet—like his house used to be, before Tai's family moved in.

Kite took the bag Alton had given him out of his pocket. Carefully, he reached in and extracted the candy. Crumpling up the bag and shoving it deep in his pocket, Kite popped the candy in his mouth. Orange really was his favourite.

Chapter V

I wish there were more girls in our group," Korel lamented that afternoon, after classes in hunter protocol and travelling instruction had ended. "It's only the three of us and … how many guys are in our group again? It doesn't matter. My point is, there are too many male trainees. It's the same in the other groups."

They were in the women's locker room and, although Tai was ready to leave, she found herself hooked into Korel and Silsa's conversation. She'd just quietly bide her time until it wouldn't seem impolite to leave.

"Yeah, it would be nice to have other girls around," Silsa agreed.

"It would be more than nice. We'd get a bigger locker room then, too. Do you know how much bigger the guys' locker room is? The H.A. is so sexist."

"There's more of them, though, so they *would* need more room …"

"Come on, Silsy. We're girls. We need more room."

"Isn't that kind of sexist too?"

Korel shrugged and yanked her auburn curls out of their ponytail. "Don't you find it annoying, Tai? Being outnumbered?"

Tai did find it mildly annoying, but she found being stuck in a locker room conversation even more so. "I guess."

"Gods-That-Remain, are you two women or not? Don't you care that we're being oppressed?"

"We're not really being oppressed," Silsa empha-sized. "It just so happens that more trainees are male."

"Yeah, because that's what the H.A. encourages! Haven't you noticed the Council's made up of almost all males? The only women on the Council are the head of plasma research and one of the unit coordinators! That's two to 10! Not even a quarter!"

"There's also the Eastern liaison," Silsa pointed out.

"She's important, sure, but only when it comes to relations with the East. She might be in on all the Council's meetings, but when it comes to making decisions about our Association she can only comment, not vote."

Silsa turned to Tai for assistance, but Tai had no desire to enter the debate. "I should go," she said instead.

Korel looked irritated at the abrupt end to one of her favourite topics, but Silsa was the one to speak. "Right! Of course! Sorry for keeping you!"

Tai waved her off and left, swinging her duffle over her shoulder. It contained the few belongings—mostly clothing—that had been in her room. All recruits scheduled to leave on their field tests had been encouraged to clear their belongings from the trainee dorms; those who passed wouldn't be returning to the Hunter Association Headquarters itself. The pass rate was apparently high.

As she was taking the steps from the main door of the Hunter Association Training Facilities—which was connected to the dorms and the Headquarters where the Council met—Tai heard someone call out to her. She paused at the bottom of the stairs and saw Gareth coming toward her, taking the steps two at a time. He, too, was carrying his belongings, although

Tai had only one not-quite-full bag, and he had two overstuffed bags. Following Gareth were Damian and Mao, not in half the hurry Gareth was.

"Are you on your way home?" Gareth asked. Tai nodded. "Perfect! We'll come with you. We're all going the same way, at least for a bit. It only makes sense."

"You just want to see Tai's house," Damian grumbled as they walked, taking a spot between Tai and Gareth. Mao, who had caught up to them, kept his gaze on the ground while walking on Gareth's other side.

"It's not *my* house," Tai muttered. All the recruits had found out Tai was staying at Regailia's manor, which apparently was a famous spot among the trainees, thanks to the history of both the house and the family.

"I'll admit," Gareth said to Damian, "that *is* part of the reason. It's a magnificent house, and perhaps Tai will finally introduce us to her family."

"And by that, he means Regailia." Damian grinned at Tai. "She's his idol, in case you didn't guess by how much he talks about her designs."

"I didn't mean that at all! I sincerely would like to meet Tai's siblings! Though I can't lie, getting the chance to speak to Regailia in person ... well, I wouldn't pass that up. Even a moment with her son would be ideal. I'd love to ask him about that sword he modified for Unit Q17's Kanta."

Tai tensed at Kanta's name. She'd thought Kanta had been kidding, originally, when he talked about being a hunting prodigy. As it turned out, he hadn't exaggerated nearly as much as Tai had thought. The majority of hunters at the Association knew his name and his unit. Unit Q17 was highly esteemed, apparently, thanks to Thalus's dedication and hard work over the years. Although he formally had the same amount of power in the Association as any other unit commander, it was obvious Thalus had more sway than his position typically would allow. He was highly respected among the other unit leaders and Council members.

"Oh, that guy." Damian wasn't as impressed by Kanta's exploits as most hunters.

"What was it like?" Gareth asked Tai.

"Kanta?" Tai responded, confused. Damian laughed.

"The katana," Gareth clarified. "But speaking of him, what was it like working with the youngest hunter in history to have killed a boss? You hardly mention him."

"She hardly mentions anything," Damian pointed out. Then to Tai, "No offence."

Gareth was looking at her expectantly. Even Mao seemed slightly interested.

"I didn't work with him." Technically, she hadn't. They'd both worked their own ways.

"Oh ... Then, did you ever witness him in action, hunting?"

She'd often been asked questions like this since coming to Hunters City, whenever someone realized she associated with Kanta. It got on her nerves, which she was sure to let Kanta know in her letters whenever she felt like it. In her last letter, she'd asked him to tone down the hunting excellence and fail a bit more, so he wouldn't be so famous back home. She'd even asked it in a moderately nice way.

Before Tai could answer, Gareth relented. "Sorry, never mind! That would involve your admitting to illegally entering a haunted premise. How impertinent of me."

"Like we'd tell anybody," Damian joked.

"I'm sure you wouldn't, and Mao here wouldn't, but I'm not nearly so sure of myself! I'd likely retell her stories about Kanta killing ghosts, not at all intending to get her in trouble, but doing so nonetheless!"

Killing. Tai still found herself frustrated when hunters used that term. She had to stop letting it get to her.

They turned onto a busy street as they neared a market, and they were divided by the crowd. Damian stayed next to Tai, taking her arm to guide her through the throng, an action which Tai did not consider necessary in any way. Still, they were in a group, and shaking him off would be rude. Even if he was grinning at her with a not-quite-Kanta-level grin.

Damian was handsome, a fairly good hunter, and not altogether irritating. But Tai found *this* irritating. This interest he had in her. Tai found it more troublesome than flattering. She wished he'd stop indulging his urges to talk to her and single her out. Tai just wanted to be left to her training—to do what was important.

When they rejoined the others, Damian held her arm a few moments too long. Tai waited impatiently until he released her, slipping her another half smile.

"Don't you have to turn down here?" Damian asked Gareth, when they reached a crossroads.

"Er, well, I guess I do ..." Gareth didn't finish, but Tai knew why he was reluctant. It would mean not passing her house. He'd evidently planned to take the long way home and keep quiet about it. Damian, however, had his own plans.

They said goodbye to Gareth. Soon afterward, Mao disappeared in a crowd, which Damian had clearly been expecting. Tai wasn't surprised by it either.

Gareth was the only member of their group Mao seemed remotely comfortable around, and, if Gareth wasn't there, Mao tried not to be either.

Damian and Tai were alone now. Tai assumed this had been his plan.

"Two weeks," Damian mused. "You've travelled for longer than that, right?"

Tai nodded.

"What was it like?"

"Tiring."

"It'll be even more tiring this time. You'll actually be hunting—we'll be hunting. I think it'll go well, though. We've got a pretty good team. For the most part."

"What?"

"Don't worry; I don't mean you. And Gareth can get distracted, but he's a solid hunter. Korel and the others too. The only one I'm really worried about is Mao. I mean, he's fast and has pretty good aim, but not much else. He never speaks. How can we work on a team with someone like that, even if it's just for two weeks?"

"Didn't you just say I hardly speak a little while ago?"

Damian smiled. "Yeah, but you're different."

Luckily, Tai spotted someone coming toward them, absorbed in his own thoughts.

"Kite!" Tai called. Startled, Kite stopped in his tracks, almost colliding with the person behind him. Apologizing, he hurried over to Tai, not looking particularly pleased. Kite rarely did.

"I'm on my way back to your house," Tai informed him. "Let's walk together."

Kite was about to protest. Then his eyes darted between Tai and Damian. When he spoke, Tai noticed that his tongue was orange. "Okay."

They resumed walking, Kite rather awkwardly as

he fiddled with something in his pocket.

"I'm Damian." Damian's voice was tighter than before.

Kite took in Damian's attire, murmuring to himself. "A trainee."

"Yeah. I'm in the same group as Tai."

"Yes. I gathered that."

Though still trying for a friendly smile, Tai saw Damian's lips twitch downward. "This is Kite, Regailia's son."

"What's it like being the son of the head of plasma research?" Damian asked.

"Not vastly different from being the son of any other working parent, I'd assume."

"It's gotta be more interesting. You have access to all the latest plasma weapons, right?"

"No. My mother's research is classified. I know about and am able to access any new equipment at the same time as every other hunter."

"You're kidding—even though you're her son?"

Kite didn't reply, as he tended to do when the person he was speaking to repeated a question he'd already answered or posed something he deemed rhetorical or common knowledge.

Tai schooled herself to keep from laughing at the expression on Damian's face. He was typically a smooth talker and could strike up conversations with most people. Someone like Kite, who was detrimental to the continuity of any social dialogue, got under his skin. She should have introduced them sooner.

"When exactly are you leaving, Tai?" Kite asked. He'd quickened their pace, she noticed, wanting to get home as soon as possible. She didn't have a problem with that.

"You're looking forward to her going?" Damian attempted to lighten the mood.

"I'm completely neutral on the subject. I'm simply asking for a fact about which I have not been informed, which may later affect me, as we live in the same building two out of seven days a week."

Damian had no comeback.

"I leave on Sunday," Tai informed them. "We're meeting at the H.A. at 9 a.m."

"That early? Regrettable."

Tai agreed. Even if she'd gotten used to the early mornings while training at the Hunter Association Facilities, she didn't enjoy them.

"How have the little twins been this week?" Tai asked.

"Better. Everything's cleared up between Grippa and that other girl."

"What do you mean? What girl?"

"Grippa got in a fight with a girl in her class last week. Paige didn't tell you?"

No, Paige certainly had not.

"Grippa's your youngest sister, right?" Damian asked.

"Yeah," Tai mumbled, still focused on Kite. "What happened, exactly?"

"Grippa apologized to the girl. The next day she went to her house after school to play, so I'd say it's all cleared up."

"Okay, but why was there a fight? Did Grippa start it?"

Kite paused.

"*Kite*. Was it Grippa?"

"Yes."

"Why would she do that?"

"She … didn't say."

"I wouldn't be too worried if I were you," Damian advised Tai. "Kids get in fights all the time, don't they? I know I used to. That girl probably spilled your sister's fingerpaint or something."

"Grippa's eight years old," Kite stated. "Her school time is spent learning mathematics, history, and proper writing—not frivolously dirtying paper that could be put to better use."

"How is it frivolous?" Damian demanded. "She's only eight. Kids should play around when they're little."

"She has four years of schooling left. In what way does that limited amount of time teach her what she'll need to know to advance in our society allow for play? Besides," Kite added, "she spends the majority of her time outside of school playing."

Tai was thankful they'd arrived at the manor. Breaking into whatever retort Damian was about to make, she said firmly, "This is us. See you on Sunday."

Damian hesitated, but then said goodbye and headed down the street. Kite stood at the gate to the manor, watching Damian retreat.

"Was that really necessary?"

"Was what necessary?"

"Having me chaperone the pair of you. I found it very uncomfortable."

Tai didn't answer, just opened the gate and started up the short path to the house. "So will you tell me now why Grip got in a fight?"

"I'm not sure I should."

Tai turned back to Kite and fixed him with her best icy big sister look, the one she used on her siblings when they were being difficult. "Tell me."

It didn't take long for Kite to fold. "The kids

were assigned a family project for their history lessons, to teach them the values of history and genealogy using familiar information. When Grippa and Alton presented, they mentioned you and Paige, and your parents and grandmother vaguely. A girl in their class had heard ... well, she'd heard from her parents, I assume, who must have picked up the rumours at some point ..."

"Rumours about what?"

"About your brother. That the group of orphans Thalus's unit brought back two years ago included an elder brother and that he disappeared and was searched for without success. This girl spoke up during Grippa and Alton's presentation and called them out on not including their brother. Grippa got angry with her and told her they didn't have an older brother, but the girl persisted. It ended in Grippa's tackling her. The teacher had to pull them apart."

"Grippa actually said she didn't have an older brother?"

"According to Alton. He told us what happened, in great detail. Apparently her exact words were 'We don't have an older brother. You aren't allowed to talk about him.'"

A shiver crawled up Tai's spine. She remembered that Grippa had had a tantrum, just over a year and a half ago, because she'd wanted Brighton to put her to bed instead of Paige. Not knowing what to do, Paige had gotten Tai, but Grippa wouldn't calm down. She wanted her older brother.

You don't have an older brother anymore, Grippa! You aren't allowed to talk about him ever again, understand? I don't even want to hear his name!

Tai took the steps quickly, reaching the door before Kite had even moved. Slipping inside, she was greeted by the sweet aromas that always accompanied Henna's tea.

"Tai!" Paige exclaimed, appearing from the sitting room and spotting Kite behind her. "I thought you were g-g-going out ..."

"I was," Kite said, hanging up his coat. "Somehow I found myself coming back."

Tai dropped her bag in the hall. She'd put it away later. "Where's Grip?"

"Grippa? She went t-t-to a friend's house. I told her this was the last weekend we'd spend t-t-together before your field t-t-test, b-b-but she must have forgotten ..."

Yeah. Tai thought. *She must have forgotten.*

"Tai!" The call came from Tai's younger brother. Alton darted out from behind Paige, who was half blocking the doorway to the sitting room. He was smartly dressed in a white dress shirt and green plaid pants. The shirt was tucked in so neatly that Henna must have helped him with it.

Tai kneeled to hug Alton. He was far too big for her to pick up anymore, so this was the best she could do.

"Henna said I can't eat any sweets if I don't finish my tea!" Alton whined as they separated.

"Did she?" Tai asked. "And who made all those nice sweets you want to eat, Mr. Alton?"

"Henna did ... kinda ..."

"Then I think she can decide whom she gives them to, and when." Tai got to her feet and ruffled her brother's hair. "Come on, Altie. I'm hungry, and I have no problem finishing my tea."

"Will you finish mine for me?"

Tai steered him into the sitting room, and Paige

and Kite followed. "Some things, Altie, you've just gotta do on your own."

The next day Tai went around the City with her family all the way to the Southern Market, where they had lunch and window-shopped. Grippa and Alton nattered away about school, and Grippa told Tai about all her new friends. But no mention was made of the fight Grippa had gotten into, and Tai didn't bring it up.

They got home late, which Henna had expected, so she served dinner when they returned. She'd brought Kite his food earlier, since he'd stayed locked in his room the whole day trying to figure out a particularly vexing project. At least, that's what Henna deduced from the amount of cursing and balled-up paper produced from his room.

Tai wouldn't have minded if Kite were present, but it was nice sitting at the table with just her siblings. Even Henna left after bringing out the food to spend her Sunday off with her son and his wife in another part of the City. Henna wished Tai the best of luck on her test and showed her where she'd stashed a package of Tai's favourite homemade foods to take with her on the road.

Tai didn't see Regailia until late that night, after everyone else had gone to bed and she was still up packing. Regailia had been absent not only that weekend but apparently the last week and weekend before. Something about the new equipment that was being developed. As she was the head of plasma research, she would be required to oversee the project, but Tai had also heard that it—whatever they were making—had been Regailia's brainchild. Tai couldn't deny she was curious about the huge undercover project, but she didn't ask. As Kite had said to Damian, Regailia's work was classified.

The lady of the house swept in when it was almost midnight. Tai didn't hear her—Regailia was notoriously light-footed, a trait her son had inherited—but Tai wasn't surprised when she found Regailia hanging up her coat in the foyer.

Regailia had become a mother young. With the death rate so much higher than it used to be, and lifespan so much shorter—thanks not only to the ghosts but the poverty that had ravaged most of the New World—families started and ended early. Regailia was in her 30s: this made her not only the youngest research head but also the youngest Council member ever.

Tai wouldn't have guessed Regailia was in her 30s. Her extremely youthful and fine-featured face made it impossible to pinpoint her age. Kite had her pale skin and black hair, although Regailia kept her hair long and wavy, and the same calculating blue eyes. Kite also had his mother's intelligence.

"Good evening." Regailia didn't look at Tai, who was setting her bags by the door. "You're leaving us tomorrow."

"Only for a few weeks. How's the project going?"

Regailia knew Tai wasn't prying for details. The older woman sighed. "It's going as predicted. Everyone knew it would be a big job when we took it on three years ago. I'm just grateful it's nearing completion."

Regailia noticed Tai's minimalist belongings. She didn't comment, but Tai felt her approval.

Realizing this was probably the last time she would see Regailia before she left, Tai took a deep breath. "There's something I want to say ... Basically,

I want to thank you. For everything. For taking me and my family in for these two years, for taking care of them while I trained, for—"

Regailia held up a hand, and Tai fell quiet. "I believe by now you know how I feel about expressions of gratitude?"

Tai nodded.

"Good. Shall we have tea?" Regailia headed for the kitchen. "Henna's sure to leave me a pot of tea should I not be home when she takes her leave. We'll celebrate your field-test passage upon your return. For now, a quiet farewell shall do."

Chapter VI

Since they'd finished clearing the ghost town ahead of schedule, Unit Q17 was taking its time getting back to Hunters City. They were making stops on the way, such as this one, near a haunted city that the Hunter Association had no hopes of clearing, because of its size. Still, as the hunters were passing through, they stayed to clear a few buildings to lessen the ghost presence in the city—to keep it contained.

Thalus wanted to clear a few suburbs and avoid the hub of the city and all the towering ruins, but Kanta convinced the commander to let him take a group into a mall. It had taken awhile, but Thalus eventually relented, mostly to get Kanta to go away.

Here they were. Not in the biggest mall, but a mall nonetheless. For the past week, Kanta, Freid, Yano, and Browen had been cleaning—as in they'd been thinning out the ghosts without sticking around for the boss. Now the mall was finally empty enough to attempt to clear. Just in time too. Their unit was moving out in a day.

Kanta stood in the mall atrium, gaze skimming the broken elevators, abandoned shops and their shattered displays, toppled benches, and long-dry fountains. An escalator was forever frozen into a staircase. They'd use it to traverse the three levels, should the boss prove adventurous.

"In position yet, Freid?" Kanta asked.

"Not yet."

Yano's voice crackled. "What's the holdup, Freidrick? We've only got three minutes!"

"I know." Freid sounded as if he was panting. "I have to change my vantage point."

"Make it quick!"

"Are you in place, Yano?" Kanta asked.

"You know it!"

Kanta glanced up to see Yano waving his automatic from just above him on the second level. Grinning, Kanta spoke into his WT. "Browen?"

"Ready."

"Okay, Freid." Kanta could just see Freid on the top level, positioning his plasma sniper, which took special plasma bullets for speed and distance. "You good?"

"Yeah."

"Just in time," Kanta murmured, as he felt the boss wake up. Someone whooped into his WT—probably Yano.

Kanta unsheathed his katana just as the boss flew up from the floor at his feet. It hovered high in the air, glaring down at Kanta with all three eyes. Then it screeched.

"Screamer!" Yano's excited voice came from Kanta's WT, now attached to his hip. "I called it! Freid, you owe me 50 bucks!"

"It was 20, you ass—"

As the boss's shriek faded, it suddenly split in two. The two halves rippled, like an image in a well, then filled in the missing parts. Two identical ghosts, both with black middle eyes, hovered above Kanta.

"Shit!" Yano exclaimed. "Who called Splitter?"

No one answered. Kanta was too busy dodging

the boss—bosses. The first dove at him and he jerked out of the way, quickly repeating the action when the second came at him.

"Yano!" Freid snapped. "Cover Kanta, damn it!"

Seconds after Freid's command, plasma rained over the first boss, which had been lining up to attack Kanta again. Its image fizzled where the plasma touched it but, except for that, the boss was unscathed. Whipping its head around, it set its sights on Yano, and flew at him. Yano backed away, firing plasma all the way.

Meanwhile, Kanta still had his own boss to deal with. Putting his katana between them, Kanta waited to see what it would do. It hovered for a second, too far up for Kanta to reach it, and then opened its mouth.

Shit! It's going to split again! "Freid—!"

A plasma bullet whizzed through the back of the boss's head, just missing its third eye. It broke its scream to search for the attacker. Another bullet sailed through its jaw.

Just as the boss flew at Freid, Browen appeared underneath it, on the second level. He'd got the boss in the stomach, leaving a gaping hole in its centre. The boss changed its course, diving at Browen, who ducked away and spun around, still firing.

"Guys!" That was Yano. "Hurry up! As much fun as I'm having, I can't distract this one on my own forever!"

"Hold tight!" Kanta shouted at his WT and raced up the escalator. Browen was close, with his back to Kanta. Kanta was in time to see Browen roll out of the way as the boss tried to soul-rip him.

Just as the ghost flew through the space where Browen had been—now ground level—Kanta rushed forward and sliced his katana across the boss's neck. The head tipped sideways but didn't disconnect. Staring at Kanta with its flickering white eyes and black eye, the ghost's head slowly straightened, phantasmal blue strands of its severed neck reaching for one another.

Kanta slid his katana through the boss's third eye. It dispersed, but didn't screech.

"Crap!" Yano, again. "Guys, it's gonna split and I need to reload—"

A shriek ripped through the air and the whole building shook. Kanta winced, waiting for the boss's new twin to appear.

Instead, what he heard from his WT was "Gods-That-Remain ..."

"Yano?" Kanta snatched the communication device from his belt with his left hand and carried his katana with his right. "What's going on? Did the boss split, or ...?"

"Or. That one. I pick *or*."

Sheathing his katana, Kanta waved for Browen to follow him and they both went to where they'd last seen Yano. They found him in the food court, which was on the second floor and only a short distance from the atrium. He wasn't alone.

"Yo." Mid poked her head out from behind Bear, waving her black pistol, which was dripping fresh plasma. "What up, bro?"

"Mid ...? MID! What the hell are you doing here?"

"I got bored clearing the suburbs." Mid attempted to wipe her pistol on the side of a toppled counter, with minimal success. "Not that you'd understand my boredom."

"Does Thalus know you're here?"

"About as much as he knows when you don't come back after a tavern raid."

Kanta marched forward. Grabbing his sister roughly by the arm, he dragged her away from the others. Bear followed, but Mid held up a hand for him to wait, and then shook off her brother. "Uh, hello? Child abuse, much?"

"Exactly, Mid—*child*. You're only 15! You're not allowed in malls, and definitely not during Hallow Hour!"

"C'mon. I can obviously handle myself. I got that boss, didn't I? Besides, Bear was with me. I was perfectly safe."

"No! No you weren't! Just because you didn't get soul-ripped doesn't mean you were safe! And that's not the point! This is against protocol! When Thalus finds out—"

"When? I think you mean *if*. The others I was hunting with thought I headed back earlier. Nobody will know any different if I go back now."

"Maybe not, but that doesn't mean I won't tell Thalus. You shouldn't be here, Mid."

"Yeah, okay. I think I got that now. But listen up, big bro, you're not gonna tattle on me to Thalus, and neither are your friends. 'Cause if any of you do, Thalus just might find an anonymous report on his desk about the exploits of Kanta and Company in every village tavern we've come across over the past 12 months."

"As if Thalus would really care about that when you've broken proto—"

"And I'll tell Tai about all the girls you've messed around with when we go back to H. City."

Kanta promptly shut his mouth. Mid batted her innocent eyes at him. "What's wrong, big brother? Don't you and the Fire Demon exchange letters weekly? Haven't you been updating her on all your latest conquests?"

"Look, Mid, if you say anything—"

"I won't," Mid promised. "And neither will you."

Kanta wasn't happy. Even if he didn't want to betray his sister to Thalus, he wanted her to get hurt even less, and if someone didn't deter her risky, rule-breaking habits, that was bound to happen sooner or later. For now, Kanta was just going to have to hope it would be later, until he could find another way to discourage Mid.

"Fine," he said between gritted teeth, receiving a smug look from his sister.

Holstering her pistols, Mid swaggered back to her rock giant. "C'mon, Bear. Let's blow this plasma stand. Our job is done."

As they left, Yano came up beside Kanta. "Hey man, I know you're pissed right now, so don't get mad at me for saying this, but your sister sure can shoot!"

"I totally agree, Bear! It was uncool of Kanta to blow up like that!"

Mid and Bear were on their way through the city, back to camp. Mid spun her pistols leisurely as she ranted.

"I mean, way to be a hypocrite, right? He's always broken way worse rules than that. Like, remember how this whole thing with the stupid siblings started? Yeah, total worse-than-what-I-just-did rule breaking on behalf of my idiot brother. Like always, Bear, you're the only one who gets me. Not like Kanta ever tries anyway—"

Mid stopped both walking and spinning her pistols. The rock giant halted just behind her, but Mid still whispered, "Hold up, Bear."

In the distance, weaving between the ruins, was a pack of hellcats. They hadn't spotted Mid yet and didn't seem to be heading in her direction. Mid stood perfectly still, watching the cats dart from one building to another. An alarming number of them—a larger pack than Mid had ever seen.

By the time the hellcats were gone, Mid's heart was hammering in her chest. She kept her voice low. "Should we keep going, Bear?"

Bear didn't move.

"I agree. Let's go wait for Kanta and the others. To escort them, of course. I mean, if they have a hellcat encounter they'll need us there. Good thinking, Bear."

Bear was content at Mid's praise.

Carefully, the two retraced their steps. Mid kept an ear out for hisses or snarls. They'd barely gotten three steps when she heard a swishing sound.

Tensing, Mid spun around. There was nothing on the road ahead of her, but she thought she glimpsed a movement in one of the buildings. On the second floor, through a crumbling window pane. A flash of colour.

"Did you see that, Bear?"

Bear didn't say anything.

"Yeah, me neither." Mid shivered. "Let's go meet the others."

Mid reasoned that fatigue was causing her to be spooked and that the movement in the building must have been her imagination. After all, hellcats weren't white.

Chapter VII

The trainees had been on the road for a week. It had taken Tai awhile to readjust to the travelling life, but she was nearly there. She still missed the real bed back at the dorms. Even if it hadn't been comfortable, it was better than blankets over rocky ground.

Their party moved with just three caravans: one for tent supplies, one for kitchen equipment and food stocks, and one for their weapons and plasma. Their group consisted of 12 trainees, two instructors, and a tech from the Association. Tai knew that this was the composition of all groups that had been sent out. Several of the group had left through the City gates on the same day, all headed in different directions for their field test.

"This is boring," Korel grumbled. It was nearly evening and they were on the road, walking by one of the caravans. "When are we actually going to start training?"

They *had* been training. Everything they'd done so far had been part of their field test, which was an evaluation not just of hunting skills but travelling adaptation and efficiency. Tai didn't say this, however. Normally Gareth would—in as kindly and as long-winded a way as possible—but he was learning how to drive a caravan, with one of their instructors. They were all being taught, in rotation.

"I'm sure we'll get to go hunting soon," Silsa said optimistically. "They just want to get us used to the road first."

"I'd get used to it if I knew when it was going to end. I'm sick of travelling and setting up tents and taking them down and walking. I want to kill ghosts!"

"You think you're the only one?" Damian asked. He was walking a little too close to Tai, while everyone else was evenly spaced out. "It's called a field test, Kor. They won't just be testing us on hunting; they're testing us on everything in the field. So stop complaining if you don't want to fail."

"I'm just saying what all of you are thinking!"

"Yeah, we know." Silsa squeezed Korel's shoulder in an attempt to placate her. "We're all tired of travelling, and we all want to hunt."

"We're not all tired. But I won't argue about wanting to hunt," Damian confirmed. "It feels like forever since I held a shotgun."

"You won't have long to wait." Gareth walked up to them, shadowed by Mao.

"Why?" Damian asked.

"Kassa told me while she was showing me how to drive the caravan. She said we'll reach our destination tonight and make camp for the next week. She said if we get there soon enough, and she and Os have time to do a preliminary check of the haunted area, we might even get to start hunting tonight!"

Korel and Damian perked up at this. Even Silsa looked excited. Tai couldn't share in their enthusiasm. Even if she had once felt that way about her own version of hunting, she no longer did. What she was doing now was her job, nothing more.

"Did Kassa give any details about the Area?" Damian asked.

"Not many. She said it's a phantom village, and

the ghost population is low enough and weak enough that it'll be a good training area."

"So they're training us to fight weak ghosts?" Damian continued.

Gareth shrugged. "A ghost's a ghost, right?"

"Are we going to get to fight any mini-bosses?" Korel asked. In a haunted area like Gareth had described, the bosses were usually too weak to be categorized as actual bosses and instead were called mini-bosses.

"Kassa said we will."

Korel clapped her hands. "This is going to be fantastic!"

"I thought you were bored and tired," Damian inserted dryly.

"When did I say that?" Korel quickened her pace. "Come on guys! You heard Gareth! The sooner we get there, the sooner Kassa lets us hunt!"

"I doubt your walking faster is going to make the horses do the same," Damian stated, but Korel just waved him off, not faltering in her stride.

Kassa and Os left the trainees to make camp and went off to check the phantom village, which they'd passed at a distance earlier. It had been difficult to make out many details in the darkness, except for the hulking outline of the wall.

The trainees had finished pitching the tents and unloading the kitchen equipment when their instructors returned. Kassa had been a trainer at the Association for years, since an injury sustained while hunting in her youth had left her with a limp. She could still train other hunters and take them in the field to haunted areas with low ghost infestation, but she could no longer function as a regular hunter. Still, Tai thought she made a good instructor. Os, in his late 30s, was younger than Kassa by almost 20 years. He'd chosen to become an instructor after five years of hunting in the field—enough experience to allow him to teach.

"We'll be taking a group of six into the phantom village tonight," Kassa told the trainees when they had assembled. She nodded to their tech. "The rest of you will stay here with Nona and guard. Volunteers?"

Korel and Damian immediately volunteered. Silsa was about to step forward, but Gareth discreetly put a hand on her shoulder. Tai heard him whisper, "Wait for it ..."

Kassa smiled wickedly at the trainees who'd stepped forward. "Thank you for volunteering. Nona appreciates it, I'm sure."

It took the trainees a moment to realize they hadn't volunteered to hunt but to stay and guard the camp. Gareth, Tai noticed, looked amused as he softly clapped Silsa on the shoulder, and then withdrew his hand.

"Get your gear and meet us by the caravans," Kassa told everyone else. "You have five minutes."

The group dispersed, leaving behind angry volunteers.

"You should have known, guys." Gareth shook his head at Korel and Damian. "After so long with Kassa, you just should have known."

At the weapons caravan, Gareth dug through their cache and produced a pair of pistols, then his own shotgun. "I agree with Damian: I've missed my baby."

"He didn't put it quite like that," Silsa reminded him.

"Then he didn't truly appreciate how heart-wrenching the separation was." Gareth stroked the side of the shotgun, murmuring, "I love you."

Tai rolled her eyes. Gareth caught her.

"Excuse me, milady. Does my affection not meet with your approval?"

"You just remind me of Kanta when you act like that."

Gareth's mouth opened in surprise, closed, and opened again. "You mean that?"

Tai continued to search for her gun, refusing to answer. She shouldn't have said anything in the first place, but she couldn't help it. Still, she tried not to bring Kanta or the others up—ever. Especially in front of Gareth, Unit Q17's number one fan.

Suddenly Tai realized someone was pushing her gun toward her.

"Yours."

Tai accepted it, glancing at Mao, who was still searching for his own weapon. "Thanks."

He didn't reply.

Heath, another trainee, had climbed into the caravan to look around. He appeared with a box, offering its contents to the others. "Goggles, anyone?"

Nobody in their group had ghost eyes, so everyone grabbed a pair. There was enough left over for all the other trainees, as well as extras. Next, the box of plasma vials and plasma bullets was circulated. Mao was the only one who needed the bullets. There were two other rifle users, aside from Kassa, but they'd volunteered to guard the camp.

Gareth fit his goggles over his glasses, scrunching up his nose to push everything in place. "Does this look extremely odd?"

"Not at all," Silsa assured him, pulling on her own goggles.

"Yes," Tai said.

"Thank you for your honesty, milady."

Tai frowned, but not at Gareth. She'd managed to yank her goggles down and pull her ponytail above them but she was having trouble loosening the strap.

"Want help?" Silsa asked.

"Yeah."

Silsa reached up to adjust the band. Just as she was about to, a memory flashed—it wasn't Silsa, but her brother, gently fixing the band of her goggles, eyes crinkled with amusement, bright green plasma splattered on his back where she'd shot him.

Abruptly, Tai pulled away. Silsa was surprised. "Sorry, was I making it tighter?"

Tai shook her head, mumbling her thanks as she tugged the strap down a little. Before Silsa could say anything else, Gareth handed out needles of Surreality Serum, the clear liquid that, if injected properly and quickly after an attempted soul rip by a ghost, could save a person's life.

When they were finally ready, they met with Kassa and Os, who led them to the phantom village. As they walked, the instructors reviewed the basic ghost-hunting protocol and tips they'd been taught in training. Outside the village walls, they stopped.

"You'll be divided into groups of two and assigned to a house," Kassa explained. "Os and I will wait in the street. Should you have a problem, call us or, should you be unable to do that, come and get us. Barring that, only come to us when you've finished cleaning the house. We'll then assign you a new one."

Kassa paired them: Tai and Silsa, Gareth and Mao, and Heath and the last of their group, Erik. Os made sure everyone had their WTs set to communicate with their partner, and their partner only. Kassa explained that she would have her own WT set on the same channel as Tai and Silsa should they need to contact her, and Os would have his channel set to communicate with the other team.

Kassa advised Gareth and Mao, "If you two have a problem, just scroll up one channel and you'll be able to contact me. Otherwise, stay on your own channel, or you'll interfere with another team."

Before they went in, Kassa added, "All of this is only a precaution; these ghosts shouldn't be problematic for you. Having said that, it's your first time hunting in the field. If you have any trouble, contact us."

Kassa waited until everyone nodded their understanding and led the way into the village.

Tai tried not to look around. It was obvious this had been a New World village because of the wall and empty plasma lanterns, which Kassa said had malfunctioned. Tai didn't want to look at the details of the houses and shops and think about the people who had lived here, who had lost their homes and probably their lives to the ghosts.

When they were assigned a building, Silsa let Tai go first. Even though her partner only had a pistol, Tai carried her automatic. It was far more cumbersome than the pistol, especially to carry around through the house, but its weight comforted her. Tai could almost imagine that the weapon was red instead of black and held something much hotter than plasma.

Tai squeezed her eyes shut and waited a moment before opening them. She couldn't think about that. That part of her life was over.

But when Tai shoved the door open and took her first step into the front hall, she couldn't help that part of her that had been trained to search. Even after two years, it was as sharp and accurate as ever.

Upstairs. The first room on the left. Something in the corner. Something small.

Over her shoulder, Tai told Silsa, "I'll take the first floor, you go upstairs."

Silsa looked like she was about to protest—they were to stay together, Kassa had said—but something in Tai's expression made her clamp her mouth shut, and nod. Silsa was on the first step of the stairs when she stopped, gasping.

"Did you feel that? The ghosts!"

It took Tai a moment to realize that Silsa had just felt the ghosts wake up, like Kanta had said he could—like he'd said all hunters could. But Tai couldn't.

"Yeah." She headed down the hall without looking back.

Even if she couldn't feel the ghosts, Tai could see them, thanks to her plasma goggles. They stood out: a pale cyan against the slight green tint of her goggles. The first one drifted through a door to her right, oblivious of her presence. Tai mistakely looked at its head, and for a split second she panicked, seeing the wispy tendrils of long hair, floating around the ghost like seaweed under water. Then it turned its head toward her. Tai caught a glimpse of a nose in the mess of ethereal cyan hair, and that snapped her out of her stupor. Before she could see the face, Tai fired her gun, shooting plasma right through the side of the ghost. It dissolved before it could scream.

Taking a breath and waiting for her heartbeat to return to normal, Tai pressed on. She'd warned herself repeatedly over the years that when the day came when she was finally hunting in the field, she couldn't look at the ghosts' faces. The rest, sure—

their torsos looked more or less the same, a vaguely humanoid form ending in wisps that hovered above the ground—but not faces.

She didn't know how other hunters could do it: kill ghosts with human faces down to the finest detail.

Tai knew it would be difficult to fight bosses without looking at their heads, but she'd have partners to help in boss fights. She could be the distraction, and they could kill. Of course, she wouldn't tell her partner her problem—or any other hunter, for that matter. Kanta had told her, after all, that all hunters went through troubles after facing their first ghosts, but they got over it. She hadn't, and she wouldn't let that get in the way of supporting her family. She'd make it work. Maybe get over it, eventually.

But not yet. For now she just wouldn't look at their faces.

That worked for the rest of the house, which she and Silsa cleaned quickly. By the time Tai was done the first floor, Silsa was waiting in the hall, eyes wide and shining with exhilaration behind her goggles.

"Done?" she breathed.

Tai nodded, sliding another plasma vial into her gun. "Let's go."

The next several houses went much the same. Tai would direct Silsa to the level or rooms opposite of where she sensed the heart. Silsa obliged. There were few ghosts, and those that were there didn't seem alert to Tai, so it went smoothly and quickly. Tai found it boring. It was like hide-and-seek, except when she found what she was looking for, she shot it with plasma. The ghosts never noticed her in time to fight back.

Silsa, on the other hand, found it thrilling. When

they finished their next house, she enthused to Tai, "Don't you find their screams amazing? I mean, really scary, but in a good way, since it means we got them?"

Screams? Tai hadn't heard any screams the whole night. In fact, it had been eerily silent. But she simply nodded.

"It's almost The Hour," Kassa said when they came out. The other pair was already there, while Gareth and Mao were still in their last house.

"Does that mean we're going back?" Erik asked.

"You've all done well tonight," Kassa said. "Os and I have decided to split you into two groups and send you back to one of the houses you already cleaned. Even if these bosses won't be as powerful as most bosses, it's still better to send you out in larger groups."

Silsa took Tai's arm when she heard this, squeezing it tightly, smiling from ear to ear. The other trainees looked just as excited. Tai envied them.

When Gareth and Mao returned, Kassa and Os broke up the pairs and put one from each in a group. Tai was with Mao and Erik. Silsa seemed slightly annoyed at being separated from Tai, and Tai was surprised to realize she felt the same.

"Don't worry, milady," Gareth whispered mock-seriously to Tai as the trainees walked back to the houses Kassa and Os had chosen. "I'll protect Lady Silsa, your royal subject, with my life."

Tai couldn't help a slight smile at Gareth's foolishness. Gareth was delighted at seeing her smile, tapping Silsa on the shoulder and gesturing to Tai. "Look! I've gotten her divine approval! Finally, after two years!"

The groups split. Silsa sent Tai an encouraging smile, while Gareth gave them two thumbs up.

"You have 10 minutes," Kassa told Tai's group. "Familiarize yourselves with the house, if you didn't hunt there before, and make a plan. Your WTs will go off at Hallow Hour. Make sure your guns are fully loaded."

Tai, Erik, and Mao entered the house Erik and Heath had cleaned earlier.

Tai felt it instantly—faint but definitely present. Not on their level, but not on the second level either. It was coming from somewhere below …

"Is there a basement?" Tai asked Erik.

"No, just the two levels. There were more ghosts on the second floor, so I think the boss will appear upstairs. We should set up there, in the hallway. One of us can wait at the bottom of the stairs." Erik said to Mao, "Use your pistols, okay? The house is too small for a rifle."

Mao already had his pistols drawn. Tai wondered if he'd used his rifle at all that night. None of the houses had really been big enough for the gun, which Mao had likely already deduced. Still, he didn't seem annoyed at Erik for stating it. He didn't wear any expression.

"Are you sure there isn't a basement?" Tai asked again. "Or a cellar?"

"Yes, I'm sure. Why?"

"I was just wondering if you'd checked the whole house."

"We checked enough."

"But what if you missed a ghost?"

"Missed a ghost?" Erik was incredulous. "How can you miss a ghost? The few that were here swarmed us when we came in. It's not like they hide."

Tai didn't respond, and Erik started up the stairs. Mao, Tai realized, watched her through his bangs.

"Something to say?" she demanded.

He kept his mouth shut and went after Erik. Frustrated, Tai followed them. In the end, Erik reasoned he and Tai should stay on the second floor and wait for the boss, since they both had faster-firing and bigger guns. Mao would wait at the bottom of the stairs, in case it tried to escape.

They had a few minutes before The Hour. Tai, positioned in the doorway of a bedroom, was trying to ignore the tugging sensation coming from floors below her.

"Hey," Erik called, from the back of the hall, "you ever hunt before?"

"What do you mean?"

"You were travelling with Unit Q17, right? You ever hunt with them?"

Tai wanted to pull her hair. Of course that's what Erik meant. It's what everyone meant when they asked her that kind of question. She was sick of it.

Before Tai could come up with an answer, Erik's eyes widened. It took her a split second to realize it was the same expression Silsa had worn on and off all night, the one that meant a ghost had awakened. In this case, *the boss*.

Erik brought his gun up, scanning the walls around them as the WT alarm blared. They heard Mao fire his gun. Suddenly, the boss flew up the stairs, right toward Erik. Shocked, Erik fired, spraying its shoulder with plasma. Where the plasma touched fizzled and the boss recoiled, swerving into the bedroom next to Tai. It went through the wall, into the room behind her. Tai whirled around in time to fire at its stomach, causing it to retreat back through the wall. A second later, Tai heard Erik shouting in the hallway. She ran out just as the boss ripped through him and into the floor. Erik collapsed.

Tai ran over to him, calling out and shaking his shoulder. Cursing, Tai whipped out her WT just as Mao came up behind her. He stared at Erik.

"He got soul-ripped," Tai explained quickly. She spoke then into her WT. "We need help—"

"They won't come," Mao said. "I just saw them go into the other house."

"Shit." Tai dropped her WT and dug the Surreality needle out of her belt pouch. Just as she did, the boss flew through the floor right in front of her. Tai jerked backward, dropping the needle and knocking into Mao, causing him to trip. The boss hovered over them, short, curly hair fizzing in a halo around its head. Tai stared at the face. It wasn't very old— maybe a few years younger than Tai herself—and had dark freckles speckling its cheeks. The eyes bore into Tai, swirling cyan and dead black. But even that couldn't keep Tai from staring at the face. There was something about it—

Just as the boss was about to dive through Tai in a soul rip, a plasma bullet whizzed over her head and through the boss's own, through its left eye. It opened its mouth, as if in a shriek, and then disappeared into the floor.

Tai felt her arm being pulled. Mao was up, and he had his rifle under one arm. "Come on. It's going to try and take us down like Erik if we stay here. We have to banish it before we help him."

Tai got to her feet. "Where is it?"

Mao didn't ask why she couldn't sense the boss. "It's flying between the three levels, not staying in one place. If it can't sneak up on us again, I think it's going to continue running away until The Hour's over."

Mao didn't add what both of them were thinking: then it would be too late to wake up Erik. But if they stayed and tried to revive him, the boss would attack again. They had to find a way to catch and banish it before The Hour was up, but Tai didn't see how they could do that. They couldn't exactly fly through walls like the ghosts could.

Then again, they didn't have to catch it, did they? They just needed to get rid of it.

"Do you have any matches?" Tai asked. All trainees were supposed to carry matches, as well as other basic survival equipment, but Tai had left hers back at camp, unsure if she'd be able to resist the temptation.

Mao shook his head. Tai turned back to Erik. He was wearing the same kind of belt as Tai, with an attached pouch for his needle and a hook for his WT and an extra pouch for plasma vials and other small items. Digging through it, Tai's heart sped up when her hand closed around a fistful of matches.

"Keep the boss busy." Tai started down the stairs. "Keep it away from me for the next five minutes."

Hopefully five minutes was all it would take. Following its heartbeat, Tai found a trapdoor in the kitchen. Seconds after she shoved it up to reveal dusty stairs winding into a dark cellar, the boss flew through the wall in front of Tai.

And right through Tai.

Catching her breath, Tai's head snapped around when she heard gunfire. Mao was in the kitchen doorway, shooting at the boss until it retreated into the ceiling. She quickly ducked into the cellar. Mao probably hadn't seen what had happened, Tai told herself, but, even if he had, that wasn't something she could deal with now.

Thanks to her plasma goggles, Tai was able to see around the cellar. It was small, and had been used for storage. Mao came down the stairs behind her, but didn't say anything. He kept his eyes and rifle trained on the ceiling.

The heartbeat was even louder now, pulling her toward one of the shelves, and a tiny wooden box. It wasn't the box itself, but what was inside. Opening it Tai found a shrivelled flower that looked like it would dissolve at a touch. But ashes would remain, and so would the boss.

Striking a match, Tai dropped the seed of fire into the box. Closed it.

At Mao's shooting, Tai turned to see the boss dive at her. Stumbling out of the way, Tai watched as the boss flew right up to the box, where it hovered, wispy blue arms reaching out as if to touch the object. Slowly, its head turned toward Tai, revealing two misty eyes crinkled in sadness. The third eye, however, continued to spit angry black fire. Then the boss opened its mouth in a shriek Tai couldn't hear and shot toward her. Just before it made contact, its face became etched with terror and, as if made of glass, shattered into a thousand pieces. Each piece dissolved into cyan mist before touching the ground. Then, nothing.

Tai couldn't move for a moment, heart hammering against her chest. She strode over to the box and knocked it off the shelf. It opened on the floor, spilling its fiery contents, which she quickly stomped out. Tai looked up to find Mao staring at her.

"We need to go wake Erik." Tai headed for the stairs. Mao, however, was standing in the way.

"How did you do that?"

Of course he wanted an explanation. Just as Kanta had.

Except Mao *wasn't* Kanta. He was quiet, reserved, and, besides that, two years younger than her. She could deal with him.

"I'm going to go help Erik. Can you move?"

Mao realized for the first time that he was in the way. He stepped aside, and Tai hurried up the stairs. She heard him follow.

Erik was still mind-deep in Surreality. Tai reached for her needle, but remembered she'd dropped it earlier. She couldn't see it anywhere in the hall.

Before she asked, Mao was kneeling on the other side of Erik, needle in hand. As Mao lined up the middle eye, Tai positioned herself to brace Erik, as they'd been trained to do. Mao slipped the needle into Erik's forehead and the liquid drained under his skin.

Mao had just taken away the needle when Erik shot up, out of Tai's hold. She hadn't been prepared for his waking so suddenly. They'd been taught to expect convulsing. But, Tai reasoned, Erik had been soul-ripped by a mini-boss without the strength to plunge their victims too far into Surreality.

"What happened?" Erik asked, dazed. "Where's the boss?"

"Banished," Tai informed him.

"How …"

"She banished it," Mao said, surprising both of them, "after you got soul-ripped."

"I got soul-ripped?" Erik was stunned.

"Yes." Mao got to his feet. "We need to report in."

He headed for the stairs without looking back. Tai got up too but waited for Erik, who was having trouble finding his feet. She didn't help him. If he hadn't been so dismissive of her questions about a third level to the house, she could have persuaded them to wait there for the boss, which always surfaced at Hallow Hour from the object that contained its heart. Then they wouldn't have been ambushed and stuck upstairs, and Erik wouldn't have been soul-ripped.

Tai remembered something. Mao had said there were three levels to the house, after Erik had been soul-ripped. Was it because he'd believed her, or because he'd known? The only way that would be possible was if he could sense something in the cellar: the boss's heart—which was impossible—or the boss itself.

Hunters didn't have senses that acute, though. They could sense the relative proximity of a boss, but they couldn't know exactly where it was, nor place it on a building level. The only person Tai knew with such acute senses was her sister—Paige.

Chapter VIII

A lmost a week had passed since the incident at the mall. Since then, Kanta had barely spoken to Mid. When he did, he wouldn't look at her, and his tone was totally dismissive. Even if Kanta hadn't gone to Thalus, his disapproval was apparent.

But Kanta hadn't paid that much attention to her before, anyway. He had his friends now—which was fine with Mid. She had her soulmate, Bear, something Kanta would never have, nor understand. Mid also had Wendy, even if he was busier than usual with tech responsibilities.

Kanta's behaviour still pissed Mid off. Not because she wanted his attention but because he was being a hypocrite. For almost a year, Kanta had been sneaking off to village taverns with his friends and staying out half the night partying. Mid not only made sure he got back in time to stay out of trouble but also did so without shunning him or showing her disapproval. Without showing the full depth of it, anyway.

Now, after Mid had done one little thing against protocol, Kanta wasn't letting her live it down. It just wasn't fair.

They were less than a week away from the port city from which they would sail to Hunters City. Thalus came up to Kanta and Mid one afternoon when they'd stopped for a break, not far from a village. Knowing they liked to do the supply runs, Thalus had fallen into the habit of always giving them that job.

Usually Mid was pleased with this but, with Kanta in his current mood, she was far from happy.

Thalus gave Kanta the list and Kanta, Mid, and Browen headed for the village. Kanta ignored Mid in favour of talking to his friend about one of their hunts at a haunted city—not the one on which Mid had intruded—while Browen kept glancing at Mid, as if wondering why she wasn't part of their conversation.

At least Kanta had only taken Browen. He probably would have tried to get Yano and Freid to come too, if they hadn't been hooked into cooking lunch. Mid was considering buying something to eat at the village. When Freid or Yano were on any duty involving food, there was no guarantee anything would be made on time. When they'd last worked together to make dinner, Freid had gotten so fed up with Yano he'd walked out before they were done. Thalus hadn't reprimanded him. Maybe their commander knew how difficult it was to work with Kanta's mischievous, loudmouth friend.

Just inside the village wall Kanta handed Mid half the list. "Meet here in an hour."

Mid read the list. By the time she'd done, Kanta was already walking away. "You want me to get the horse feed? I can't carry that on my own!"

"Sure you can. Besides, you like doing stuff on your own."

"Bear was with me!" Mid yelled at him. Kanta kept walking. Browen leaned in and said something, glancing uncertainly back at Mid, but Kanta just shook his head.

Mid balled up her hands, crushing the list. What right did Kanta have to act like this? Just because she'd done something he didn't like, something that could have been a *bit* dangerous. But she'd been fine, and Bear had been with her. Mid wasn't a 12-year-old junior hunter anymore, stumbling through haunted houses she'd divided up with her big brother, searching tirelessly for a boss to kill. Mid was 15, an official field trainee, allowed to clean small buildings on her own with Bear, and she *had* already killed her first boss. That one in the mall had been her fifth! Kanta needed to treat her with respect and realize that Mid could take care of herself.

Besides, if he'd taken her along on the mall clearing—which Thalus likely would have allowed, with some begging—she wouldn't have had to sneak in. But Kanta had wanted his guy time.

Just like now. Kanta would rather hang around with his friend than explore the village with his little sister. He and Browen probably wouldn't even pick up their half of the list until they were just about to leave, instead wasting time in a tavern, even if it was the middle of the day.

Mid was furious as she went through the village, buying supplies with the money Thalus had given her. It took her longer than she'd expected to find everything on her own, and, by the time she had only the horse feed left, she knew she wouldn't have any time to look around. Kanta had given her the longer part of the list.

Fine. Mid could play that game too. Next time Kanta went out with his friends and didn't come back with them, she wouldn't go get him. He could cover his own ass.

The village stables were, as expected, located at the back of the inn and tavern. Almost every town and village had stables as most travellers owned horses that would need food and rest. Horse feed could be purchased at the stables, although sometimes the proprietor overcharged. That was fine. Mid was in a bartering mood.

She walked around the back of the inn. As she did, a caravan came into view, parked in front of the stables, horses harnessed and waiting.

"I'm sorry you have to go so soon." A deep, male voice came from within the stables.

"It can't be helped," a younger male voice replied. "Hunters were spotted nearby this morning. Boss says we need to move out."

"I understand. Any idea when you'll be back in these parts?"

"Not that I can say. You folks should be good though, for a while. You have enough to last you the next six months. If we aren't back by then, someone else is bound to pass through."

"I hope you're right."

The two men exchanged farewells, and Mid ducked behind the caravan just as the young man left the stables. He was tall and broad, with cropped golden hair and a square jaw. He climbed into the driver's seat and took up the reins. Mid backed up as the horses took off at a trot, pulling the caravan away. As it left, Mid stepped forward, trying to peek into the back of the caravan. All she could see were large metal containers.

What had that been about?

Questions swirled through Mid's head, and she immediately wanted to tell Kanta. She shook off the urge. Whatever it was, it probably wasn't that important. Kanta would say it was nothing and call her a kid for being concerned. If Kite was still with them, she could have talked to him about it, but he wasn't, and she didn't want to bother Wendy with something that might have just been a trivial conversation.

That left Bear. She'd discuss it with Bear. He might have some ideas.

Mid waited a moment before entering the stable, making sure her plasma goggles and any other obvious hunter signs were in her bag, just in case.

Chapter IX

During the week, after she dropped off the little twins at school, and before she picked them up, Paige worked at a florist's shop near the Eastern Market. It was one of the more expensive shops in the market; flowers were becoming less common all the time in the New World. Still, the demand was higher than Paige had expected, and the shop was in excellent condition. It even had glass window displays.

The job was a good way for Paige to earn money so that she and her family weren't entirely dependant on Regailia. It also kept her busy. She enjoyed taking care of the flowers and arranging them. She'd gotten to know the regular customers. Her employers, an older couple with no children of their own, treated all their workers kindly.

Paige also liked the florist's shop because it reminded her of her mother, who had been a herbalist. Of the children, Paige had been the only one interested in her mother's work, and she hoped one day to become a herbalist herself. She still remembered the afternoons of her childhood when her mother had taken her outside the village walls to the small forest down the road. She had shown Paige what to collect for certain cures and ointments, which herbs had what properties, and what was poisonous and should not be touched or eaten. During those afternoons her mother had taught her how to make charms, for luck, protection, good health—but sometimes for evil.

"Curses are real, Paige," her mother had insisted. They'd been sitting on a blanket of leaves in the forest, their harvest for the day spread before them. Her mother had picked up a small speckled mushroom. "This is poison, but only to the mind, and only when properly employed with other elements. It is only part of the poison."

"Poison for ghosts?" Paige had asked unsurely, for her mother had been teaching her how to make charms that would dispel and harm ghosts.

"No, not ghosts."

Paige's mother had showed her how to make the poison charm but would not explain how it worked. She'd merely said, "If any human causes you harm or unhappiness, darling, then you need only give them this charm—slip it into their pocket, or hide it in their room—and they will cause you unhappiness no more."

Paige had been curious but couldn't bring herself to ask any questions. After all, why would a living person ever try to harm her? Weren't ghosts the bad ones?

Months after that lesson, when she and her mother had been in the forest again, her mother had asked, "Paige, are you happy?"

That had been after the death of their grandmother. Although Paige was still mourning, she was adjusting. She still had the rest of her family, and, all things considered, she had thought she was happy. Especially when she was out in the forest with her mother. Paige liked the forest.

She'd told her mother all of this.

"Good," her mother had said, wearing a more serious expression than usual. "I'm going to show you how to keep that happiness."

That afternoon, they had collected not the usual

herbs and mushrooms but flowers. Her mother had brought some blossoms from their home garden as well. When they had reached the clearing and sat down, Paige watched her mother sort the flowers into piles. She pointed out each pile to Paige, naming the flowers and explaining their properties, from healing to charm potential. Then she took a petal from each pile and put them together in a napkin, which she handed to Paige.

"You must let them dry. Then, grind them up together into a fine powder. Sprinkle this powder on the ground that is causing your unhappiness."

"What do you mean?"

"If someone is causing you unhappiness, then you sprinkle this powder where they dwell, and leave for a night. All your troubles will be gone in the morning."

"Will it hurt them?"

Her mother had given her a sad smile and reached over to tuck a stray strand of hair behind Paige's ear. "Darling, you must understand, your happiness is the most important thing, not the happiness of other people. In the end, your only responsibility in life is to keep yourself happy. And you must do whatever you have to—no matter how hard it seems—to preserve that happiness."

Paige hadn't understood her mother's words, but she'd nodded and put the petals away. Maybe one day, when she was older, she'd know what her mother meant, or have the courage to ask her.

The next night, Paige and the little twins had gone to a sleepover at a friend's house, since their father was in the middle of one of his curse-induced fits, rambling nonsense and thrashing about while wailing his dead sister's name. Tai and Brighton had been out late at their grandmother's house, putting the finishing touches on the interior, oblivious to trouble at home.

That night, while Paige was away playing with her friends, her home had caught on fire. Her mother and father had perished in the flames. So had the petals.

Paige shook herself, realizing she'd been staring at the same bouquet for ages, hands poised to add some fireweed. Paige paused and assessed the bouquet. She'd used some of her mother's favourite flowers. Deciding against the fireweed, since her mother had never been partial to it, Paige wrapped up the bouquet and positioned it in the centre of the display case. Someone knocked on the window in front of her and Paige started, almost tipping over a row of flowers. Seeing a familiar face, Paige offered a sheepish smile.

The bell over the door chimed as Paige climbed out from behind the display. She was just in time to meet a regular, a man with light brown hair and dark blue eyes. He was in his early 30s and visited whenever he was in the City selling his wares.

"You've done a lovely job." Basil gestured to the display. "As usual."

"Thank you. I didn't know you were in the City."

"We arrived last night," Basil explained, referring to his travelling companions, who helped him run his stall. Paige had met Basil in the market, attracted by his stall, which sold remedies that reminded her of those her mother had made.

"How have you been?" Basil looked at the bouquets. "How's your family?"

"Good! I—we've been good. My sister left for her field test the weekend before last. I haven't heard from her yet, but I'm sure she's doing well."

"You're worried?"

"Yeah," Paige admitted, twisting her apron in front of her. "I know she'll be fine, but … I can't help it."

"I understand. My family worries about me when I leave for the City. It's to be expected."

Paige had expected to be worried about Tai, but she still didn't like that she felt that way. She knew that her sister could handle herself, and had been doing so for years.

"That bouquet you just put out, in the display? Before I leave, do you think you could make a similar one for me?"

"Of course. Would you like me to add anything? Baby's breath?"

"No, it's perfect as it is. Those are her favourite colours."

Paige didn't ask who he meant. Basil often mentioned a woman back at his town, whom Paige assumed was his wife. When he spoke about her, Basil's face took on a dreamy expression.

"You love her a lot, don't you?" Paige had asked him once, then chastised herself for being so impertinent. Basil hadn't minded, though.

"Yes," he'd said. "I'd do whatever she wanted of me."

Paige had found that very romantic. She couldn't recall ever meeting an adult like Basil, who seemed so happy and dedicated in his relationship. Her parents had certainly never acted that way, not that she could remember. Then again, her father had been spiralling toward insanity even before Paige was born. What her parent's relationship had been like before the curse took effect, she would never know.

"She'd like you," Basil told Paige. "If you ever want to take my offer, I'm sure the two of you would get along."

Paige gave him an apologetic smile. After learning that Paige had both experience and interest in herbalist work, Basil had offered her a job at his stall. Paige had been excited, but when she learned it would involve travelling from town to town, she had to refuse. She couldn't leave her family. Basil had understood.

He understood now, too, seeing Paige's expression. "I know you can't. I'm just saying it's too bad, and if you ever change your mind …"

"I'd like to, but I don't think I will. If you ever need someone to help while you're in the city, though, I'd be happy to."

"Yes, thank you. I might need your help one of these days. Come visit our stall this week. We have a few new products on which I'd like your opinion."

"I will! And I'll make you that bouquet, when you need it. I'm not sure it'll last until you get back home, though …"

"That's okay." Basil smiled, a smile Paige found comforting. "She doesn't mind if they're shrivelled. She says she prefers them that way, if I'm the one bringing them."

Basil left, waving at her through the display case. Paige had just enough time to wave back before another customer came in, and she returned to work.

Chapter X

Five days had passed since Tai had killed the boss. In that time she'd gone back to the ghost village twice, and the hunting had gone smoothly. The first time she was paired with Gareth; the second, Korel. The groups she'd been put in for taking out the bosses had included Silsa once. She hadn't hunted with Mao again. She hadn't spoken to him.

He hadn't approached her. Instead of feeling relief, Tai was unnerved. Kassa and Os hadn't taken her aside to ask any questions. Mao couldn't have mentioned her strange behaviour to them, and none of the others had brought it up. Had Mao kept it to himself?

It was their final night in the village, which by now was almost entirely cleared. Kassa and Os wouldn't be going with the trainees this time; it was a final test to see how they could function on their own. Both instructors stayed with the tech to guard camp, dividing the 12 trainees into two groups to clear the remaining buildings which were the largest and likely to have the strongest mini-bosses. Tai's group was assigned the conjoined inn and tavern, the other group the village hall.

Tai's team included Silsa, Gareth, Damian, Korel, and Mao. She tried to find an opportunity to pull Mao aside, but it was impossible. He was glued to Gareth, while Damian seemed determined to keep Tai in his line of vision, as this was the first time they'd hunted together.

"What a shabby place." Korel kicked at a tavern stool as she shot a ghost with her pistol. "No wonder the villagers abandoned it."

"They didn't necessarily abandon it," Gareth pointed out, reloading his shotgun. "It's possible the majority was caught in the ghost invasion, and the ghosts we're banishing at this moment are the villagers in question."

"Thanks, jerk. Now I feel bad about this."

"I don't see why. All ghosts were once people but retain none of their former memories. We aren't hurting the humans themselves, because they no longer exist as individuals."

"How exactly do you know that?" Korel demanded. "Did you interview a ghost?"

"I read it at the archives. The documents there really are fascinating. When we return to the city, I'd be happy to show you the articles."

"How could I pass that up?" Korel responded dryly.

"More plasma, less talking." Damian shot a ghost Gareth had missed. They'd entered through the tavern and hadn't had time to explore before the ghosts converged.

"I'm pulling my weight!" Korel snapped. "I've taken down six already!"

Damian frowned, but didn't reply. He hadn't gotten as many, Tai realized. A moment later, Gareth shot the last ghost and everyone lowered their weapons.

"There were a lot of them!" Silsa wiped her forehead with her sleeve.

"This is the tavern," Damian emphasized. "If I was trapped in a village full of ghosts, I'd want to spend my last moments here."

"Whatever." Korel pushed herself up on a stool to reload. She tried to jam her plasma vials into the magazine, but was having trouble. "Gareth, help me with this."

"Yes, ma'am." Gareth pushed himself up next to Korel. Taking her gun, he was about to accept the vials but pointed out, "Those are the wrong kind."

"They're the ones you gave me when you handed around the ammo."

"Ah. My mistake, then."

Korel swatted his shoulder. "What am I supposed to use if my gun's not working?"

"I could loan you mine—"

"I don't want your dumb shotgun!"

"*Dumb* shotgun?" Damian also used a shotgun.

"Yes! Dumb! Automatics are so much better …"

Tai checked her WT. They still had plenty of time before Hallow Hour to strategize for the boss and explore the rest of the inn. For now, though, the others were distracted with their own conversation. Even Silsa was completely absorbed.

This was probably the best chance she'd get.

Mao still hadn't moved from where he'd shot his last ghost, busily filling his pistols and checking that his rifle was fully loaded. He didn't notice when Tai came up behind him.

"Can we talk for a sec?"

Mao, surprised, nodded, and slung his rifle over his shoulder. He followed Tai.

Standing in the inn's front hall, Tai closed the tavern doors as quietly as she could and then turned to Mao. "Have you told anyone about what happened the other night?"

Mao shook his head.

Tai glared at him. "Are you lying?"

"No. I haven't told anyone."

Tai believed him. She relaxed a bit. "Good. Don't tell anyone, okay?"

"Why?"

He would ask questions. Tai squared her shoulders. "Because it was nothing."

"Which part? When you killed the boss or survived a direct soul rip?"

Tai froze. He *had* seen that.

"Just forget that night," Tai said coolly, giving Mao an icy look. "Whatever you think you saw, and whatever you think happened, didn't."

It was one thing to explain how she could kill ghosts with fire, but something else entirely to talk about her immunity to ghosts. It was something about which everyone, including Kanta and her younger siblings, were oblivious. Tai didn't understand it either, so she'd never spoken of it to anyone.

"Are we going to have a problem?" Tai hissed, when Mao remained silent.

The tavern doors opened.

"What are you guys doing out here?" Damian asked, as he and the others came into the hall. He frowned as he looked at them.

"Just going to explore the rest of the inn," Tai said quietly. "You were all busy talking."

"Is that a polite way of saying we weren't doing our job?" Gareth walked over to stand between Tai and Mao, clapping both on the shoulder. "Because I couldn't agree more! It's a good thing you two are here to pick up our slack!"

"What slack?" Korel headed for the stairs. "Silsa, let's look around the second level."

"Okay. You coming, Tai?"

"Yeah."

"So this is guys against girls now, is it?" Damian asked.

"No," Korel replied. "It just so happens the better team is all female!"

"Team?" Tai asked Silsa quietly.

"In the tavern we decided we'd have a contest: divide up and see which group could take out the boss."

That didn't sound smart to Tai, especially as they were all beginners. She thought Silsa would agree, but the other girl looked excited.

Silsa started up the stairs behind Korel, who was waiting at the top. Seeing that Tai wasn't following, Korel asked, "Are you on our team or betraying us for the guys?"

"Of course she's betraying you." Damian sounded smug as he came to stand too close to Tai. "It's not like the boss is going to be upstairs anyway."

"In all the houses I've cleared this week it has," Korel insisted.

"Yeah, but this is an inn, not a regular house. Obviously the boss is going to be the innkeeper, and the innkeeper's rooms are always on the first floor."

Korel said to Tai, "You agree with him?"

"No." Tai stepped away from Damian. "I think it's going to be in the tavern."

"The tavern?" Damian demanded. "Look, I know I said the whole village probably fled to the tavern, but do you honestly think one of them is the boss? The innkeeper probably ran this place his whole life, so he's bound to do the same in the afterlife."

"There you go, being sexist again!" Korel called.

"How do you know the innkeeper was a he? And you're still wrong! The boss will be up here!"

Damian shouted back at her, but Tai had already turned to go to the tavern, from where she could sense the beat of the heart. It was stronger than it had been in any of the other buildings, and she'd located it immediately, hidden in a glass behind the bar, probably the last one from which its victim had drunk.

It almost physically hurt to see the boss's item in plain sight yet unable to destroy it. She'd left her matches at camp again, knowing that, after the other night, she'd definitely use them.

"You're really going into the tavern?" Damian asked. "You'll lose, you know."

"It's a matter of who kills the boss, isn't it? Even if I pick the right spot, I could still lose. The ghost is not going to stay in one place for us."

Tai usually didn't say this much, but Damian irritated her. He was either surprised by her comment or by the fact she'd actually made it, giving Gareth a chance to speak up in the silence. "Why don't we split into three groups, then? That would make it even more exciting! I'll take the tavern with Tai—"

"I will. I agree with her. I also think it's in there."

"All right ..." Gareth was taken aback by Mao's input. Damian, meanwhile, was glowering at Mao. Mao ignored both of them and walked past Tai into the tavern.

"Good luck," Gareth added after a beat, as Tai left. As she closed the door, Tai heard Damian growl, "Why are you wishing them good luck? Don't you want to win?"

Tai and Mao were alone again. She waited for him to say something, assuming that was why he'd joined her, but he remained silent. Unsure what else to do, Tai got her gun ready and waited. It wasn't like they had to explore the tavern, which was just one big open space. They'd see the boss as soon as it appeared. Still, Tai walked around, taking in the tables and bar, trying to keep from looking at the glass.

Unable to stand the silence any longer, Tai asked, "Why do you think it's here?"

Mao hadn't moved from his spot by the bar. "Because you do."

Tai looked at him sharply, and he met her eyes. Tai realized Mao's eyes really were pale. So pale they were almost glowing.

Their WTs went off. Tai yanked her goggles up, as did Mao. The devices beeped 12 times—then went silent. It was The Hour.

Mao aimed at something behind Tai, and fired. She turned around just in time to see the boss, hovering over the glass, swerve away from Mao's bullet. Tai levelled her gun and fired at its belly. In her last two boss fights, Tai had distracted and injured the bosses, but hadn't once aimed for the head. Her teammates had to banish the bosses. Mao would have to do it this time, too, if one of the others didn't get it first.

Actually, it would have to be Mao, Tai realized, unless the others came in, because the boss wasn't running. Instead, it circled around Tai and dove at her from behind, a move none of the other bosses had seemed sentient enough to attempt. Tai couldn't dodge out of the way, thanks to the tables on either side of her, and instead dropped to the floor. The boss flew so close over her head she could have reached up and touched it.

Tai jumped to her feet and fired at the back of the

boss, which had stopped a few feet away, hovering in the air. She was fine with shooting the boss like this, when its back was to her and all she could see was its hair, short and thinning. Another of Mao's bullets whizzed through the back of the boss's head, close to the third eye. Its head whipped around before Tai could look away and its lips curled in a snarl.

Tai had seen that expression on that face before.

Tai was so shocked her gun clattered to the floor. The boss set its sights on Tai, opened its mouth in a mute screech, and then dove at her, face contorted in rage. Tai heard Mao's gun behind her and a plasma bullet shot through its third eye. It jerked backward, as if physically hit, and then exploded in a cloud of blue smoke.

Vaguely, she heard the others shouting and calling out as they came into the tavern. With shaking fingers, Tai reached down to pick up her gun.

She'd suspected but hadn't allowed herself to consider it. Hadn't allowed herself to look hard enough to know the truth. Everything had felt so familiar, but she'd reasoned it away. Now, she couldn't.

The boss Mao had just banished had the face of her old mayor's son. Warren.

This village—dark and abandoned and haunted— had been *her* village.

Chapter XI

Unit Q17 had reached the port town. Thalus checked the group into the Hunter Association-funded inn, which was specifically for hunters passing through, and arranged for their caravans and horses to be housed at the inn's huge stables, as they wouldn't be taken across the water to Hunters City. The horses, cared for during the two months the hunters were in the City, would be ready when the unit returned.

As much as he enjoyed his job, Kanta looked forward to his break. Especially as Tai would be in the City.

"She's out on her field test right now," Kanta said aloud, as he and the guys walked through the port town that evening. Their boat was scheduled to leave early the next morning, and they had free time until then. "She'll probably be back by the time we get to the City, though."

"Who's this, again?" Yano asked, adjusting his bandana.

"Tai," Freid emphasized. "Who else?"

"What do you mean?" Kanta demanded.

"Come on, Kanta," Freid pointed out. "She's the only girl you ever talk about. I'm still surprised you two aren't together. Tai must have more sense than I gave her credit for."

Kanta sent him a dirty look, while Yano exclaimed, "Hold on! You aren't together? All this time I thought you guys were, you know, an *item*."

"No. We're friends. Good friends. That's it."

"That's it? Didn't she travel with you guys for, like, half a year? And nothing happened?"

"Plenty happened," Freid muttered under his breath, but Kanta elbowed his ribs.

"Nothing happened. Not how you mean, anyway."

"Not for lack of trying, I hope," Yano retorted.

"He tried all right," Freid put in, earning an elbow to the gut. "Gods, Kanta! It's true! Don't deny it!"

Kanta ignored him, saying instead to Yano, "Tai and I are friends now. That's all that matters. We're close, but like you and I are close."

Yano looked hurt. "You wouldn't date me?"

Kanta couldn't help laughing at that, but it was partially due to the face Freid made. Even Browen looked amused.

The streets became busier the deeper the hunters went into the town, despite the fact that night was coming on. It wasn't so surprising in this port town, which Kanta had been to many times before. It was highly populated and hosted many guests, thanks to the commerce and trade the port offered. It had a thriving nightlife, with several streets closer to the port dedicated to inns and taverns.

They searched for a party to crash.

"Hey, look," Yano whispered, jabbing Freid's arm, as if this could get everyone's attention.

"Can you guys stop hitting me tonight?"

Yano ignored him. "See those girls? Looks like they're coming over."

Yano was right. Ahead was a group of three girls, who had just finished talking to some slightly older boys. One girl, whose hair was dyed an unusual blue, was looking at them. At him, Kanta realized.

The girls, led by the blue-haired girl, who was

slightly taller and older than the other two, came over to them. Kanta noticed that all three had half a dozen or so red ribbons tied around their arms. The blue-haired girl had a ribbon around her neck too.

"Hey there." She stopped in front of Kanta. "You boys heading anywhere special tonight?"

"That depends," Kanta said, giving her The Grin. The girl seemed to like it. She untied a red ribbon from her own arm and reached up to tie it around Kanta's upper bicep. He watched her curiously.

"That's your key," she explained.

"To what?"

"Follow the red and find out."

She and her friends left without another word. Kanta glanced over to see if the other guys had been given their own ribbons.

"You heard her, chief," Yano said excitedly to Kanta. "Follow the red!"

"Yeah, but what does that mean?"

Browen pointed to a street lamp bearing an identical red ribbon. "That, I'm guessing."

The ribbons led to a small tavern spilling light, voices, and music. Red ribbons were tied all over its signpost.

"I think this might be it," Kanta agreed. The man outside the door, seeing their ribbons, let them in. The inside was full of people, all fairly young, all dancing or talking or singing. Music—the likes of which Kanta hadn't heard before—was coming from somewhere, but the player and his or her instrument were hidden in the crowd.

"I don't know what I expected," Kanta shouted at Browen, "but it wasn't this!"

Browen nodded, not even attempting a reply.

Yano shouted something to Kanta, which he couldn't hear, and disappeared in the crowd, dragging a reluctant Freid behind him. Kanta and Browen followed them.

Half an hour later Kanta and Browen were talking to a girl whose father owned one of the boats the hunters sometimes used. Browen had just asked if the ship was leaving tomorrow, if it was the one they'd be taking, when someone tapped Kanta's shoulder. Thinking it was Yano or Freid, who'd ditched them earlier to hang out with the guitarist he'd found in one of the booths, Kanta was surprised to see the blue-haired girl.

"Glad you could make it," she said.

Kanta flashed The Grin again. "Clever, what you did with the ribbons."

"Thanks. Enjoying our little get-together?"

"This is supposed to be little?"

"*I* think so. Then again, my friends say I'm tough to please."

"Tough to please, hmm. Well, my friends say I like a challenge."

"Do you? And who *are* you, exactly?"

Kanta dug in his pocket, drew out his ID, and passed it to her. As she read the information it contained, her dark brows rose in surprise.

"Kanta." She handed his card back. "You're a hunter."

"Pays the bills."

"I bet it does."

"What about you? Are you going to tell me who you are?"

"Maybe. If you impress me enough."

"Now that's easy—" Someone grabbed his arm. Glaring over his shoulder, Kanta found Freid behind him. "What?"

"Just come with me."

"If you want to leave then go ahead—"

"Just come, Kanta." Not waiting to make sure he followed, Freid plunged back into the crowd. Assuring the girl he'd be back in a minute, Kanta hurried after Freid.

They stopped in front of a booth. Before Kanta could ask what was going on, he saw who was sitting beside Yano, glowering at her lap.

"What the hell?" Kanta yelled. "Mid!"

Mid's head snapped up, eyes wide on her brother. They narrowed when Yano gave her shoulder a shake. "Found her squirming through the crowd. Figured you'd want a word."

"Yes. I do."

Yano slid out of the booth, and Kanta dragged Mid out behind him. He didn't let her go, pulling her toward the back of the tavern, where he'd seen an exit.

"I can walk just fine without you pulling me!"

"I know you can walk. I'm just worried where you'll walk next without my pulling you."

Mid didn't protest again. Kanta shoved the back door open, leading them into a small backyard with a bench. A brick wall and gate offered privacy from the back alley.

"Why are you here?" Kanta demanded.

"I followed you guys when you left the inn."

"Followed us? Why the hell would you do that?"

"I was bored."

"So you've been here this whole time?"

"No. They wouldn't let me in without one of those dumb ribbons. I had to get one from a lamppost, but it took awhile to find one low enough for me to reach. Your friends found me as soon as I got in."

"Good. Does Thalus know *you're* here?"

"Does Thalus know you're here?"

"This isn't funny, Mid."

"I'm not trying to be funny! This isn't how a hunter should act, Kanta! Going off to stupid clubs with your guy friends and partying all night and—and it's like you don't care anymore!"

"Of course I care! Gods, you can be such a child sometimes! Hunting isn't the only thing! I need to have more to my life than that!"

"And this is so much more, is it? This is what life really is to you?"

"Maybe it is! Either way, it's my decision, so back off."

"Fine! Go ahead and screw up as much as you like. I won't do anything!"

"That's all I'm asking!" Kanta turned back to the tavern. When Mid followed, he jabbed a finger at the back alley. "Oh no, Midgard. You are not coming back in here. Get your ass back to the inn right now."

"Why should I? If you can do what you want, then so can I!"

"Try again. You're 15. Maybe when you're my age—"

"You were doing this kind of thing long before you turned 19!"

"Just get out of here, Mid!" Kanta roared. "Just leave! I'm sick of having my kid sister around all the time!"

Mid gaped at him, but Kanta didn't stick around. He went back inside, slamming the door behind him, and immediately dove into the crowd. When he reached the spot where he'd been before, the blue-haired girl was gone.

"Looking for me?" Kanta turned to find her behind him.

"Yeah. Wanna dance?" His fight with Mid had left him charged with energy. Dancing seemed a better use of that energy than, say, punching the tavern wall.

"Yes, actually, I do want to dance. That's your second point."

"Second? What was my first?"

"You came back. One more point, and I'll tell you my name."

"How am I supposed to get that point?"

"Tell me something impressive. Some hunting feat. Or something about Hunters City. I've always wanted to go there. I hear they throw the best New Year's celebration."

"They do. It goes on for several days, and New Year's night they throw a huge party at the H.A. Headquarters. Hundreds of people go, and all the big-shot Council members and their families are there, so they don't spare any expenses."

"Sounds amazing. Are you going?"

"Yeah. I always do."

"Tell me about the parties," the girl prompted, leading Kanta toward the dance floor with a gentle hand on his arm.

"If you tell me your name. I've earned that third point. You look impressed."

The girl rolled her eyes, but smiled. "My name's Mina."

Mid stood where Kanta had left her, hands in tight fists at her sides. She was embarrassed at being caught, both by Kanta and his friends, but more than that she was angry. Angry at what Kanta had said.

Angry for how he'd been treating her. Angry at him.

Fine. If he didn't want his kid sister around, she wouldn't be.

Mid went out the back gate and had just started storming down the back alley when she heard the tavern door open again. Assuming it was Kanta, returning to apologize for being a colossal jerk, Mid peeked back around the gate. It wasn't Kanta, but two young men, one with dark skin and hair, whom she'd seen playing the guitar inside, and one with dark blonde hair.

She heard one of them say, "We got a good turnout tonight."

That voice. Mid doubled back and glanced over the top of the gate. The blonde guy. He was the same one who'd been at the stables in that vilage.

Ducking out of sight, Mid pressed her back against the brick wall and listened.

"Mina and the girls did a good job," the blonde continued. "Boss'll be pleased. Did you manage to get anything out of those guys sitting with you?"

The other man's voice was too low for Mid to hear his reply.

"The Boss is really gonna like that." It sounded like the blonde sighed. "I've missed this place, you know. Life on the road is nice and all, but it's great to put my feet up for a bit, let you guys handle things."

Another reply Mid couldn't hear.

"The raids? Oh yeah, they went swell. Don't make that face, Kam, we were careful—and no, we didn't kill anyone this time. I wish you'd let that go. It was an accident, and it wasn't even me."

More mumbling.

"Yeah, I know. Haine can be a loose cannon, but I've got it under control. Besides, the Boss has faith in him. That's all that really matters, and he was on his best behaviour when we worked together. Don't get me wrong—I'm glad he's still out on a job. He can have a real violent streak. See, there was one incident on the road: bandits trying to steal our plasma haul and he …"

Mid went rigid. Plasma?

"Yeah, I guess we should go back," the blonde replied to something the other had interjected. "I'll tell you the rest of the story later. Anyway, Mina got us such a good crowd. If we don't work them right, she'll have a fit."

There was some shuffling of feet and then the tavern door closed. Mid stayed where she was, head spinning. Plasma traffickers. They had to be. The kind of people that attacked the Plasma Fields and sold their plunder under the table. That's what had been in those metal containers she'd seen in the blonde's caravan. Illegal plasma.

Mid had to get back to the inn. Had to tell Thalus.

Spinning around, Mid was about to dash down the alley but bit her tongue on a scream. A girl, maybe Kanta's age or a little older, with a blonde pixie cut and very dark eyes, stood behind her in the alley shadows.

"Gods-That-Remain! Is it necessary to sneak around alleys at night like that, lady?"

"And how exactly would you describe what you're doing?"

"Well … um … uh." Mid suddenly remembered the situation she was in. "Hold on, did you hear those guys? The ones there just then talking about weird stuff."

A second witness could help, Mid figured.

"Weird stuff?"

"Yeah, plasma and raiding and stuff. Wait, okay, in this day and age it's not all that weird. But still. Weird for the circumstances, you know? Did you hear them?"

"I did. Did you?"

"Uh … yeah? Obviously."

"Ah," the girl sighed. "That's too bad, then."

"Too bad?"

"Yes. For the circumstances." The girl pulled something from the back of her belt and aimed it at Mid. A gun.

"And—weird as it might be," the girl informed Mid, "this doesn't take plasma."

Chapter XII

Kassa and Os had been so impressed by the trainees during their field test that they stayed at an inn one night on the way back to Hunters City rather than getting in one more camping tutorial. Kassa told the trainees they could stay up as long as they liked and unwind at the tavern but warned them not to cause any trouble or complain of lack of sleep the next day. Anyone who complained, she promised, would walk the entire way back, with no caravan-driving breaks.

Tai and her group were sitting at one of the booths; the other trainees were at a table in the centre of the room. The tavern was busier than Tai had expected it to be, but she should have known that, since the town was so close to Hunters City, there would be travellers on their way to and from stopping here all the time.

The booth was shaped like a half-circle. Tai sat between Silsa and Damian. She'd hoped to sit at the end, not liking being boxed in, but Damian had slid in after her. Their legs touched, which made Tai very uncomfortable, but she didn't have room to move.

"I don't really care what group I'm assigned to for field training," Korel announced. She was sitting between Silsa and Gareth, idly circling the rim of her glass with her index finger. "I do care when our food gets here. What's taking so long? Heath and the others got their order 10 minutes ago."

"Seeing how much you complain about trivial stuff, it's a good thing you're not gonna complain about your training unit," Damian stated. "Besides, you've gotta pass your field test before you think about training."

"Of course I passed. We all passed. Why else would Kassa be in a good mood?"

"I dunno. Could mean we failed," Damian offered. "She does enjoy our misery."

"She wouldn't let us stay at an inn if we failed," Korel answered. "She'd make us do another night of field training. What about you, Sil? Is there a group you want to be assigned to?"

"I'd, um, like to be in the same unit as my brother and aunt. At least for training."

"Right. I forgot about that." Korel turned to Tai. "I guess you're hoping to officially rejoin that unit?"

Tai shrugged, not wanting to mention Kanta's assurance she would join the unit.

"Unit Q17," Gareth mused wistfully. "My dream unit. Tai, think you could put a good word in for me with Commander Thalus? I'd be your eternal servant."

"If you make that kind of offer, she's more likely not to help," Damian pointed out. "'Sides, what's so great about that unit? No offence, Sil. I know you wanna join for family reasons, but aside from that it's no different than any other group."

"What?" Gareth spluttered. "How can you say that?"

"Actually, I agree," Korel put in. Noting Gareth's open-mouthed look, she explained, "What? I do! It's not that special, even if it has a well-known commander and hunter prodigy. It's the same as any other unit."

"Exactly," Damian added. "I'm with Kor. I don't care where I'm assigned."

"What about you, Mao?" Silsa always tried to include everyone.

Before Mao could reply, not that it was likely he would, Damian said snidely, "He's obviously going to join his father's unit."

Mao's hands tightened around his glass. No one except Tai noticed. Their attention was focused on Damian.

"Can't say I blame you," Damian went on. "If my father was some big-shot commander, I'd wanna join his unit. It'll be a nice set-up for sure."

Mao knocked over his glass. Everyone reacted as if it was an accident. Tai wasn't so sure.

"Oops." He stood up. "I'll get something to clean it up."

"Get our food while you're at it," Damian called as Mao walked away. "Doubt he'd be able to carry half our order, even if it was ready. I still can't believe he can use a rifle, with those stick arms."

"Damian." Gareth's voice echoed disapproval.

"What? It's true! That rifle probably weighs more than he does!"

Damian's leg pressed closer to Tai's as he talked. Whether it was on purpose, or he was just relaxing further into the seat, Tai didn't care. She got up, too. "I'll go help."

"With what?" Damian asked.

"Our order. Can you move so I can get out?"

Damian smirked. "Why not just climb over me?"

"Just move, Damian," Korel snapped. "Gods, you're such an asshole sometimes."

Damian ignored her. Frustrated, Tai tried to get around him, but there really wasn't much room, so she had to step over his legs.

Out of the booth, Tai strode toward the bar, her face burning. She'd help Mao with the drinks—then she was going up to bed. She wasn't about to sit back down, not with Damian there. At first she'd been able to tolerate him, but she was sick of him now.

Mao was leaning against the bar. His hands were still clenched, fingers curling and white-knuckled over the wooden counter.

"Are you okay?"

Mao turned to Tai, startled. This close, Tai could clearly see that Silsa had been right about his droopy right eyelid. It was only slight, but noticeable.

"Yes." Mao's attention went back to the bar as he retracted his still-shaking hands.

Tai didn't know if she should press it or not. Before she could decide, Mao said, "I can handle my rifle just fine."

"What?"

"It's not that heavy. I adjusted to the weight a long time ago."

"I never questioned—"

"I know. I just wanted to say it to someone."

The bartender left the kitchen and came over to them.

"Can I help … Gods-That-Remain!"

It took Tai a moment to recognize the bartender with his hair grown out and the start of a beard masking his face.

"Tai," he breathed. "Is it really you?"

"Roge …?"

"Gods-That-Remain," he whispered again, using the counter to steady himself. "How … Why … What are you doing here?"

"I …" Tai wasn't sure how to respond. How could

she explain everything that had happened to her over the past two years? "Why are *you* here? Wasn't the village …?"

Tai couldn't finish, but she didn't need to.

"You know about the village?" Roge asked.

"Yeah, I … What happened? When did it … when did …?"

"When did the ghosts attack? A year ago. It'll be a year ago in two weeks." Roge's eyes were hooded. "A year since they all died."

Tai swallowed.

"I can't believe it's you," Roge continued. "You grew your hair. It looks nice."

Tai couldn't bring herself to say anything.

"I never thought I'd see you again, after … well, after that night. I've always regretted it, my role in that, what Warren did. You'll be happy to know he's dead."

Happy wasn't the right word, Tai thought.

"I guess this is the world's sick sense of irony," Roge went on. "Reuniting us like this. We're two of the last ones left. Barely anyone escaped. Marny didn't."

"Marny?"

"You might not remember her. She worked at the baker's. She was a few years younger than us. Short, with curly hair and a really sweet smile. She was so nice—nicer than most people. And so optimistic, even after most crops failed last year. She was sure we'd get through it. She was always so sure and so happy. She made me happy too, when I got over your leaving. I'd never really noticed her before—I was so caught up in you, even though you didn't even consider me a friend anymore. I don't know what was wrong with me, but Marny woke me up. We were engaged, you know. She wanted to get married last summer, but

I wanted to wait until she was older—it was what her parents wanted, and I wanted to impress them. I should have married her when she wanted. I should have given her that wedding, that one last memory. I'd proposed that spring, and she'd been so excited, even though I was too poor to buy her a ring. The entire village was too poor—there weren't even rings to buy. But she was happy with just a flower."

"A flower?" Tai's voice was scratchy.

Roge was too lost in his own world to notice. "Yeah. I proposed with a flower I took from my mother's garden. You remember that garden, don't you? We dug up all her flowers when we were kids, that one time."

"Yeah. I remember."

Roge offered Tai a sad smile. "Like I said, it's ironic. We did such a horrible thing to you and your family, and in the end we all paid for it. Maybe you guys really were cursed, and we brought that curse on ourselves."

Tai tensed.

"How is your family? Are they okay? How's Brighton?"

No one was allowed to say that name anymore.

"Tai?" Roge asked. "What's wrong? Nothing happened to him, right?"

"Who's Brighton?" Mao asked. Tai had completely forgotten about him.

Evidently so had Roge. "Ah, I forgot you were with someone. My name's Roge. Tai and I come … *came* from the same village. Are you two … are you together?"

"No! I mean yes, we're together, but in a group. I'm a trainee now, Roge, with the Hunter Association."

"You became a hunter?"

Tai nodded.

"How could you do that?"

"What?"

"Don't act like you don't know," Roge snapped. "You're one of them now! You're one of the people who destroyed our village!"

"I don't understand what you—"

"We couldn't pay our taxes, Tai. The taxes for the plasma lanterns—we couldn't afford to pay them! We tried to get them to give us time to pay them back, but they refused. We ran out of fuel for the lanterns, and that's how the ghosts from the city got in! Not because of an accident, or because the lanterns broke—it was because the Hunter Association wouldn't help us! They knew this would happen, and they still refused to help! They did this! Hunters did this! *You* did this!"

Trembling, Tai stepped away from the counter and rushed out the back exit, bumping into other patrons on her way.

Outside, Tai slumped against the wall of the inn, trying to catch her breath. The night air was cool compared to the stuffy heat of the tavern but was no comparison to the chill inside her chest.

It had been the Association's fault her village had been destroyed, that almost everyone she'd grown up with was dead. She'd been training with them when it happened. Roge was right. It was her fault. Maybe not directly, but she wasn't blameless. Not when for years she'd renounced the hunters, and then, as soon as she turned around and joined them, this happened. She'd betrayed her beliefs, her village, and the one person who'd always warned her off the hunters— her grandmother. She was a traitor.

Tai heard someone come out. She didn't look up as whoever it was came over next to her, afraid it was Roge with more accusations.

"Are you okay?"

"Yes." Tai realized she'd asked him the same thing only moments ago and she, too, was lying.

Mao sat down next to her, keeping a slight gap between them, like he did whenever he sat beside anyone. "The phantom village we cleared, was that your village?"

"How did you know that?"

"Your conversation." Mao had his legs stretched out, hands resting in his lap. "When did you last see your village?"

"Over two years ago."

"Can I ask why you left?"

"You're asking if you can ask?"

"Yes."

Tai considered. After a moment, she drew her legs up to her chest, resting her cheek against them. "It's not a good story, just so you know."

"I'm not looking for any kind of story. That's not why I'm asking. Why did you leave your village?"

"We were forced out, my siblings and I. They accused us of witchcraft and being cursed. They burned down our house, and banished us. That was when we started travelling with Unit Q17."

It was a minute before Mao said anything. "You feel bad for them? The villagers who died?"

"Yeah."

"Isn't that a waste?"

"What do you mean?"

"It sounds like they destroyed everything you had. If Unit Q17 hadn't been there, what would you have done?"

"I ..." Tai didn't have an answer. There wasn't anything they could have done; the closest villages were too far away to travel to without proper gear, which they didn't have in the first place. They hadn't even had money at that point—everything having been destroyed in the fire, and they wouldn't have been let within the walls.

"When I say it's a waste, I mean they don't deserve your emotions," Mao insisted. "Including that man in there. They didn't spare any for you, when it mattered. They left you for dead. You don't owe them anything, least of all your sympathy."

Tai hadn't expected this from soft-spoken Mao.

"Don't think about it anymore." Mao got to his feet. "I'm going to bed. If Damian's hungry, he can move his lazy ass and get his own food."

Tai hadn't expected that from Mao either. Realizing she was staring at him, Mao simply offered her a hand. Hesitant at first, Tai took it and let him pull her to her feet. His hand was only a little larger than hers, making them a comfortable fit.

They walked around the building. It was dark, and the village was deserted. The only noise except for their footfalls came from inside the tavern.

"They weren't entirely wrong." Tai admitted. "The villagers. They were wrong to banish us, but we weren't normal. We lived outside the wall, but more than that ... there was evidence of a curse."

Tai didn't know why she was saying this. Maybe it was the stress and exhaustion from the events of the past few days. Maybe it was because she wanted to believe Mao—that she didn't owe anything to the villagers, that she shouldn't feel like she did. But Mao didn't know *everything*. If he knew about the curse, would he call her blameless? And if he would, could Tai herself forget about this—about how her village had perished—and completely move on?

"There was a curse," Tai explained. She was sure now it was exhaustion. "There *is* a curse. They were right about that. My family's cursed. I'm cursed. But it never harmed them, the village, and never would have. It only ever harmed us."

Tai stopped—and Mao stopped with her. "We never did anything wrong. It isn't our fault our family's this way. We didn't … we didn't choose this. We didn't want it. I don't want it." Tai caught her breath, as she realized how true it was. "I don't want it any-more. I can't handle it on my own."

Tai was horrified when she felt her eyes stinging. She blinked hard. She couldn't cry. She *wouldn't*. Not after going two years without her twin, five years without her parents, and six without her grandmother, and not shedding a tear. Tai didn't cry, because that would mean she was breaking. It meant she was giving up.

Her grandmother had taught her not to cry, taught her what crying meant. Her grandmother had taught her a lot of things—Tai had thought *everything*—and it *had* been everything. Back when the curse was worth it. Back when anything was worth it as long as she could kill the ghosts.

But it wasn't everything. Not anymore. Not with her brother gone and this curse a time bomb between them. How could she ever let him go, really let him and the past go, when she knew that one day she would go insane, without really knowing for sure? What about Brighton? How could he live knowing the same might happen to him, that Tai might die and he would lose his sanity? And the little twins, their lives wouldn't be any better. Tai didn't want her abilities if it meant the curse. It wasn't worth it anymore.

Mao slipped his hand into Tai's again. "Can I ask you to tell me everything?"

No. She couldn't. She couldn't tell him—someone she'd been acquainted with for two years but was only just starting to know. She *couldn't*. That wasn't something Tai, the family head, keeper of all secrets and solver of all problems, would do.

But that was just it. There was *nothing* she could do. Not about what had happened to her village, not about her brother's choosing to leave, not about the curse. Nothing. She was powerless, and she was sick of pretending otherwise. She was sick of keeping it all in, hoping she could change it one day. That day would never come.

And what she'd said was true: she couldn't handle it on her own. Not anymore.

"Okay," Tai whispered. "You can ask."

Chapter XIII

$\mathbf{M}$id was sure her brain was malfunctioning. "Okay, just checking … but you said that that gun takes plasma, yes?"

"No." The girl waved her down the alley with the gun. "Quickly and quietly, please. There's a side entrance."

Mid backed up as the girl approached. "Uh, we're going in again?"

The girl didn't reply, simply stared at her down the length of the barrel. Normally Mid could interpret no-replies pretty well. This was not one of those times.

"See …" Mid kept backing up. "I can't go back in 'cause I just sort of got kicked out. By my big bro. Who's a hunter. A really big important hunter. Who would so attack anyone who even parts his sister's hair the wrong way. And his weapon doesn't take plasma either. Well, it sort of does, but it can be used for the metaphysical and the physical. So—"

"Door." The girl gestured to the side of the building.

"Oh I see. Yes. That is a door."

The girl gave her a pointed look.

"And I guess I'm opening it." Mid turned the knob and slipped inside. She was in a hall, with a few doors on either side, one at the end, and a staircase. She couldn't see the tavern but could hear the music pounding through the wall. "Uh … an inn?"

"Something like that." The girl closed the door behind her—click.

"Oh … Wait, did you just lock the door?"

"I don't see how that matters."

"It totally 500 per cent matters. And I heard a click. Did you lock the door?"

"Quiet," the girl hissed, stepping toward Mid.

Mid squealed and tripped up in her hurry to back away. "I'd be more concerned about someone hearing a gunshot than a girl screaming if I were you!" Of course Mid was confident that her screaming could out-volume a gunshot, but this was not the time to announce that.

"Gunshot?" The girl furrowed her brows.

"You know! From your non-plasma-taking threat weapon!"

"No one's going to get shot."

"So you're saying that doesn't take bullets?"

"No. It does," the girl sighed, holstering her weapon. "Look, just calm down. If I need to shoot you, I can, but mostly the gun's just for show. Or emergencies."

"Okay, you just said you could shoot me waaaaaay too passively for me to feel comfortable!"

"The safety's still on."

"That doesn't make me feel comfortable either!"

"We need to talk. Quietly." The girl offered a hand. Surprised, Mid shoved it away and jumped to her feet, careful to keep distance between her and the girl.

"What you just heard, out back—it's not as bad as you think—"

"It's not as bad? Are you trying to downplay illegal plasma smuggling?! Oh, shit, you're a smuggler too, aren't you?"

"I was going to say: it's not as bad as you think—

it's worse. As a hunter, you should know that."

"Uh, did I say I was a hunter?"

"You did. It's fine. It makes this easier."

"It's fine? Okay, thanks for your approval."

"Please listen to me. As a hunter, you must be aware of the lack of plasma fuel being delivered to waypoint villages. Without the fuel, their lanterns go out, leaving the towns vulnerable."

"I know how the lanterns work, thanks. Also, you're totally wrong; the H.A. keeps everyone's lanterns filled."

"That's what they tell you, isn't it? I'm not surprised. That's what most of the Council members believe is happening as well."

"What are you talking about?"

"The corrupt Council members and their hunter conspirators. A small but powerful sect within the Hunter Association is corrupt and hiking up taxes for particular villages, then holding out on lantern fuel. Extortion, if you want to bottom-line it."

"Are you kidding? If you wanna make me believe stuff like that, you'd better start swinging that gun again."

After the words left her mouth, Mid realized sass, especially firearm-related sass, probably wasn't her best move right now.

"That conversation you overheard," the girl continued, "was between my cousin and another of our members, Kam. Kam's family used to live in a village much like that—one being extorted by the corrupt individuals of the Hunter Association. Eventually they couldn't pay the inflated taxes anymore and the lanterns ran out of fuel; Kam is the only survivor of his village. His entire family perished in the ghost invasion. His mother, his father, his aunt, his cousins. His little sister. When he first came to us, he'd have nightmares; he saw his little sister get soul-ripped. He used to dream about that all the time, waking up calling his sister, trying to get to her to save her in time. He still lives with that. He always will. He's not the only one like that here. Everyone helping us has been affected by the corruption in some way. I won't lie to you: we do plan raids on the Fields. But it's to acquire more fuel to distribute among villages that can't pay their taxes anymore. We don't sell it ourselves; we're not out for profit. We're out for change. Everything I'm saying right now, I realize, are just words. There's no strong evidence behind them. I don't have pictures or official records as proof of the corruption. But words are all I have right now."

"You have a gun," Mid reminded her.

The girl unholstered the gun. She emptied the chamber on the floor in front of Mid and tossed the unloaded gun to Mid, who just managed to catch it.

"If you have questions, ask them." She held Mid's gaze. "Barring that, don't report us to your commander. I realize you have responsibilities—all hunters do. But we have responsibilities, too, to the people, just like you. I'm not going to say anything more than that. It's your decision. What will you do?"

Mid was hesitant, turning the gun over in her hands. Even unloaded, it felt heavier than her plasma pistols. "If I say I'll inform on you anyway, you'll just charge me or something, right?"

"If you plan on informing on us, I doubt you'll tell me that. It's simply a matter of if your answer will be a truth or a lie."

"And if it's a lie?"

"Then my group and I will clear out long before you reach your commander. Squads may be sent after us, but we've dealt with such things before. We'll avoid them and continue our fight."

"You'll probably clear out when we're done here anyway, won't you?"

"Probably. It's not solely my decision; the entire group decides."

"And if it was your decision?"

The girl's lips twitched in a half-smile. She shook her head. "If it were my decision—if over the course of everything, we'd been adhering to my decisions—we wouldn't be creeping around in the shadows like this. The corruption must be weeded out—for the good of everyone. We'd stand and fight."

"Fight the H.A.?" Mid's heart hammered in her chest. This girl, maybe five years older than Mid, was talking about rebellion.

"The corruption." The girl clarified.

"So … so if it's only a few corrupt people, why don't you work with the H.A.? It's stupid that one bad person surrounded by good people still has that kind of power."

"I'm afraid it's not that simple. The Association is set up to protect those at the top. Of course, the system was styled with the assumption that those at the top would be good. Unfortunately, some people can work any system, and there are those in the Association who have. They've made themselves untouchable."

"So you're just gonna go around handing out free plasma until you're caught? You won't stand up to them at all?"

"I've told you already that it's more complicated than that. But, again, as I've said, *I* would. More than anything I wish we could stand up against this, but we're just citizens. Bandits, in the Association's official eyes. We'd never make it to Hunters City, let alone the Association, to make our case to the Council about their interior corruption. And the hunters closest to the Council, those who have a chance to make a change, don't understand that a change must be made. So for now, yes, we'll do what we're doing and hope to avoid capture, at least long enough to save another village. Another person."

Mid stared at the girl's determined gaze and set jaw. She was certain, strong, brave. She'd make the kind of hunter Mid had always dreamed she herself would become. But she was also against the hunters.

"What if you could find a way to do it?" Mid asked. "To, I dunno, talk to the Council or something? Get them your message?"

"There isn't a way."

"There has to be!" Mid exclaimed. "And ... my aunt's on the Council! I mean, I know she's not corrupt, but she's on the Council and maybe ... maybe ..."

The girl was clearly taken aback by Mid's words. Mid caught her breath. What was she doing? To divulge so much information to a smuggler with hatred for the Hunter Association ... but she couldn't deny it. What this girl was saying rang true for Mid. If there was possible corruption in the Association, she—as a hunter, a protector of the people—wanted the issue explored. She wanted to know for sure. Especially if it could be causing the deaths of so many people, the destruction of so many villages. That just wasn't right. And as a hunter, Mid had to do what was right.

"I appreciate it," the girl finally said. "But it's best you don't get involved more than this. I would just appreciate your silence, though."

"Why can't I? I'm sure I could help. Or, you

know, find a way for you to talk to someone. I may not be that important in the whole H.A. pecking order, but I know some super-important people! Some super-important non-corrupt people."

The girl seemed to consider it. "You ... what's your name?"

"Midgard!" Mid struck a pose. "Hunter Trainee of Unit Q17!"

"Midgard, hmm? You can call me Summer. Look, I'm still not sure. You're awfully young—"

"Young? I'm already 15!"

"Still, it wouldn't be right to involve you to such an extent. But ... look, as I said, we're a group. Maybe, sometime in the future, we may need your help. If we ever find a way to appeal to the Hunter Association—if that happens—I'll try to get word to you."

"Just send something to my aunt's!" Mid exclaimed. "She's the head of plasma research, FYI. Regailia. Maybe you've heard of her?"

"I have. She's a remarkable woman. To have someone like her vouching for us ..." Summer's brown eyes shone. "That would be remarkable."

"Then let me talk to her for you!"

"As I said, I'll be in touch if the need arises. For now, please keep quiet for us. That's all I can really ask for." Summer stepped aside, nodding to the door. "You should get back to your unit. I realize you aren't a child, but being a trainee they'll likely still be keeping close tabs on your activities."

"True enough. Oh yeah. Here." Mid tossed Summer the empty revolver. "You know, for future shows you might need to put off and stuff."

"Thanks." Summer holstered the weapon. "Safe journey."

"You too." Mid unlocked the door and cracked it open to the cool night air.

"Oh, and Midgard?"

Mid glanced back.

"Thank you for hearing me out, and for offering your help. I've always known it, but it feels good to verify there are still honourable hunters out there."

Mid's cheeks burned and, with a mumbled thanks, she hurried outside.

Honourable. Midgard, Hunter Trainee of Unit Q17. Honourable Hunter.

Mid liked that.

Chapter XIV

Hunters City loomed in the distance over the water. It looked nothing like the haunted cities in which Mid and the squad banished ghosts. The buildings were much smaller in Hunters City; only the Hunters Association Headquarters had more than two stories, and it had only three. Mid still couldn't fathom how the Old World had built their insanely tall skyscrapers—Kite and Wendy had often attempted to explain it to her, but they'd gotten entirely too technical and Mid always had to walk out during the explanation.

As the largest settlement in the New World, Hunters City also had the highest population. That, along with its access to water and high-level anti-ghost security, made it a crucial economic hub for the New World. Of course, being the hunters' central stomping ground and base also helped the city's economy.

The extensive harbour was immediately ahead, filled with tiny fishing vessels and larger shipping boats. Mid could see sailors milling about the docks, moving crates or transporting their catch of the day. Watching one sailor teeter on the plank connecting his ship to the dock, Mid's gut clenched. She wished, not for the first time, that the overland route to Hunters City wasn't so long and so dangerous.

Mid hated boats. When she was younger, she'd had nightmares that Bear had sunk through the boat or fallen overboard, lost beneath the watery depths.

She had gotten over those nightmares but not her dislike of sailing. Mid and her queasy stomach were grateful when the boat reached the port in Hunters City.

Thalus had to report to the Hunter Association before he could return to the manor, so Mid and Kanta grabbed their belongings and went on without him. Unfortunately for Kanta, his friends were all taking different routes home and, unfortunately for Mid, Wendy lived in the opposite direction. The siblings were forced to walk home together, just the two of them, and Bear. Mid was more grateful for her rock giant than ever. Seeming to know just what Mid expected of him, Bear walked between the two, carrying Mid's luggage. She hadn't even offered, on Bear's behalf, to have Kanta's bags carried; her brother wanted to do his own thing, after all. That could include carrying his bags.

Kanta and Mid didn't say a word to each other. Mid refused to let an awkward silence fall, however, and chattered to Bear the whole way, mostly about all the stuff she wanted to do over their break. What she really wanted to do was to discuss her encounter with Summer. But she could hardly do that with Kanta standing right there and, besides, she'd already given Bear the overview.

"You'll be my date for the New Year's Ball, right, Bear?" Mid asked. Bear, of course, said he would. They went together every year. It was tradition.

Finally, they arrived at the family manor. Mid, glancing at her brother, wasn't surprised that he looked as excited as she felt. Probably more.

"She might not be back yet," Mid couldn't help pointing out. Kanta ignored her, hoisting the strap of his bag higher on his shoulder. He opened the gate and strode toward the house. Mid followed.

"Hey!" Kanta called, opening the door. "We're home!"

There was a clattering sound in the kitchen. The next thing they knew, Henna was in the hall, a huge smile spreading across her face. Kanta tossed his bags aside and enveloped Henna in a hug. Henna laughed happily and patted his back.

"I'm so glad you two are back! You three!" Henna amended, pulling back and smiling at Mid and Bear, whose head was mere inches from the ceiling. She swatted Kanta lightly on the shoulder. "Back in the porch right now, young man, and take off those filthy boots! You're tracking mud through my spotless hall!"

"It's fine, Hen. The wood's too dark to notice." Kanta grinned as Henna swatted him again.

Kicking off her shoes, Mid ran forward, knocking into Henna with her own hug. Henna returned it eagerly. After a moment she pulled away, keeping her hands on Mid's shoulders. "Let me get a good look at you."

"I grew, right?"

Behind Henna, Kanta rolled his eyes, but Mid ignored him.

"You certainly did, dear! Why, you'll be taller than me in no time!"

"Are you the only one home, Hen?" Kanta asked.

Henna faked indignation. "Am I not enough?"

"'Course you are. I just want to know how long I'll have you to myself."

"You think yourself quite charming, don't you, lad? Well, you'll have me to yourselves awhile yet. Young Kite's still at the labs, as is his mother. The twins won't be off school until 3 p.m., and Paige will return with them."

"What about Tai?" Kanta asked hopefully.

"She hasn't returned from her field test yet."

"Do you have any idea when she'll be back?"

"Sorry, lad. Now don't make such a long face. She'll be back soon enough. Why don't I get some food into the two of you? No doubt the boat ride made you hungry!"

"No doubt!" Mid loved Henna's cooking.

"Mid definitely made enough room while she was on the boat," Kanta muttered. Mid flushed at the memory. She couldn't help being prone to seasickness.

"That's not much of a surprise," Henna told them. "Your father never could handle boats, nor Miss Regailia. Their parents had a job getting them anywhere, when they did decide to travel. Those two would come home with horror stories, moaning about how rocky the boat was. They never turned down a snack after a voyage, though, not when I asked them."

"They were bad with boats?" Mid asked. "Aunt Regailia and our father?"

Henna smiled at the memory. Sometimes Mid forgot that Henna had been around when her father and aunt were growing up. Henna didn't often tell stories about them.

Turning her attention back to the siblings, the older woman clapped her hands. "All right, then. Let's fill you two up, since you've already made room."

"Hey, I didn't get sick," Kanta boasted. "Just Mid."

"Yes, well, you always did take after your mother more," Henna said dismissively and headed to the kitchen. "Now, are we in the mood for herbal or black tea?"

Chapter XV

"Why can't I go to my friend's house?" Grippa demanded as they walked down the street. She refused to walk next to Paige and her brother but instead trudged ahead and scuffed her shoes in a way that would wear them down, which Paige often asked her not to do. She did it now for exactly that reason, Paige was sure.

"I told you, Grip," Paige explained. "Tai will be home soon, and it would be nice if you were there to greet her, considering you weren't when she left."

"I did see her before she left," Grippa whined. "'Sides, is she going to get home today?"

"She might."

"But you don't know for sure!"

"Yes, but we won't know for sure. She'll get back soon, though. It's just for the rest of this week, Grippa."

"I wanna go to Vikki's house."

Vikki—another new friend. Lately every friend Grippa mentioned was a name Paige hadn't heard before. Surely her little sister must have run out of female classmates to visit by now.

"The gate's open!" Grippa exclaimed, as they approached the manor. "If it's Tai and she's back, can I go to Vikki's house after saying hi?"

"No. And it might not be Tai. Kite could have left the gate open."

"He wouldn't do that," Alton added.

"He could've, Altie." Paige didn't want to get their hopes up, in case it wasn't Tai.

"No, he wouldn't. He always complains when you leave the gate open."

"He d-d-does? He's never said anything …"

Alton shrugged. He'd given all the input he had to offer.

Grippa, meanwhile, had run ahead. Paige hurried to catch up with her sister, careful to close the gate behind them. Seconds later, she heard a squeal of delight from Grippa in the porch. Paige's heart leaped. Was it really Tai?

Paige went inside and found Grippa bouncing around a familiar rock giant, not their elder sister. When Alton saw Bear, he discarded his schoolbag in the hall like his twin had, and ran up to him. Two years later, Bear was still one of Grippa and Alton's favourite things.

"Bear? What's going on? I heard something annoying." Mid appeared in the kitchen doorway. "Oh. I was right."

Mid looked different: slightly taller but just as thin. Her hair, much longer, was tied in two long tails as opposed to her former stubby ones. Her face had become more angular too, Paige noticed.

"You look the same," Mid informed Paige. "Besides the short hair. And the fat."

"F-F-Fat …?"

"Yeah." Mid waved to indicate Paige's figure. "You like Henna's cooking, clearly."

Paige reddened. She'd filled out and gained more curves where she'd once been scrawny, but she hadn't put on that much weight.

Then again, compared to Mid …

"What's going on?" Kanta appeared behind his sister, carrying a cup of tea. "Who are you being an intolerable brat to now?"

"You're the one who's intoler—"

Before Mid finished, Kanta saw Paige in the hallway. "Paige!"

Handing Mid his cup, Kanta pushed past her and walked up to Paige. Before Paige knew what was happening, he was hugging her. It wasn't a long hug, but enough to stun her.

"You look great. Grown up."

"I d-d-don't look that d-d-different."

"Don't be ridiculous," said a voice behind her. "It's been a year. Of course he'd think you look different."

"Kite!" Mid yelled. She'd already deposited Kanta's tea somewhere, so she was free to dash down the hall and launch herself at her cousin. She stopped short, however, when she saw him behind Paige.

Mid's mouth dropped open. "You're not Kite!"

"What are you talking about?"

"Gods-That-Remain!" Kanta laughed, half amused, half shocked. "Are you taller than *me*?"

"If you're still 5-foot-9, then yes. Now can you all move so I can get inside my house?"

Paige stepped out of the way. Kite didn't get far, as Mid blocked his path. "What the hell is this, Kite? Height is not allowed! I thought we agreed on that!"

"Yes, well, apparently my genes did not."

"No way, Boy Genius," Kanta said. "Genes can't explain this. You've become a monster. You experimented on yourself, didn't you? I've always told you not to do that, no matter how tempting it was."

"Now I remember why I didn't miss you two."

"Hey!" Mid hit Kite's arm. "Take that back! I'm your favourite cousin! You were obligated to miss me!"

"Can we move this into another room, preferably the kitchen? We skipped lunch today to keep working. I'm hungry."

"Sure!" Mid latched on to Kite's arm, dragging him down the hall. "Henna went out to pick up some stuff for a big dinner, to celebrate my homecoming, but she made some tea."

"Of course Henna made tea, but is there any food?"

"It's your house, isn't it, Kite? You should know the answer to that better than me ..." Mid's voice faded as they disappeared into the kitchen. The little twins and Bear moved into the living room where they could better play. Paige and Kanta were alone.

"How have you been?" Kanta's voice was softer.

"Good. Really good."

"You guys are happy here?"

"We are. Really happy." Knowing Kanta would want to hear about her sister, Paige said, "Tai's happy too. At least, as happy as she can be. And she ... she doesn't know anything. She's been normal, and she's doing well as a trainee. I think she's moving on."

"I'm glad. What about you? Are you moving on?"

Paige hadn't expected him to ask about her, so she was pleasantly surprised. "I don't really know. I haven't been thinking about it as much, and things feel lighter so ... maybe that means I'm moving on."

"You're not stuttering."

"I don't much, not anymore."

"It's weird. In a good way. You really do seem different, you know. Again, in a good way. And don't listen to my sister. You look great."

Paige ducked her head, afraid she was blushing. "Thank you."

"Don't thank me, it's true." Kanta gave her a mischievous grin. "The guys must be falling over their feet for you."

Harven's face popped into her head and Paige quickly looked away, sure she was blushing now.

"Ah, so there *is* a guy. He'd better be treating you well."

"We're n-n-not—" Paige clamped her mouth shut. She wasn't about to start stuttering again after Kanta's comment. And talking about Harven would definitely make her stutter.

"Never mind," Kanta assured her. "I've got plenty of time to find out about this mystery guy and question him."

"You can't!" Paige wailed, horrified at the thought.

"Hey, I've gotta make sure he's good enough for our Paige." Clapping a hand on her shoulder, Kanta steered her toward the kitchen. "For now, though, let's forget about it and have some tea. If I'm right, Mid dumped my last cup, and I was actually enjoying it."

Chapter XVI

They'd been home for two days, and, while about a dozen training groups had returned, Tai's had not. Kanta was getting anxious.

He'd told Paige he would pick up the little twins from school that day, partly to take his mind off Tai's delayed return, partly to give Paige a break. Yano went with him. He'd agreed to watch his step-siblings so that Ike and his mother could spend time together. The two had decided to make it a play-date and take the kids to the market.

Grippa was telling Yano's siblings some far-fetched story about what had happened in her class that day, swatting at Alton whenever he tried to deny her insane facts. Whenever Kanta saw her do that, he'd call out to her to stop, and Grippa would give him a sheepish look, promising she would, but minutes later she'd be hitting and poking her brother again.

"They get along worse than mine do," Yano commented. Yano's little brother was a year older than the little twins, his sister a year younger. With their dark eyes and hair and tanned complexions, they took after their mother. Kanta couldn't see fair-skinned and light-haired Ike in them at all.

"So did you hear about the Plasma Fields?" Yano asked, as they slowed by a stall selling toys and trinkets the kids wanted to look at.

"No. What happened?"

"Mom told me that apparently a report came in around a month ago that a Plasma Field was raided.

Sounds like it was close to where we were at the time, too."

"Are you serious? What about the sentries?"

"Knocked out and tied up. Didn't see much, apparently. The raiders attacked at night, wearing hoods and masks. They took almost 20 sheepworth of plasma. Drained them."

"Gods ..." Bandits and plasma smugglers' raiding the Fields had always been trouble, but lately they were getting bolder.

"It gets worse," Yano continued. "There was another raid, six months ago. A sentry was killed. Same raiders too, apparently—or at least wearing the same disguises. Guy who got killed managed to rip off a raider's mask, one of the witnesses said, and he must have seen the raider's face, because the raider shot him."

"*Shot* him?" Kanta repeated. It was almost unheard of that someone carried a gun that used anything but plasma.

"Yeah. Right in the middle eye, too."

Kanta was speechless, horrified that one living person would kill another the same way he'd kill a boss.

"Mom told me something else, even weirder."

"I'm not sure weird is the right word ..."

"It is for this. Apparently a pack of hellcats—a giant, beyond-average pack—have been wandering through city and village ruins lately."

"What's so weird about that? Hellcats hang around haunted areas anyway. I mean, I guess if the numbers are that big ..."

"No, see, the weird part is, they've seen a human with them."

"That's ridiculous."

"I thought so, too, but there are eyewitnesses! Apparently they said—"

"Kanta, I want this." Grippa held up a glittery pink bracelet. "It's my most favourite thing ever. Please can I have it?"

"Why don't you ask for it for New Year's?"

"Paige would buy it for me."

"No she wouldn't," Alton said from behind Grippa, still poking through one of the jewellery stall bins. Grippa turned and smacked her brother on the shoulder.

"Come on, Grip, none of that." Kanta tugged her from her brother. "Play nice."

"If I do, can I have this?" Grippa held up the bracelet again.

"No. Put it back where you found it."

"Kanta's mean," Grippa muttered, replacing the bracelet.

"I know I am, Grip. In fact, I'm so mean I'm treating you all to ice cream."

Grippa immediately brightened, and the other three children perked up. Finished with the stall now that ice cream had been mentioned, the children ran ahead of Kanta and Yano, discussing and debating flavours.

"Are you going to treat me, too?" Yano asked playfully.

"No way. You can pay for yourself."

Yano mimicked Grippa's pout and tone. "Kanta's mean."

"Kanta's still not paying for you. Better get out your coins and start counting."

Chapter XVII

Tai couldn't explain the relief she felt when she and her fellow trainees finally reached Hunters City. Kassa and Os had sent them all home, asking them to report in on Friday to receive their field-test results and to find out whether they'd start field training after winter break. The check-in was required, but it was more formality than anything else because, as Korel had said, it was obvious they'd all passed. Still, Kassa and Os needed to submit reports on each trainee and how they'd fared, which would then be reviewed and officially accepted or rejected. All trainees would receive a pass or fail.

Tai collected her bags and joined the others. They didn't talk much; they were all tired from the journey. Korel and Silsa were the first to split off, heading in a different direction than the others.

"I think when I get home I'll take a nap," Gareth announced. "A three-day nap. I'll wake up for Friday."

Tai thought it was an excellent idea.

Gareth didn't attempt to stick with the group and pass by Tai's house this time; he simply waved to the others. "I'll see you all on Friday."

That left Damian, Mao, and Tai.

"Want me to carry one of your bags?" Damian asked Tai. "You look tired."

"I'm fine."

Damian was quiet a moment, then he asked Mao. "Where do you live, anyway?"

"On the other side of the market."

"Oh right," Damian said. "I forgot."

Mao didn't reply.

This was the first time Mao had kept walking with them. Tai usually walked home alone, having left before the others, but sometimes they'd catch up with her and they'd walk together. If Gareth stayed to walk the long way home, so did Mao, but, if he left, Mao darted off into the crowd soon after. Despite being as tired as the others, Damian managed to look annoyed that Mao wasn't keeping with his typical habit.

"I can't believe New Year's is a week from Friday." Damian attempted conversation again. "It doesn't feel like we were gone that long."

Tai disagreed. It felt like they'd been gone forever. She didn't say this, sighing instead as she readjusted her bag. The weight was bothering her, especially how it was dispersed. She was used to all the weight being against her back.

"Are you sure you don't want me to take that?" Damian asked.

"Yes," Tai answered. "Besides, you already have two."

"I'd be fine."

"*I'm* fine." She wished the manor wasn't so far from the city gates. Like Damian, she was carrying two bags, and they were hurting her arms and shoulders. But she didn't need someone carrying her bag for her. She was fine.

Mao reached over, hooked his fingers under the strap over her shoulder, and tugged. Tai looked startled as her bag slid off her shoulder into his hold.

"She said she doesn't need help." Damian snapped at Mao.

Mao didn't look at him but fixed the bag on his

shoulder. "Just to give you a break," he explained to Tai. "I only have one bag, and it's light."

Tai was about to protest, but her shoulder already felt better. Maybe a short break would be okay, Tai thought, as she fixed the strap of her remaining bag across her chest, dividing the weight over her body.

"Why do you only have one bag?" Damian demanded, annoyed. "Where do you store all your gear?"

"I don't have my own gear."

"Are you kidding? You don't even have your own gun?"

Mao didn't reply.

"Didn't your father get you one?" Damian pressed. "It's weird for a commander's kid not to have his own gear. He must have at least gotten you a gun!"

"I didn't want him to get me anything." Tai noticed Mao had clenched his jaw.

"You're a *hunter*. What kind of hunter doesn't want his own gear? Your father probably could have gotten you the best, with his connections. Are you even serious about hunting?"

Mao stopped abruptly. Shrugging Tai's bag off his shoulder, he held it out to her. "Sorry. This way is shorter. I'm leaving now."

Tai took her bag back and, before she could say anything, Mao ran down a side street, hurrying away from them.

"That way isn't faster," Damian pointed out. "Not if he lives on the other side of the market. It's faster to go straight through."

Tai watched as Mao disappeared behind a corner.

"Want me to take your bag now?"

"No!" Tai snapped, throwing the strap over her shoulder and rushing ahead. Startled, Damian tried to keep pace. He caught up, but Tai didn't slow down. At the manor she marched through the gate without a word, shut it behind her, and strode up to the house. She didn't stop until she was inside, when she closed the door and leaned her back against it, exhausted. Anger coursed through her.

Tai stayed where she was until her breathing returned to normal. She didn't call out as she took the stairs. She wanted to drop off her bags, and maybe wash up, before worrying about anything else. She hadn't showered nearly as much as she would've liked during the past few weeks, since hot water was only available at the towns they'd passed.

Tai walked down the upstairs hall, bedroom doors on each side. She was just about to walk by Kite's, when she heard voices inside.

"... you don't even want to tell your favourite cousin about the cool new gadgets you're inventing?"

"How many times do I have to tell you it's not a matter of *if* I want to tell anyone or not—it's classified."

"Classified. If you ask me, that's a pretty vague word."

"In what way?"

Tai knocked on the door before the exchange could continue, figuring she should let someone know she was home. The door opened. Mid, Kanta's little sister, stared up at her. Tai stared back.

"Ah, Tai," Kite said from behind Mid, where he was sitting at his desk. His chair faced the bed on which, taking in the rumpled sheets, Mid had been sitting. "You're back. How was the field test?"

"It was fine."

"Good."

"What the hell happened to your hair?" Mid asked.

"I grew it out. It's easier to tie up."

"Yeah, sure, but that's not okay." Mid flicked her own hair. "Mine's long now too. Cut yours."

"Excuse me?"

"Cut. It. We can't both have long hair, and I like mine long. Cut your hair."

Tai turned to Kite. "I just wanted to let you know I'm back. I'll be in my room."

Kite nodded, and returned to the scattered papers on his desk. Tai started down the hall.

"Yeah, good to see you too!" Mid yelled, then in a slightly lower volume to Kite, "Is no one happy to see me?"

Tai heard Kite's faint reply. "Maybe if you didn't start insulting people as soon as you saw them …"

"It's called honesty, Kite—"

Tai closed her bedroom door on Mid's voice, still echoing down the hall. Dropping her bags, Tai crossed the room to open her drapes, letting sunlight spill in. She saw Bear in the back garden, helping Henna hang out the laundry.

Tai unpacked her bags, knowing if she left them she'd put it off for weeks. That task done, she grabbed a set of fresh clothes from her drawer and went into the washroom that joined hers and Paige's rooms. She showered and dried her hair as best she could with her towel, then returned to her bedroom in sweatpants and tank top. Dropping onto her bed, Tai stretched out and stared at the dark wooden ceiling. It was made of the same wood as the rest of the manor, which gave the house a dreary, lonely ambience. Tai didn't mind, although Paige and the little twins had difficulty adjusting to the dreariness at first, lighting lamps and candles in their rooms. Tai had one lamp, on her nightstand.

Rolling off her bed, Tai crouched down to reach under the bed. She pulled out a long wooden box with a bronze lock—one of her first purchases after becoming a trainee. Tai reached into the drawer of her bedside table and dug out the key hidden below some stuff. She fit it into the lock and opened the case.

Sunrays shone through the window behind her, lighting the object before her a fiery crimson. Tai's finger traced over the familiar letters embedded in the weapon. When she was younger, she'd tried copying that exact hand but could never reproduce it. Her own writing was too chunky, too unrefined. Brighton had copied it perfectly.

Tai slammed the case shut. Falling back on her haunches, she pressed her palms against her eyes. All she could see was Brighton, the soft, secretive smile he'd share with her across a room full of people, or when they were just on their own, telling her without a word that he was with her. The way his eyes twinkled when he heard her laughter after telling a joke that only she would understand. His voice, calling out to her throughout the day, even when he knew all it would take was a look, and he'd have her full attention. He would still call her name, just because he could. Just because he was Brighton.

She'd told Mao about Brighton. She'd started talking and hadn't been able to stop. He'd been quiet, watching her, listening, waiting for her to finish or to continue even when she paused for minutes at a time. When she had finally done, he didn't call her ghost-killing methods crazy or the curse crazy. He didn't comment on any of it.

After hearing Tai's story, he'd said, "You think your brother left because of you."

Tai hadn't said that, not in so many words. But it was true.

"That could be right." Mao had surprised her. The few times she'd dared share her worries with Kanta, he'd tried to reassure her that it wasn't her fault. "You'll probably never find your brother, so you won't know for sure."

"I already gave up on finding him. He doesn't want me to find him."

"But you still *want* to find him."

Tai couldn't deny that. "I just want to know why he left. That's all."

"You're lying."

Tai had been too startled to respond.

"You want to make sure he still loves you. That he regrets what he did. He doesn't. If you really want to move on, accept it. He doesn't love you. Maybe never did."

"That's a horrible thing to say."

"It's what you're thinking. Isn't it?"

Now, Tai shoved the case back under her bed, tempted to throw away the key altogether. If she kept coming back to her flamethrower like this, kept looking at it, how would she ever move on? She kept her past under her bed and its key in her bedside table.

Tai squeezed the key in her hand so tightly it left an imprint in her palm. Could she throw it away? Could she throw it all away—every ghost she'd killed, every lesson her grandmother had given her, every smile she'd shared with her brother?

A knock sounded at her door. Startled, Tai dropped the key into the drawer and slammed it shut just in time: her door was flung open. Tai barely had time to register what was going on before she was enfolded in strong arms.

"Kanta—" Tai broke off in a surprised yelp when he picked her up, feet dangling above the ground.

"Gods, Kanta! Put me down!"

Kanta laughed, and Tai could feel his hair brush against her stomach, where her top had ridden up. Tai saw Mid pass by the open doorway. She glanced at them, made a gagging motion, and went on.

After spinning her around, Kanta set Tai down on the floor behind him, so her back was now to the door. He was grinning like an idiot, ghost eyes glowing even more than normal. He wasn't even using The Grin.

Tai yanked her top down over her stomach. "What the hell was that?"

"Sorry." Kanta was slightly breathless. "I just couldn't help it."

Tai tried to scowl at him, but he looked so ridiculously happy a smile tugged at her own lips. "Fine. I'll let you off. Just this once."

"Gods, I forgot how amazing you are. I can't believe I kept away for a year."

"If you start talking like that, I'll kick you out of my room. I can't believe you barged in like that. What if I'd been changing?"

"That would've been okay." Now Kanta flashed The Grin. "Besides, I knocked. That counts as fair warning."

Tai rolled her eyes, unable to stop smiling.

Kanta calmed down. When he spoke, his voice was softer. "How have you been?"

"Do you honestly think I wrote to you all this time just so you could ask me such a stupid question as soon as we met in person?"

"Right, that was very inconsiderate of me." The Grin again. "So how about we take advantage of this *in person*? We're already in your room …"

"You haven't changed at all." Tai took his hand

and tugged him toward the hall. "Let's go get something to eat."

"Why not work up an appetite first?"

"Never mind what I said. You have changed. You've gotten worse." Tai closed her door behind them. "I haven't eaten since this morning. I'm starving."

"It's a good thing we brought back some food, then."

"We?"

Kanta grinned, taking her hand again and pulling her down the hall. "You'll see."

Kanta led her down to the living room, where a young man wearing a tiger-print bandana was sitting cross-legged at the coffee table, dividing up sweets among four children. Two were her siblings.

"Tai!" Alton scrambled to his feet and rushed to his sister. He tackled her with a hug that almost made Tai trip. Steadying herself, she laughed and ran her hands through her little brother's hair.

"How was your test?" Alton asked, tilting his head to look up at her. "Did you kill any ghosts?"

"Yeah. Tons."

"Did you kill a boss?" Grippa asked. She stayed where she was, guarding her small pile of candy and idly licking a red lollipop. "It's only really cool if you kill a boss."

Tai was hurt that her younger sister hadn't greeted her with a hug too, but she pushed away the feeling. "I killed a boss."

Grippa sucked her lollipop, although she did look impressed.

"Tai." Kanta gestured to the young man who watched her with interest. "This is Yano. I don't know if you remember him. I introduced you guys last year. He's part of our unit now."

Tai didn't really remember—Kanta had introduced her to a bunch of hunters when they'd arrived two years ago and during his break last year—but she did recall the name from Kanta's letters.

Yano got to his feet and offered Tai his hand, which she took. "Nice to meet you, again. Kanta talks about you all the time. As in, we tell him to shut up but he never does."

"You're exaggerating," Kanta insisted.

"I'd be exaggerating if I'd said Kanta's mentioned you once or twice." Yano, looked Tai over with approval. "I can see why we couldn't get him to shut up."

Tai took back her hand. "I can see why you and Kanta are friends."

"Is that a good thing?"

Tai didn't reply.

"I'm home!" Someone called from the porch. A moment later, Paige stood in the doorway. She smiled when she saw Tai. "You're back."

"I'm back."

"Are you … Did everything go okay?"

"It went fine."

"So this is the sister," Tai heard Yano say to Kanta, "I understand why you wrote—"

Tai glanced over in time to see Kanta elbow Yano in the ribs, shutting his friend up with a gasp. At Tai's look, Kanta explained, "He talks too much."

"Tai!" Alton tugged her sleeve. "Kanta bought us candy! Do you want some?"

"He bought you candy? Did you thank him?"

"Yep! We thanked him for the ice cream too!"

"Ice cream *and* candy. How nice of him."

"Kanta's not nice," Grippa contradicted. "He's mean. But that's okay."

"I wanted to treat them," Kanta explained.

"But not me," Yano added. "He didn't want to treat me."

"Who would—" Kanta started, but Henna came in. She took one look at the children and candy strewn over the coffee table and shook her head. Then she saw Tai.

"Excellent, you're back! How are you, dear?"

"Hungry." Tai knew Henna would welcome such an answer, and she was right. The older woman clapped her hands together to get everyone's attention and asked if all her guests would be staying for dinner.

"That was the plan." Yano earned an annoyed look from Kanta. "What? I wanted to give Ike and my mother a night alone. You think I want to go back in the middle of what grown-ups do when kids aren't around? They haven't seen each other for *months*."

"Point taken," Kanta said.

"We'll eat early," Henna announced. "Keep those treats for after dinner, if you would, please, and don't leave wrappers lying around. There's a bin in the kitchen for garbage, in case you were wondering."

The children picked up the candy wrappers, pocketing their unopened candy.

"I'll help you," Paige offered, as Henna headed to the kitchen. The older woman waved her off.

"Spend some time with your sister. I've been cooking in this house for 45 years on my own. I can handle another hour."

After Henna had gone, Kanta ushered Tai toward the couch. "While we wait, I want to hear all about this boss you killed and which of my techniques you used."

"I use a gun. You use a katana."

"Variations on the technique, then." Kanta sat next to her. "Come on, let's hear all the details."

Tai looked from him to the other expectant faces around the room. Even the little kids were giving her their full attention, anticipating a good ghost story to tell their friends later. This gave Tai pause. If it had been just Kanta, or maybe even Paige, she might have told them what had really happened. How she'd panicked and instead of waiting for help had gone ahead and used her old methods. How, even if it had worked perfectly, she still regretted it, because it had opened an ache in her she'd been trying to forget. But it wasn't just them, so when Tai told the story, she told the one she and Mao had told Erik and their instructors: she'd killed the boss by shooting its third eye.

Tai felt terrible for lying to them but also for being relieved that she didn't have to tell the truth that she couldn't, not with Kanta's friend and the kids around. She felt guilty because she didn't know if, even if she had been alone with Kanta, she could have brought herself to talk to him about it. They'd been separated for so long, after all, and even if they seemed the same, they weren't. Tai knew *she* wasn't.

The girl Kanta had met two years ago, who hated hunters and wanted to burn every ghost in the world, had become the one who locked her flamethrower in a case under her bed because she didn't like the memories it inspired—the girl who didn't let her younger siblings speak their older brother's name because she didn't want those memories either, the girl too tired of her past to deal with it anymore.

She'd become that girl, and she didn't know if she was ready to share that with Kanta, someone who had known her before, when she was stronger. It would mean facing how much she'd changed, how much losing her brother had changed her. Tai didn't think she was ready to do that yet. Maybe never.

Chapter XVIII

I passed!" Gareth sang out. "Unit Q17 here I come!"
It was Friday morning. Tai had gone to the Hunter Association Headquarters as she was supposed to, where she met up with the others. Their results had been posted, listing the names of all trainees who would start field training at the end of winter, although they hadn't yet been assigned their units. That would happen a week before hunting season started.

"Would you shut up?" Korel told Gareth, when he continued twirling around and cheering at the bottom of the building's steps. "We all knew we were going to pass. It's not that big a deal."

"Just leave him, Kor," Damian insisted. "There's no point in trying to calm him down. He's already in Q17 dreamland."

"He could stop being so loud about it."

"I'll be as loud as I like! Oh, but I've just had a brilliant idea!"

"Like shutting up?" Korel asked.

"Much better than that! We should all go out tonight! We ought to celebrate!"

"Actually, that sounds pretty good," Damian agreed.

"We already celebrated, back in that town," Korel pointed out. "But I guess we could call this an official celebration."

"Silsa? Tai?" Gareth asked. "You'll both come, yes?"

"Definitely!" Silsa smiled at Tai. "You'll go too, right?"

After two years of rigorous training and summer lessons, going out for a night with her fellow trainees seemed the least Tai deserved.

"Yeah. I'll go."

"There are lots of plasma smugglers, right?" Mid sat, feet tucked under her, on Kite's bed. "Why do they do it? Smuggle the plasma, I mean. What would they need it for?"

Kite had turned his chair to face her when she came in, accepting that it was better to hear her out than to try to make her leave, since that would take even longer. There was no way Kite could make her leave, even if he was a giant now, which Mid still hadn't adjusted to. She was glad he was sitting down, making his height less obvious.

"Most smugglers purchase it to sell to villages who wish to avoid paying the appropriate taxes to the Hunter Association."

"Are the taxes that high?"

"They're accurate. The Council decides the tax rates, taking into account the needs of the populace as well as the needs of the Association."

"The needs being …?"

"Salaries, for the most part. Upkeep of the training facilities, the headquarters. Really, Mid, this is all obvious. You should know it."

"I do. Sort of …"

"Why the sudden interest in plasma smuggling?"

"Uh … just, I overheard Thalus talking about it before we got back. He and Mist, talking about it, or something."

"Has there been an influx of raids? Were Thalus and Mist discussing that when you eavesdropped?"

"It's so weird that you call your father by his first name."

"Thank you for giving me your opinion on that, yet again. Is that what *my father* and Mist were discussing when you were eavesdropping?"

"Eeew. That sounds way too strange. Go back to being a cold, indifferent son."

"Just answer the question, Mid."

"Dunno! Something 'bout that, maybe! And I wasn't eavesdropping!"

"That, I do not believe."

"Ugh! Never mind! I'll go ask Wendy about it."

"Why didn't you do that in the first place?"

"Because Wendy's doing family stuff and meeting with the Tech Association this week. I didn't want to waste his time on info I could get from you."

"I have important things to do with my time too! The project I'm working on right now—"

"Is classified. Uh-huh."

"I was going to say, due to be completed by next Monday."

"That close to New Year's? Don't you get a break?"

"When I've completed this project, which is kind of hard to do with your bothering me every hour." Kite turned his chair back to his desk. "If you're really so curious about smugglers and their issues, go to the archives and look up raid reports."

"Fine." Mid pushed herself off Kite's bed. "But don't run to me for company when you've done your precious project. I'll be busy."

"Whatever. Straighten my bed before you leave."

Mid rumpled the covers, letting Kite's door swing open behind her, which he hated. Kite called for her to close it, but Mid stomped down the stairs.

Thalus hadn't been to the house since their unit had returned to the City. He'd stayed at the Association, presumably in one of the dorms they kept for commanders, to deal with some *official* business. Just like Regailia, who was still away on her own classified business. Everything about this family was classified lately. No one included Mid in anything.

Then again, Mid had her own classified business now. She and Bear did.

The little twins were at school, and Paige was at her job at some dumb flower shop Mid had never visited. She contemplated dropping by, just so she could make fun of it later, but stopped, horrified with herself. She was so bored she actually considered visiting Paige for fun? She'd be swapping hunting tips with Tai next.

Ashamed of herself, Mid searched for Bear. As expected, she found him in the back garden, bathing in the sun. When they were home, Bear usually spent most of his time in the garden, staring up at the sky.

Mid watched Bear for a moment before hopping down the steps. Bear looked at her as she approached but didn't move a rock muscle.

"Heyya Bear." Mid stood beside him. Hands on her hips, she tilted her head to the sky. "Anything interesting up there?"

Bear was unsure of a response.

"There aren't even any clouds. That's no fun. If there were clouds, then I could understand. I wish I could see what you see, Bear, whatever that is."

The sky was an endless expanse of deep blue, with the blazing sun at the centre. Mid tried looking straight at it a moment, but then blinked away, her vision spotty.

"Let's go to the market," Mid said decisively after her sight had recovered. "Maybe we can visit Wendy after. I know I was telling you earlier how busy Wendy is, but I haven't spoken to him since we got back, and he's probably missing me loads. Like you would, Bear. Except you'd miss me more because I'm your favourite, right?"

Mid was sure Bear inclined his head.

"Of course I'm your favourite." Mid strode to the back gate. "I'm everyone's favourite. But only you are willing to admit it, Bear. Only you really appreciate me. That's why you're *my* favourite. You're the favourite's favourite. Be proud of that, okay?"

Bear probably nodded.

"Good, let's spend the money I took from Kanta's room this morning. Don't feel bad, Bear. He deserves it. He doesn't properly appreciate his favourite—me."

As Mid was about to open the back gate, she noticed a ribbon tied around a fence post in the fence—a red ribbon.

"Seriously?" Mid looked down the back alley and could hardly contain her giddiness when she saw a red ribbon on a neighbour's fence a few metres away.

"Remember that thing I was telling you about, Bear? With the ribbons?" Mid untied the ribbon from the fence and tried to tie it around Bear's arm. It went halfway. "We'll just have to get more and tie them together."

Mid followed the trail of ribbons, collecting all of them. She tied enough together for an armband for Bear and two for herself. The last ribbon was sticking out of a mailbox at a house recently put up for sale.

Digging into the mailbox, Mid found a letter at the end of the ribbon. It was short, without recipient or sender indicated. It apologized for so quickly taking her up on her offer and asked to meet up at a certain tavern that night.

"So, Bear." Mid pocketed the letter and ribbon. "I know Kanta's typically the one doing this sort of thing, but ... are you up for a dip in the local night-life?"

Kanta had taken Tai out to lunch after she'd returned from the H.A. with news of her success. They were sitting in a diner in the market, finishing their meals.

"So I was talking to the guys this morning." Kanta didn't have to elaborate. Thanks to all their letters, Tai knew who "the guys" were. "And we were thinking of going out tonight, you know, to celebrate."

Tai, about to put her fork in her mouth, paused.

"Browen's bringing Silsa," Kanta added. "You won't be the only girl, if that bothers you."

"It doesn't. It wouldn't." Tai laid her fork down. "The other trainees and I were ... well, we were going to celebrate on our own."

That surprised Kanta. He wasn't sure why. Of course the trainees would celebrate. He just hadn't thought Tai would have gotten to know her fellow trainees well enough to be invited along, let alone want to go. She hadn't mentioned the other trainees in her letters. Not really.

"I don't have to go," Tai insisted. "I mean, I can go with you guys instead. Or you could come with us. I'm sure they wouldn't mind ..."

"No, that's okay. You guys should celebrate on your own. It's what I did when I completed my training, even if I was on the road when that happened. You should go."

"Are you sure?"

"Yeah. You go." Kanta gave her a half-hearted grin. "We can go another time."

Chapter XIX

Tai felt guilty when she left the manor that night. Kanta had wanted them to spend time together, and she'd refused. They'd have plenty of time later, Tai reassured herself. They had the rest of the break to spend together, and after winter she'd be joining their unit, so what did one night matter?

She repeated this as she walked down the street. She hadn't put on anything special, just a pair of jeans and a black T-shirt. She'd also thrown on her trainee jacket as the nights were colder, although it wasn't yet cold enough to require a thick coat and hat.

The tavern she was headed for was near the Eastern Market, which had the best nightlife in the City. She'd agreed to meet her group there at 8 p.m. Both Damian and Gareth had offered to walk with her, as Korel and Silsa lived close to the Eastern Market. They hadn't wanted Tai to walk alone, but she'd refused, not just because she thought she was fine on her own but because she'd assumed Kanta would be with her.

She may have been wrong about that last part, but she was right about being fine on her own. She reached the tavern without any difficulties.

This tavern was much larger and busier than the last one she'd been in. Painted in a rich red, with matching upholstery for the chairs and booths, and similar hues for the lampshades on the ceiling lights, the tavern had a red glow. Red, like her flamethrower.

Tai searched the crowd for the others, hoping she wasn't the first to arrive. She didn't wait long. Gareth waved from a corner table, where everyone was already sitting. Tai pushed through the crowd toward the table.

"Pull up a chair," Gareth greeted her.

"Good luck," Korel said. "I had to steal mine."

"We could share," Damian offered.

Tai tried not to show her disgust, quickly looking for a free chair.

"I told you we should have sat at a booth," Korel said.

"None of them was free," Gareth replied.

Silsa tugged at Tai's arm and pointed. "Over there. That table has one."

Tai retrieved the chair. Then she realized who was missing. "Where's Mao?"

"Who cares?" Damian muttered.

"I don't know." Gareth hadn't heard Damian's comment. "He said he'd come. Perhaps he's running late."

Gareth waved over a waiter and ordered food for all of them, while Damian and Korel told Tai about their plans to go to a club after eating. Damian and Korel argued about which club they should attend.

"Did Browen offer to take you out tonight?" Tai asked Silsa.

"Hmm? No, he didn't. He might have, but I told him about our plans almost right away. I was really excited when I got home. I think I annoyed him a bit."

"You should be excited!" Gareth interrupted. "We should all be excited! I'm excited!"

"We *know* you're excited," Korel stated. "You can stop making it so damn obvious now. You'd better not be this embarrassing at the New Year's Ball or I'm not coming near you."

"New Year's!" Gareth exclaimed. "I forgot it was so close! Something else to be excited about!"

Korel sighed.

"We should all go together again this year." Gareth turned to Tai. "You didn't come with us last year, did you?"

Tai shook her head. She hadn't known them well then, but she would have gone with her family and Kanta's anyway, as she would this year.

Gareth shot up in his seat, waving his arms and almost knocking over his glass, which Korel caught just in time. "Over here! We're over here!"

Tai saw Mao weaving toward them, head down and his shoulders more slumped than usual. When he reached their table, he didn't say a word.

"Chair …" Gareth looked around the tavern. "Chair, chair, chair …"

"Aren't you going to offer to share?" Korel asked Damian.

"You're so funny, Kor."

"Here, you take mine, Mao." Gareth slid back from the table. "I'll find another."

Mao sank into Gareth's chair. Silsa pushed a drink from the centre of the table toward him. "We got this for you, but it might be warm now …"

Wordlessly, Mao accepted the glass. He didn't drink from it, just set it in front of him. He kept his head bowed, bangs hiding his face more than usual.

"Are you going to tell us why you're late?" Damian leaned heavily on the table. "Were you waiting that whole time for Daddy to come home and praise you?"

Mao's eyes snapped up, narrowing so much his right eye was barely open.

"Back off, Damian," Korel warned.

"Oh, come on, Kor. You know it's true. Everyone does. The only reason he became a hunter was to please his father. So? Is he pleased with you yet? Has he accepted his little bastard?"

Gareth came over, dragging a stool. "Hey, I kinda found a chair—"

Mao pushed to his feet and strode off. Damian watched him, smug.

"What happened?" Gareth asked.

"Damian's a complete asshole, that's what!" Korel explained. "How the hell could you say something like that to him? It's not his fault his father cheated on your aunt! Stop blaming him!"

Tai hadn't heard this before.

"Oh, don't worry, I blame his father plenty," Damian continued. "But it's not like Mao is innocent either. If he hadn't come back, my aunt never would have found out. I'm glad she did—she's better off without that bastard—but he still didn't have to come back and publicly embarrass her, show everyone her husband had cheated. He was the proof. He destroyed her life and her honour, all because he wanted the benefits of being a commander's son."

"You don't know that." Korel's tone was weaker.

"Oh yeah? Why else would he have shown up after 14 years? He obviously found out who his father was and decided to cash in."

"Shut up!" Gareth yelled, surprising everyone. The stool shook in his hands. "You don't know what you're talking about, Damian. You never do."

"I know a hell of a lot more than you. You think whatever he tells you is the truth, just because you're his only friend? You don't even like him, Gareth. You're nice to him because you have to be."

"That isn't true!"

"Of course it is. Your older brother's in his father's

unit, right? That's why you look out for him, because it's good for your brother if you do and bad for your brother if you don't. You might even benefit from it, get accepted into that unit, be one of the commander's favourites since you helped his illegitimate son make it through training … yeah, that sounds like a nice set-up."

Shaking, Gareth opened his mouth to reply, but nothing came out. Korel reached up and squeezed his arm, glaring at Damian. "Do you want everyone to hate you?"

"To be perfectly honest, I could care less. Our training's done, and so is this stupid charade of all of us getting along." Damian got up. Tai was shocked when he put a hand on her shoulder and said, "You coming?"

Tai gaped at him. "Are you serious?"

"Right," Damian sneered, pulling his hand back. "I forgot. You and the bastard get along now. Well, I hope you enjoy his company, because you just lost your chance to ever enjoy mine."

After saying this, Damian left. The others stared after him, stunned. Then Gareth dropped the stool he was holding and shrugged into the jacket he'd left at the table. "I have to go look for Mao. Make sure he's okay."

"I'll come with you." Korel grabbed her own coat and followed Gareth out. Silsa and Tai left the tavern with them. They said goodbye and Silsa wished them luck before the pair took off down the street.

"That didn't go like I thought it would," Silsa remarked. "So much for celebrating. I hope they find Mao. Damian shouldn't have said those things."

"Is it true? Was Damian's aunt married to Mao's father?"

"Sorry. I keep forgetting you've only been here a few years. It happened almost four years ago when Mao showed up and his father took him in. Damian's aunt found out about the affair then and split up with him. Damian gets along really well with his aunt—she's the only other actual hunter in his family—so he's always kind of carried a grudge."

Kind of. Tai didn't think that quite captured Damian's grudge.

"It was a huge scandal at the time," Silsa explained. "At least, in the city, but it blew over and no one's really talked about it since. Mao's father is a high-ranking commander. No one wants to get on his bad side."

"Except Damian."

"Yeah …" Silsa shook her head, as if to shake the whole horrendous night. "I'm heading home now. Do you mind?"

"No, I'm going home too."

"Did you want to come back to my place? Since it's late, you don't want to walk all the way across the city by yourself."

"Thanks. I'll be fine."

Chapter XX

"I still can't believe she blew you off," Yano said, as he and Kanta carried their drinks.

"She didn't blow me off. She had plans with the other trainees."

"Yeah, and she blew you off for them."

Kanta refused to comment. They got through the crowd to Browen and Freid, who were waiting by the wall. The four had decided to stick with their plans and go to a city club, even if they weren't celebrating anything. The place they'd chosen was packed, mostly with hunter trainees, dancing to the music echoing through the room.

"Don't look so depressed," Yano ordered Kanta. "Flash your lady-killing grin."

Kanta gave Yano a withering look.

"Okay, that's not your grin, but it could probably still kill. In a bad way." Yano slapped him on the back. "It's not like she dumped you! Get over it!"

"We aren't together."

"Exactly, so, even if she wanted to, she couldn't have dumped you!"

"As much as I enjoy talking about Kanta's problems, can we not?" Freid asked.

"For once I agree with Freid," Kanta said.

"It's boring," Freid added.

"Not so sure I agree with that."

"Hey, look at it this way, Kanta," Yano insisted, "at least the other trainees like your girlfriend enough to invite her."

"Tai isn't my girlfriend," Kanta said, still thinking about Yano's comment. Apparently Tai's fellow recruits did like her, and she liked them enough to go along. The Tai he knew would have just refused if she didn't enjoy their company. Yet she'd never mentioned the other trainees in any of her letters; at least, not like someone would a group of friends. She'd only ever written about Silsa by name, and that was because Kanta knew Silsa. He didn't know anything about the others. He didn't even know how many there were. Tai wasn't obliged to tell him any of that, but Kanta wondered why she hadn't told him, whether she'd intentionally kept it back or not.

By the time Kanta had tuned back into the conversation, Yano was describing his and Browen's own graduation celebration, which, according to the extensive, likely inflated details Yano was supplying, was more on the wild side.

Listening to him, Browen winced. "Can you not remind me? My little sister's out tonight, so I'd rather not think about all the stupid stuff we did at our celebration party."

"I forgot that your responsible older brother self surfaces when we're home."

"I can't help being worried. Sil's only 17."

"Browen, we were 17 when we finished training and that didn't stop us from doing anything." Yano waved at Kanta. "He was even younger."

When Browen glanced at him, Kanta shrugged. "I was."

"You understand, though, right? You'd be worried if it was your little sister."

"Browen, I wish my little sister wanted to go out to parties. I'd rather deal with underage partying than premature soul-ripping. Besides, you shouldn't worry about Sil. She's a smart kid. And Tai's with her, if something happens."

Browen relaxed slightly, but Yano asked, "And you're not worried about Tai? What if she hooks up with one of the trainees?"

"That wouldn't happen."

"What if it already has?" When Kanta glared at him, Yano shrugged. "Look, all I'm saying is we've been gone a year. Sure, you guys wrote letters to each other, but that doesn't make up for being together in person. You of all people should know that."

"What do you mean?"

Freid spoke this time, annoyed. "Don't be an idiot, Kanta. How many girls have you fooled around with since you last saw Tai? And did you tell her about any of them?"

"Why would I do that?" Kanta asked. "It's not like any of it was serious."

Freid was disgusted. "You can be such an ass."

"Thanks. Next time you feel like hanging out, ask someone who isn't such an ass."

"Not a problem." Freid edged away from them into the crowd.

"What's wrong with him?"

"What isn't wrong with Freid? He's the uptightness of uptight." Yano stared at something near where Freid had disappeared. "Hey Kanta, isn't that the ribbon girl from the port town?"

"Ribbon girl …" Kanta followed Yano's gaze. At first Kanta didn't recognize her, with her bright red hair pulled up in a messy bun, but then she turned and he saw her face and hazel eyes, with a beauty mark just below the left one.

She spotted Kanta, too, and her red painted lips perked up in a small smile. She said something to the blonde guy beside her before weaving through the crowd. In moments, she was in front of Kanta, smirking up at him. "Isn't this a surprise?"

"Yeah, it is." Kanta was slightly dazed. "Your hair's different."

"Like it?" Mina twirled a strand around her finger. "I wanted something more fiery."

"Suits you."

"I think so."

"I thought you didn't come to Hunters City."

"Would you believe me if I said I came here hoping to see you?"

"I'd like to."

Mina laughed. "I lied. When I told you that back at the club, I was lying."

"Why?"

"I wanted to give you opportunities to impress me."

"That wasn't necessary. I'm impressive enough on my own."

"Maybe. But I wanted to hurry up the process. I'm not a patient girl."

Kanta gave her The Grin. "Isn't patience a virtue?"

"I've always preferred sins to virtues." Mina took his hand, tugging him toward the crowd. "Let's dance."

Kanta glanced toward his friends before he followed. They'd already gone. He let Mina lead him onto the dance floor.

Chapter XXI

Tai walked home, trying not to think about the disaster her night had turned into, but she couldn't help it. How had she missed the tension in the group all that time? She'd noticed that Damian tended to be mean to Mao, but she'd thought it was just his cocky personality. She hadn't realized it went any deeper.

She walked down the street that she, Damian, and Mao had gone down the day they came back, when Mao had taken her bag. That made her think about her night again, especially when she remembered how Damian had actually pushed Mao to leave.

Tai paused when she reached the alley Mao had gone down that day. It was the one he always took to avoid walking with them, she assumed, the way that Damian had said would take longer. No wonder Mao would go that way, even if it was longer, if it meant getting away from them.

Hesitating a moment, Tai went down the alley. She was too curious to pass it up, now that she was on her own, and it would probably lead her home eventually.

The alley was much darker than the street, but Tai didn't mind. She'd killed ghosts at night in the city near her village, and that had been even darker, all the streetlights toppled and smashed. She'd adjusted to the darkness and the quietness. It didn't bother her anymore.

The alley wasn't completely quiet, Tai realized; scuffling sounds came from up ahead. Suddenly on high alert, Tai edged around the corner of the alley, which led to a longer back alley behind the buildings, where people put their garbage. Two streetlamps gave enough light for her to see a group huddled halfway down the alley. Three, Tai thought first, but realized they surrounded a fourth. It took Tai a moment to realize they were beating up this fourth person. She hurried toward them, keeping to the shadows of the alley wall. As she went, Tai slid one of her daggers out of her boot.

Just before she reached them, the tallest one spotted her. Before he could call out, however, Tai grabbed the burly one in front of her by the back of his coat, jerking him toward the wall. At the same time she used her other hand to smash his head against the bricks, stunning him.

The tall one threw a punch, but Tai ducked, thankful for all the self-defence classes the Association forced on its trainees. Tai kneed her attacker once, eliciting a gasp from him, and then kneed him again. The tall man's legs crippled under him and he fell to his knees, bringing his head level with Tai's stomach. Gripping the back of his head, she slammed his forehead against her raised knee and let him go as he fell to the ground.

Dealing with the tall one had taken longer than she would have liked. Tai spun to take on the third man when she felt an arm wrap tightly around her neck.

"You're interrupting," a hot voice said in her ear.

Tai hadn't wanted to use her dagger. Sliding the weapon from her sleeve, Tai sliced at the third man's arm. It wasn't a deep cut but enough to surprise her attacker, who yelped and released her. Tai whirled around, facing him, keeping the dagger between them. She couldn't distinguish many details in the darkness except for the man's medium build and longish hair.

He spat at her feet, pulling back his hand from where he'd gripped his wound. "If that's how you wanna play ..."

As the third man slid a knife from his belt, Tai tensed. What should she do? Reach for her other dagger? Two against one would help. Or should she throw the one she had and wound him? Her aim was good. But even so, would that give the person under attack enough time to escape? Was he capable of running, or had he been beaten too badly?

Tai wanted to turn and check on the victim, whom she'd yet to get a good look at, but doing so would leave her back open.

Then the third man said, "Hold her still a sec, will ya?"

The next thing Tai knew, someone had grabbed her arms, yanking them behind her. Tai was so startled she dropped her dagger, which clattered to the ground. It took her a split second to realize she'd been grabbed by the first man she'd taken out. Apparently, he hadn't been *completely* taken out.

Tai tried to break from his hold, but he was much stronger than her. She'd only knocked him out before because she'd had the element of surprise on her side.

"I'm glad you did that." The man with the knife ran a thumb along the blade of his weapon as he approached her. "Gives me an excuse. If Charney asks, I'll just say you started it. Couldn't be helped. You were wild."

The third man was in front of her now and Tai got a better look at his face. He didn't look much older than her: he had a youthful, innocent face. There was nothing innocent in his smirk, however, or the curve of his slim brows. Light from one of the streetlamps caught his hair, colouring it a dark, almost burnt, red.

He brushed Tai's bangs out of her eyes with his knife, leaning in as he smiled at her, his green eyes bright, but not ghostly. He whispered, "Wild ones are my favourites."

Tai fought to break free.

"Are you going to lie there all day?" The redhead snapped at the tall man still groaning on the ground. "Get up, if you want to get paid."

Grimacing, the tall man pulled himself to his feet and stumbled over.

"Good. Help your idiot colleague." The redhead gestured toward Tai with his knife. "Take off her jacket. We don't want blood on it, and I tend to be messy."

Tai struggled harder. She almost got away when they released her arms to yank off the jacket. With two of them, and without her weapon, they quickly pinned her again.

"Isn't that better?" The redhead slid his knife against Tai's neck. "I bet you were hot after playing around with us."

Tai strained against her captor's hold to snap her teeth at the redhead. He pulled back from her, laughing. "You really are wild! Just my type. You've got a nice face, too." He leaned in, even closer, as he brought his knife to her cheek. "Too bad I have to ruin it," he whispered.

Just as Tai felt the blade bite into her flesh, someone tackled her assailant, knocking them both to the ground. There was a flash of silver in the light, and

Tai realized it was the dagger she'd dropped.

Before the redhead could do anything, Tai's dagger was being pressed to his throat. "Drop your weapon or I'll drop mine on your pulse."

Tai recognized that voice. His back was to her, but taking in his dark hair and thin frame, Tai knew who it was.

The redhead smirked, even as he glared, dropping his knife.

"Tell them to let her go," Mao said, adding snidely, "*if* they want to get paid."

The man laughed and waved his hand at the men holding Tai. They released her.

"Pick up his knife." Mao did not take his gaze from the man.

Tai slid it into her boot, in case one of the others tried to take it from her.

"Isn't this comfortable?" the redhead said. "Why don't you and the girl switch places, kid? No offence, but I'd rather have her on top of me."

Anger flashed across Mao's face and he pressed the dagger so that it drew blood.

The redhead let out a coughing laugh. "Touchy, aren't you? Maybe we should have roughed you up a bit more. There's still time."

A click sounded in the alley. Tai's gaze darted to the other two men. The burly one was pointing a gun, safety off, at Mao.

"You might want to get up," the redhead said.

Furious, Mao got to his feet. The redhead easily picked himself up. He grabbed the dagger out of Mao's hand, sheathing it in his belt, where his own knife had been. Then he punched Mao in the stomach. Tai jerked forward, but stopped when the gun swerved to point at her. The redhead punched Mao again, causing him to fall to his knees. He then grabbed Mao's hair, wrenching his head back to make him look up at him.

"That was just something to remember me by," the redhead hissed. "Next time, we'll have even more fun."

Letting go of Mao he walked to the other man. Taking the gun from them, he went over to Tai. She was frozen as he pressed the weapon against her head. Fear coursed through her. She'd never been so afraid of a human before.

"What's wrong?" For a moment his face really did look innocent. He clicked the safety back on the gun. "Better?"

Tai's heart hammered in her chest. She should have kept the knife out, even if it wouldn't have done anything against a gun. She should have kept it out.

"I think I like you even more like this." He leaned in to her ear. "*Terrified.*"

Tai couldn't help jerking back from him. The redhead laughed, pulled the gun away, and sauntered down the alley, the other two falling in step behind him wordlessly.

The redhead hadn't gone far when he turned back to Tai. Patting her dagger, he called, "We'll switch, until next time. Then I'll take both. Look forward to it."

He turned away again, laughing as he and the two men disappeared. Tai was still frozen, watching the spot where they'd been swallowed by the shadows.

"Tai …"

Mao's voice broke through her stupor. Tai hurried over, dropping to her knees so that she was at his level. She realized they'd also taken his jacket, which he'd been wearing earlier at the tavern. He had bruises on his arms from where he'd been grabbed.

Careful to avoid his bruises, Tai put a hand on his shoulder, using her other hand to brush back his bangs to get a better look at his face. His left eye was almost swollen shut, making it the smaller of the two, for once. His lip was split, and his nose had bled.

"Why did you do that?" Mao asked.

"Why did I do what?"

"Get involved!" He was angrier than he'd been when he'd spoken to the redhead. His voice then had been cold, distant. Now it was hot and furious. "Why would you come down an alley, on your own at night, and attack a group of armed men? Are you insane?"

"You obviously came this way too, on your own."

"Yeah, but I didn't join a fight—one where I was outnumbered and outweighed!"

"I helped you! If I hadn't come—"

"If you hadn't come, they would have beaten me up a bit more and left! They just wanted to rob me! It was because of you that things got this bad!"

Tai felt like she'd been the one punched. Getting to her feet, she said, "I understand." And walked away.

"Tai, wait!" Mao called. He pushed himself up with a wince. "It was my fault. That's why I'm mad. If I hadn't left like that and come down the alley …"

"Why were you back here?"

"I was going home."

Tai had assumed that, but she didn't understand why Mao wouldn't take the shortcut if Damian wasn't there. "Then why did you take the longer way?"

"Because I was going home."

Tai took a step back toward him. "Can I ask?"

Mao's fleeting half-smile was humourless. "I

don't know why you'd want to. The others told you already, didn't they? Damian told you."

"About your father and his aunt? I only found out tonight."

"I wish you hadn't. The others pity me enough already, if they don't hate me, like Damian."

"They don't hate you. They're worried. Gareth and Korel went to look for you."

"That's only because Gareth has to if he wants to get himself and his brother in my father's good books. And Korel doesn't care; she just takes my side over Damian's because he rejected her a year ago, and she sticks to Gareth sometimes to make him jealous. Silsa's just as bad, in her own way, but at least her attempts to be nice are simply out of pity. Damian's really the best of them, even if he's an arrogant, self-righteous ass. At least when he bothers to talk to me, everything he says is true."

Tai didn't know what to say to all of that—didn't know how to rebuke any of it, or make Mao feel better.

"See? You shouldn't have asked."

"I didn't," Tai said. "Not yet. Why do you want to put off going home?"

Mao was silent, and for a moment Tai didn't think he would answer. "Damian was wrong. Not about everything, but he was wrong when he said I was waiting for my father to get home to tell him my results. He already knew my results, since he's a commander. But that's not the point. I was late meeting you guys because I lost track of time, not because I was waiting for my father. It was the opposite. He was waiting for me. I didn't go home, not at all. I wandered around all day, after our results were released. I didn't want to go home and talk to him. I still don't. He'll be mad by now that I didn't come home. Not worried. Mad. That'll be easier to deal with than earlier, when he would have been in a good mood, satisfied that his bastard brat finally succeeded at something. I'd rather face him when he's angry, if I have to face him at all."

Tai was at a loss for words again. Mao sighed. "Sorry. Here I am complaining about my father, when your parents died. I must seem like an ingrate. I guess I am, because most of the time I find myself wishing *I* was an orphan."

"What about your mother?"

"She's gone."

"I'm sorry."

"Don't be. Did anyone's being sorry ever make you feel better?"

"No … Are you going home now?"

"*Home.* It's funny, isn't it, how most people think of it as a comforting word. Yeah, that's where I'm going. It's not like I can stay out all night, especially after what just happened."

"Couldn't you go to Gareth's?"

"He'd just try to convince me to go home. We both know my father would be pissed at him and his brother if I spent the night there instead of going back to him."

"There's really nowhere else you can go?"

"No. Not since they evicted us from the dorms. I'll walk with you to your house. It's not like I can take the long way anymore, since those guys went in that direction, so it'll be on my way."

They left the alley in silence. Back in the street and under the lamplight, Tai could make out Mao's bruises and cuts more clearly. She wondered fleetingly if she'd have bruises, too, but her thoughts quickly returned to Mao. It made sense, now, how quiet and reserved he was all the time, always seeming to separate himself from their trainee group. It was because he didn't view them as his group, just hunters who knew about his father.

Tai wanted to know more about Mao's father, and their relationship. It wasn't good if Mao would go to such an extent to avoid him. She wouldn't pry, though, since Mao clearly didn't want to talk about his father. He didn't even want to see him.

They still had a ways to go when Tai asked, "Why don't you stay with me?"

"What?"

"Come back to the manor. You can stay the night. There's lots of room."

"I couldn't do that."

"Of course you could. Besides, do you think going home beaten up like this is going to make facing your father any easier?"

Mao glanced down at himself as if this hadn't occurred to him.

"It would just be for one night."

"But ... don't you live with other hunters, and one of the Council members? If my father found out—"

"Like I said, there's lots of room. No one would have to know." Normally, Tai wouldn't be so pushy. She wouldn't even offer. But she felt compelled to help Mao. Maybe because he'd listened to her on the road outside that tavern. He'd told her not exactly what she needed to hear, and not what would comfort her, but his opinion. Even if it had been blunt, it had helped. It had made her see things in a way she hadn't before.

Tai didn't think she could help Mao in that way,

but she'd do what she could. Which was why, when he still didn't look convinced, she added, "Do you really want to go home and deal with your father with everything else that's happened tonight?"

"I thought you'd tell me to face my problems."

"Why? I don't face all my problems, in case you didn't detect that in my story."

"You deal with them."

"Yeah, well you don't need to deal with yours. Not tonight."

Mao hesitated a moment. "All right."

Chapter XXII

K anta had spent the rest of the night with Mina, mostly dancing, sometimes just talking. Mina didn't speak much herself but was intent on keeping Kanta talking about himself and his life as a hunter. Kanta wasn't a stranger to citizen curiosity about hunters, and he certainly wasn't tired of retelling the same hunting stories. After all, how could he pass up the chance to talk about himself for an hour?

When Kanta yawned halfway through one of his own stories, he realized he'd been talking for more than an hour.

"It *has* gotten kinda late," Mina said. "Way past The Hour."

"Seriously?" Kanta checked his watch. "Shit, I should go."

"Sorry, should I have stopped you? I didn't know you needed to be somewhere."

"It's not that, it's just ..." Everyone at home would be asleep by now. He didn't want to stumble through the house, wake them all up, and be interrogated about his late-night activities. Even though he'd just been out dancing and talking, Mid would blow it out of proportion and maybe even allude to his partying habits in front of Tai.

"Go on. We'll see each other again soon, I'm sure."

"Will your hair be another colour?"

Mina laughed. "You never know!"

Kanta left Mina at the table where they'd been

sitting. He searched the crowd, which had begun to thin. The atmosphere had mellowed, along with the music. Kanta couldn't find Yano or Browen, but he did find Freid sitting with some people at a booth, looking like he was about to fall asleep.

"Made new friends?" Kanta asked.

Freid glanced from Kanta to the people around him. Two people were kissing at the back of the booth, and the rest were chatting quietly or staring moodily around the club. Freid slid out of the booth.

"Can I stay at yours tonight?" Kanta asked.

Freid was exhausted but managed to make a face. "No."

"Come on, Freid. It'll be a blast." Kanta slung an arm around his protesting friend's shoulders and led him out of the club. "Besides, that's probably the first time anyone's ever asked you that. You aren't in any position to refuse."

Chapter XXIII

Mid had always loved exploring Hunters City. It was, in fact, the only thing she liked to do there. Exploring its winding streets and back alleys with Bear kept her sane every year over the huntless holidays. Now, it came in handy.

After sneaking out of the manor, Mid met up with Bear in the backyard. The two took a series of alleys until they reached downtown. Although those who would recognize her and report to her family were likely in their homes asleep, Mid didn't want to take any chances, and stayed off the main roads. Besides, it wasn't as if she had to worry about shifty people in the alleys; Bear was with her.

When they reached the back of the bar, Mid and Bear had to part ways. "I'm sorry Bear. I don't think they let rock giants in. Racist, I know. We'll take them to task later. Right now I need to meet Summer. You wait here for me."

Mid took a step toward the back door and Bear followed.

"Bear, seriously, I'll be fine. Quit worrying. If anything going wrong, I'll call out and you can come crashing through the wall, all Superman-like."

Mid patted Bear's arm and ducked into the club.

The lights were low and, although there were people inside, there weren't as many as Mid had expected. Most were sitting in booths, tired. A few couples were swaying slowly on the dance floor. Mid couldn't understand why her brother wasted his time in this kind of place when he could be out hunting. It was downright boring.

Mid spotted a blonde sitting in one of the booths, with her back to Mid. As Mid approached, she heard a voice that wasn't Summer's say, "He wouldn't shut up! Seriously, I was waiting for something useful and all I got was bluster and gloating and it felt like my ears were bleeding. If he even said anything useful, I didn't hear it, because of all the blood in my ears. At least I got it. If I hadn't, it would've been for nothing—"

Mid passed the booth, discreetly trying to peek back to see if it really was Summer. It was, and slumped next to her was a girl with bright red hair. Mid's attempt at discretion fell flat as both Summer and the red-haired girl caught her looking.

"Good, you made it." Summer gestured to the other side of the booth. As Mid hesitantly sat, Summer turned her attention to the other girl. "We can continue this later."

The girl blinked at her, and realization dawned. "You're trying to get rid of me?"

Summer waited patiently.

"But that would involve getting up! I'm so tired, and so comfy. Just let me stay here." The girl hooked her arm around Summer's and she cuddled up to the blonde. "I'll fall asleep and won't hear anything. Actually, I'm asleep already."

Summer extracted her arm from the other girl's grip. "Now, please."

Sighing, the girl pushed herself up. She punched Summer's shoulder weakly and grumbled something about the blonde being evil and slunk across the dance floor.

"That was …?"

"Part of our group. She can be a bit much for some people, especially when she's in a whiny mood. Besides, I think it's best for now that we talk one on one. Don't you?"

"Uh, I guess. So yeah, what's this about anyway?"

Summer glanced around but the closest booths were empty and the nearest dancers out of earshot. Still, she leaned across the table. Mid mirrored her actions.

"We're going to do it," Summer said. "We're going to take a stand. My encounter with you got me thinking more about it, how we have to inform the public and the rest of the Hunter Association so that they're aware of the corruption. We at least have to try. I've managed to convince the others. We're going to do it."

"How?"

"We've decided to do it at the New Year's Ball. All the hunters will be gathered. All the Council members. It's the perfect time to reveal what's really going on. In that environment, our unveiling of the truth will have an explosive effect."

Excitement coursed through Mid. "Could that work? Would they believe you?"

"Whether they believe us or not, the truth will be out. Someone—someone official, with far more power than us—will investigate what we've said, and then they'll uncover the truth themselves."

"But what'll happen to you guys?"

"Imprisonment. Possibly worse."

It was rare enough someone was imprisoned in Hunters City, but …

"Worse?"

"The H.A. has a reputation, in respect to its corruption. Anyone aware of the corruption, and attempting to do anything about it, or anyone who gets in the way of their extortion, disappears, even if they've been imprisoned."

"They'd actually do that? They'd actually *kill* you?"

"Remember what I told you about the villages? They've been killing hundreds, possibly thousands, of people, for years. All for money and power. They certainly won't hesitate to kill more to preserve the empire they've so carefully crafted."

"But you can't do it then! I mean, if they're gonna kill you—"

"We have to do it. As a hunter, you risk your life fighting ghosts to protect the people. I may not be a hunter, but what I'm doing is the same: fighting a threat—fighting evil—even at the risk of my own death to protect the people."

Mid didn't know what to say. All she could think was, despite the truth of Summer's statement and all the remarkable hunters Mid herself had known, she didn't think she'd ever met anyone stronger than the woman in front of her.

"There's one hitch," Summer admitted. "That's why I got in touch with you. We're aware that the New Year's Ball is strictly for hunters and their guests only. It's going to be nearly impossible to sneak in. Having attended the Ball before, do you know any possible way for us to get in? There won't be many—me and a few others. Enough to get everyone's attention and say what needs to be said before we're taken away."

Mid couldn't believe Summer was really asking for her help. Her mind raced, trying to come up with something—anything—remotely useful.

"My ID!"

Summer looked confused.

"My hunter's ID!" Mid clarified, digging it out of her pocket. Even in Hunters City she couldn't shake the habit of carrying her ID everywhere, since she always needed it on the road. She knew Thalus and Kanta did the same, so she didn't feel too silly about it. "My ID doesn't have my picture on it. And even if the people checking IDs know me, you can just say you guys are my guests or something. I always go with my aunt and uncle, and they have their own IDs, so I don't need mine to get in if I'm with them."

"I'm not so sure. If we used your ID, you could be connected to us. You know how dangerous that would be."

"And you know I'm a hunter. Like you said, hunters risk their lives fighting evil, for the people. I'm prepared to go face to face with an ugly, screaming boss, so lending my ID is no biggie, right?"

The corners of Summer's lips twitched into a small smile. She took the ID. "Thank you, Midgard."

"It's fine. I mean, you guys are doing the tough stuff, right?"

"It may seem that way, but without this," Summer held up the ID, "our work would be moot. All it takes is one little detail in a plan to go awry and everything falls apart. In light of that, thank you again. This really does mean a great deal to me, to us."

Mid preened. "You're welcome! Anything else I can do?"

"As I asked before, just keep this to yourself, but aside from that," Summer pocketed the ID, "countdown to the New Year."

Chapter XXIV

It was after noon the next day when Paige went to her room for a shower. She'd put it off all morning, afraid of waking her sister, with whom she shared a bathroom. Tai still hadn't risen. She didn't know when Tai had gotten home the night before, but it was after Paige had gone to bed. It must have been late, because her sister didn't often sleep in.

Paige couldn't put off her shower any longer, even if she risked dealing with a grumpy, sleep-deprived Tai. She had plans to meet with Harven after lunch, and she wanted to look her best.

Paige didn't bother to knock—normally she would, in case Tai was in there, but since her sister was asleep it didn't matter—and just opened the door.

There was someone in the bathroom, not long out of the shower by the looks of it—a young man, dark hair still wet, wearing only a towel around his waist that reached just above his knees.

Paige would have shrieked if the sight hadn't rendered her mute.

He stared at her, surprised.

"Sorry," Paige squeaked, before shutting the door. She ran out of her room as fast as she could.

Tai was awakened by pounding footsteps in the hall. Groaning, she rolled on her back, rubbing her eyes as she blinked groggily at the ceiling.

It had taken her forever to get to sleep, and twice her dreams had awakened her. She just couldn't shake off the redhead, how he'd pushed the barrel of the loaded gun against her head. Tai had been afraid before—afraid of dying—but never like that. Even when he'd held the knife to her throat hadn't been as bad. There was something more natural, to her, in the thought of bleeding out. He would have slit her throat, and she would have known when he was about to do it. She would have felt the blade cut into her skin and, as blood poured from the wound, she would know she was dying.

With a gun, it would have just happened, with no warning. At any point last night, when she'd stared him in the eyes, he could have pulled the trigger, and she would be instantly gone. Even now, in her hazy, sleepy state, a shiver ran up her spine.

He hadn't pulled the trigger. Tai kept telling herself this. He enjoyed her terror and taken her dagger, insinuating they'd meet again. Tai was almost glad they'd exchanged weapons, if it meant they'd be reunited. If that really happened, Tai intended to make him regret not killing her when he had the chance.

Until then, Tai would keep his knife, as a reminder. She wouldn't let herself feel that terror again—no matter what she had to do.

Her bathroom door opened and Mao appeared. The night before, Tai had shown him to the guest room next to hers. A door connected the two, and she'd told him if he needed the bathroom for anything, he could just come through her room. Normally a heavy sleeper, she was sure she wouldn't hear him. Apparently, she'd been right, even if she had heard whoever was running down the hall. Probably one of the little twins. Kite never made that much noise and Paige knew to tread lightly when Tai was sleeping. Or it could have been Kanta or

Mid. For a moment, she'd forgotten they were back.

Tai sat up, realizing there was something different about Mao. He'd taken a shower. His hair was still damp, making it longer than usual, so that his bangs reached to his nose. But what caught Tai's attention was what he was wearing. Or not wearing.

She'd never thought about Mao's physique, since he wasn't as tall or broad as the other guys in their group, but she'd been wrong to dismiss him as weak. He'd gone through the same training as the others and had the muscles to prove it. He might not be as toned as Kanta, but Kanta flaunted his physical perfection with tight shirts and short sleeves, so Tai was used to it. Tai wasn't used to Mao in that way, which, she told herself, was why she stared at the abs etched in his stomach longer than she should have. And she was tired. That was also a reason.

"I think I just saw your sister."

Tai hoped Mao hadn't noticed her momentary distraction. Or the pause it took her to find her words. "Um … what?"

Mao nodded toward the bathroom. "She just walked in. I think I startled her."

If he'd managed to startle Tai, he'd probably made Paige faint. At least, this was what Tai was thinking until she realized this might be a huge problem. She'd meant to get Mao in and out without anyone knowing. Not that they'd likely mind she'd let him stay over, but she didn't want them asking questions, or misinterpreting anything. Which Paige might do, after seeing Mao half naked in their shared bathroom.

"Did she say anything?"

"No," Mao answered. "I don't think I've ever seen you like this before."

Tai figured he meant her dishevelled post-sleep

appearance. That was when she remembered that she'd worn only a white tank top and a pair of sweatpants to bed. As discreetly as possible, Tai pulled up her knees to block her chest.

Not sure what she should say—if anything—Tai was saved the trouble when Mao added, "This is the first time I've seen your hair down."

Tai blinked, startled. Was that true? Sure, she always had her hair in a ponytail for training, but she must have let it down at some point. Why would Mao notice that?

"Do you want to borrow some clothes?" Tai gestured to his bare torso. She averted her eyes, her cheeks burning. She wasn't really blushing over this, was she?

Mao didn't seem embarrassed by the situation, which Tai found annoying. "I don't really want to put on what I was wearing last night. Do you have anything?"

"Yeah, I'll grab something from Kanta's room."

"I forgot he lives here."

"Only for two months a year. The rest of the time he uses this place for storage." Several dark spots on Mao's stomach caught Tai's attention. "I'll get them in a minute. Come here."

Mao walked over to her, stopping at the side of the bed. Tai leaned forward to inspect his bruises. From far away, they hadn't seemed so bad against his tanned skin, but up close they looked horrible.

Not entirely aware of what she was doing, Tai brushed a finger over a bruise near Mao's belly button. He tensed.

"Does that hurt?"

"No."

"Don't put on a brave face. Tell me if it hurts."

From her position, Tai could see under Mao's bangs, where his cloudy eyes watched hers.

"It doesn't hurt."

How he said it reminded Tai of how close they were and how intimate this situation might appear. She immediately dropped her hand, but Mao caught her wrist. He brought her fingers back to his bruise and made them press harder.

"*That* hurts."

Tai snatched her hand back and climbed out of bed. "Sit down. Back in a sec."

Mao did as she said. Tai hurried into the bathroom, grabbing her shirt from the night before. The bathroom was still steamy from Mao's shower, but, besides the towel he'd taken, he'd put everything back as it was.

Tai pulled her shirt over her tank top and went through the bathroom drawers until she found some salve Henna had bought for bruises. She made sure Tai and Paige's bathroom was well stocked, as Tai usually bore bruises of some sort from training.

Before she left the bathroom, Tai caught her reflection in the mirror. Her eyes were glazed and her cheeks rosy. Her hair was a mess. Tai started to grab the brush lying on the counter, but stopped and shook her head. What did it matter if she was a mess? Still, she combed her fingers through her hair before she left the bathroom.

Mao was still sitting on her bed, looking around her room with quiet interest. As she walked over, Tai discreetly kicked the pile of last night's clothing, which included her underwear, under her bed, hoping he hadn't noticed them.

Sitting next to Mao, Tai turned to face him, legs

crossed. She twisted the cap off the salve and was about to dip her fingers in, when she paused. He could apply it himself.

"Here." Tai passed him the jar. "For your bruises."

Mao accepted it without comment and applied the cream.

"How did you sleep?"

"Not very well. The bed was comfortable, but …" Mao shrugged. "After last night, it was hard. And my body hurt."

"I'm sorry."

"What for?"

"For interfering. It was dumb. They beat you up more because of me."

"I didn't get mad at you because *I* got hurt."

Mao didn't elaborate, and she didn't want to press him. Instead she asked, "Why do you think they took our jackets?"

"My money was in mine. But since they took yours too … I don't know. They're high quality. Expensive to make. They might make a profit selling them."

"I guess … but they didn't take my money. It was in my jeans, not my jacket."

"Would you have wanted them to dig through your jeans?" Mao asked, almost tersely. Tai's face heated again. "Forget it. It's over. We won't see them again."

Tai picked at the hem of her sweatpants. She wasn't so sure, though.

"You're thinking about what that asshole said, aren't you? He was just being arrogant. Someone like him will probably get himself killed before the year is over. Hopefully it's slow."

Tai was startled by the loathing in Mao's voice,

which had taken on a dark, hostile quality she hadn't heard before. She didn't find his hatred unappealing.

"I don't want someone else to kill him," she said. "That wouldn't be fair."

"You'd rather he get dragged before the courts?"

"No." Tai opened her bedside table and took out a knife. It was of a much more expensive make than her dagger, albeit older, with little chips along one side of the blade and the hilt wrapped with worn tape. The guard, however, was in perfect condition and, aside from the chips, the blade was deadly sharp.

"I'd like to use this, I think." Tai tilted the blade so that it caught the sunlight streaming through her window. She never closed her blinds when she was home, even at night. "It would be fitting. His own knife. He's probably used it to kill before. He seemed that kind of guy."

Paige would have been horrified to hear Tai admit these desires. Kanta would have been concerned, and then tried to reason with her and help her come to terms with the fear and anger still swirling inside her.

"It's the least he deserves," Mao stated flatly.

Tai dropped the knife back in her drawer, noticing that Mao had finished with the salve. "I'll put some on your eye for you. It works for black eyes."

Mao handed her the jar, and Tai scooped a bit of cream with her finger. Pulling herself into a kneeling position next to him, Tai brushed back his damp bangs. Mao watched her with his quiet gaze and obediently closed his eyes as she gently massaged the cream into the purpled skin around his left eye.

She could study his face more closely, like this, when he wasn't watching her. He had thin, smooth black eyebrows, a small, rounded nose, and a hint of high cheekbones. He had no facial hair, unlike Kanta, who'd developed a close relationship with his stubble. It looked good on him, Tai had to admit, but she preferred someone cleanly shaven. Besides, Kanta's stubble was scratchy. He'd gotten her to touch it, exclaiming it felt as good as it looked, when Mid had been telling him he looked dirty with facial hair. It had felt prickly against Tai's fingers, and she hadn't entirely liked the feeling.

Mao opened his eyes. "What are you doing?"

Tai had her fingers on his chin, which was smooth and hairless. She snapped her hand back. "There was, um … a bruise."

Mao didn't question this, but Tai was sure he didn't believe her. He'd know if he had a bruise on his own face. But she couldn't come up with anything else. She didn't even know the real answer herself.

"You've got a bruise too." Mao dipped his fingers into the cream, still on Tai's lap, and reached to her shoulder. Gently, he nudged back the loose neck of her shirt and strap of her tank top underneath, and rubbed in the salve. Tai wondered if she actually did have a bruise there—had anyone grabbed her by the shoulder?—but, for whatever reason, she didn't look down to check. Mao's fingers felt warm on her skin but also created a tingly sensation, as he rubbed smooth circles over the spot. When he was done, Mao gently pulled her strap back into place. The whole time, Tai felt frozen in place.

"There. How does that feel?"

"Better," Tai said. The spot hadn't hurt, in the first place. She felt a little dazed.

Mao's lips tugged up into a smile, surprising Tai. Had she seen him smile before?

"I should get your clothes," Tai murmured. "I should, um, get you some clothes."

"Thanks."

Tai got up and wobbled a bit. Mao caught her arm, steadying her. "You okay?"

"My legs fell asleep." Tai wondered if it was true. "Wait here until I get back."

Mao let her go. Tai left her room, closing the door behind her. After she got Mao something to wear, she'd sneak him out. He could return the clothes later. Kanta wouldn't even know anything was missing. And she'd talk to Paige and make up some believable explanation without going into detail about what had happened.

In the midst of making plans, Tai realized she was rubbing her shoulder. She dropped her hand. What was wrong with her? Probably spooked from the night before and everything that had happened. And tired.

That was why she was acting strange, Tai told herself, as she unconsciously reached to rub her shoulder again.

Chapter XXV

It was almost 1 p.m. when Kanta got home. He'd awakened less than an hour before, thanks to the late night. After shaking Freid awake to tell him he was leaving, Kanta started home. Freid, who had bags under his eyes, had growled at Kanta for waking him up, muttering something about never talking to him again. Kanta treated it as sleep-talk.

Finally at the manor all Kanta had to do was to sneak up to his room and change before anyone noticed he was wearing the same clothes he'd been wearing the night before. Even if he'd stayed at Freid's for the night, slinking back home as he was doing would insinuate otherwise. Mid wouldn't believe his story, for sure, and he didn't want Tai doubting him at all. It was best to get in unnoticed.

Kanta quietly opened the front door and slipped into the foyer. Just as he was about to enter the hall, he heard footsteps on the stairs. Cursing, Kanta stayed still, hoping whoever it was would go into the kitchen or living room, or anywhere but toward the front door. However, that was exactly where they went. And it was exactly the last person he wanted to find him.

Tai jumped when she saw Kanta, evidently shocked, then dread washed over her face. That caught Kanta off guard, since it was the expression he was probably wearing.

Then he spotted the person behind Tai. The guy behind her.

The three stood there, not saying a word. Then Kanta noticed something.

"Is that my shirt? Are those my *clothes*?"

"Shit, Kanta. I can explain. He was just borrowing them—"

"He? Who is he?"

Tai was miserable as she turned to the guy. "You can just head home. I'll—"

"No he can't. Not in my clothes, anyway. Take them off," he ordered.

"Gods, Kanta. It isn't that big a deal."

"Take them off. *Now.*"

"Kanta!"

"What? It doesn't matter, does it?" Kanta realized his voice was rising and was unable to stop it. "I'm a guy, and you've probably already seen what's under there."

Tai went white, then red. At first Kanta thought it was because she was embarrassed, but then she glared. An icy glare. "What the hell is wrong with you? He's a friend, okay? He stayed here last night because … I don't owe you an explanation, especially when you're acting like this!"

"It's my house!" Kanta yelled. "You owe me a dozen explanations, and they better be really gods-damned good ones!"

Tai recoiled, shocked. Kanta regretted his words— Tai had always been sensitive about accepting their hospitality, always pointing out it wasn't her home when others referred to it as such—but Kanta was too angry to take back what he'd said. He deserved an explanation, not just because it was his family's house but because … because …

Because she'd loaned this guy his clothes, damn

it.

Tai grabbed the hand of the guy behind her, tugging him into the foyer, past Kanta. "I'll talk to you later, when you're ready to at least pretend that you're mature."

Kanta grabbed her arm, trembling with anger and something else, unsure of what to say.

Finally, he settled on waving at her with his free hand. "Do you want to borrow some of my clothes too? Or are you fine with walking through the City in your pajamas?"

"I'm pretty sure I am." Tai tried to shake him off but he wouldn't release her. "Gods, let me go, Kanta!"

Kanta hesitated. Maybe he should. He wasn't finished, but he couldn't formulate all of what he wanted to say. Not now. Maybe it was best to let her go—

Before Kanta could reach this decision, Tai's "friend" reached over and pried his fingers off her arm. He didn't even say anything to Kanta, just turned his attention back to Tai when he was done, actually pulling her toward the door.

"Wait right there—" Kanta shouted, when someone came into the hall behind them.

"My, my, what do we have here?" Right behind Henna were the little twins, watching the scene curiously. "Surely you three aren't leaving?"

"Only two," Tai snapped. She paled when she noticed her younger siblings.

"I'm sure you can put that off, at least until after lunch," Henna insisted. "This is the first chance we've had to meet any of your friends, Tai. You won't let him leave without being fed, will you?"

Kanta knew Tai would cave before she said it.

Leaving now, after a shouting match her brother and sister had likely heard, would create a bad impression. She had to make sure they knew nothing was wrong, even when everything was.

"Fine." Tai dropped the guy's hand.

"Excellent," Henna said, not in her usual cheery tone. "We'll set the table. Kanta, why don't you change?"

Despite all the negative feelings rushing through him, Kanta was grateful to Henna. She knew he'd been out all night and needed to change, and though her tone indicated she didn't approve, she wasn't about to blow the whistle on him in front of Tai, who'd left before him last night and didn't know that he was wearing the same clothes.

The little twins, however, were not so subtle. Both had been up when he'd left.

"Didn't you wear that yesterday, Kanta?" Alton asked. "Why are you wearing it twice in a row? Do you really like that outfit?"

"Yeah. I do."

"I never wear stuff twice in a row," Grippa complained, "even if I really like it."

"Maybe when you're older," Kanta managed before heading up the stairs. He refused to look back at Tai, but he had a feeling she was glaring at him, because his back suddenly felt cold.

Kanta reached his room and stayed there a moment, trying to calm down. It wasn't any use. Rage burned inside him. Sure, it wasn't like he and Tai were in a relationship, but, for her to bring a guy back to the house he also lived in, was too much.

He changed, noticing that Tai had made sure nothing looked amiss in his closet. He wouldn't have

noticed the shirt and pants missing if he hadn't run
into the guy wearing them five minutes ago. She
clearly hadn't meant for him to find out her "friend"
had borrowed them. She hadn't intended for him to
find out about her friend.

As he walked down the hall, Kanta's mind
flashed to his conversation with Yano and the others
the night before. Yano had suggested Tai might hook up
with someone at the trainee party, and he'd dismissed
it. He hadn't thought Tai was that type of girl. She'd
seemed almost above dating, as if she didn't need
companionship in that way. They'd known each
other for over two years and nothing had happened
but occasional flirting, always from Kanta. She'd
grown more receptive lately but never let it get far.
He hadn't thought she'd let it get far with anyone.

By the time Kanta reached the dining room, he'd
worked himself up again. Everyone was already sitting
down. Tai was next to her friend, across from Paige.
The little twins sat on Tai's other side, and Kite and
Mid were at either end of the table. Mid was extremely
pleased and didn't bother to hide it.

"Where's Henna?" Kanta noticed that the food
was already laid out.

"Gone to the market," Kite replied. He'd brought
his papers, riddled with equations, to the table, which
he never did unless Henna was gone. She deemed
work at the table rude and would have disposed of
the papers permanently. "We're out of something."

"Oats," Paige said, almost sheepishly. "I forgot
to pick them up yesterday. We don't usually run out,
so I'm not used to picking them up."

"That and the fact that Harven was working,"
Kite added.

"H-H-How d-d-did you know that?"

"Just guessing. But now I know."

Paige reddened. Kanta sat next to her, ignoring the pair across from him.

"I w-w-won't forget again ..."

"It wasn't that you forgot, you were distracted, and it's unlikely you'll be able to keep from being distracted again." Kite scribbled something on his sheet of paper. "The only way to solve the problem is to not give you new tasks you'll 'forget' to do."

"Back off, Kite," Kanta said. "Give her a break."

Tai snorted.

"Something to say?" Kanta snapped at her.

Tai glared.

That was when Mid chose to make her move, which Kanta had been anticipating, and dreading. Folding her hands in front of her on the table, Mid leaned forward, smiling slyly. "So, Tai, who's your friend? I don't remember your talking about him before."

"That's because we don't talk," Tai answered.

Mid was momentarily put off. Kanta filled the silence. "Actually, I'd like to know too. We haven't been properly introduced, have we?"

"Oh, you want an introduction?" Tai asked. "You have manners now?"

"I have manners, all right. I'm just selective who I use them on."

"Grow up, Kanta."

"Maybe later."

"Gods, you can be such a—"

"I'd appreciate an introduction," Kite broke in. "Wouldn't you, Alton? Grippa?"

Tai tensed but schooled her face into a calmer expression. Kite's reminder of her younger siblings had worked.

"My name's Mao." It was the first time Kanta had heard his voice. It sounded soft. Weak.

Kite was interested in the guy's name. "Your father's a commander?"

"Yes."

Kite contemplated this for a moment but then returned to his equations.

"How do you guys know each other?" Mid asked.

"From training." Tai stabbed at the food on her plate without eating it.

"Oh!" Mid brightened, then to Mao. "Do you know Silsa?"

Mao nodded uncertainly.

"She's a friend of mine!" Mid explained, waving in Kanta's general direction. "And my brother, I guess. More so me. You'll figure out pretty quickly I'm the friendlier one, and just all around more likeable. My name's Mid—Midgard, but I just go by Mid. I'm sure Tai's mentioned me. So how old are you?"

"Seventeen."

Kanta, who was in the middle of pouring himself some water, spilled some on the table. Sure, the guy looked like he could be 17—even younger, maybe—and it was only a two-year age difference, but it still startled him.

Mid rose her eyebrows at Tai suggestively. "A younger guy. I never would have guessed you'd be into that."

Tai looked like she wanted to murder Mid.

"Into what?" Grippa asked.

"Ignore Mid," Kite said to the little twins. "She didn't get much sleep last night, so she might say things that don't make sense right now."

"Oh, I got plenty of sleep." She directed her next comment at Tai. "You and your friend here, on the other hand, I'm not so sure about."

"Did you have trouble sleeping, sissy?" Alton asked Tai.

"A little. But don't worry, I'll sleep fine tonight. I can't say the same for Mid, if she keeps talking. She might wind up with a … headache."

Mid was more amused by the threat than anything else. She started talking to Mao again. "So why do you have those bruises on your arms? What happened to your eyes?"

"There was a brawl last night at the tavern," Mao offered. "When we were trying to leave, I got caught in it."

"You do look roughed up, like you'd been in a brawl. But I'm not so sure about the location."

"Okay!" Tai said loudly. "Grip? Altie? Are you guys done? No, you don't have to finish your vegetables. Why don't you play outside? It's nice out, and that's where Bear is, right?"

The little twins nodded and excitedly dismissed themselves. Rarely did they get to skip eating their greens to play with Bear. After the back door in the kitchen shut, Tai turned to Mid. "What's wrong with you? They're eight!"

"Exactly. It's not like they'll understand." Mid batted her eyelashes at Tai. "Now we can have a straightforward, detailed conversation. Isn't that great?"

Paige quietly left the table. Only Kanta noticed. Kite didn't seem to be paying attention to anything anymore, lost in his equations. Mao kept his gaze down, which annoyed Kanta. His entire silent presence was annoying Kanta.

"So, Tai, is this really the first time you've had some-one over?" Mid asked. "Or have your sneak attempts just succeeded in the past? Have there been dozens of 'friends' we don't know about?"

When Tai refused to answer, Kanta spoke. "That's a good question."

"Isn't it?" Mid beamed at him. "We're gone for a year, so how would we know what Tai gets up to? I mean, she doesn't know what we get up to either, right, Kanta?"

Kanta had forgotten that Mid wasn't just targeting Tai here. He also risked being in his sister's spotlight. They hadn't exactly been on good terms lately.

"Then again, it's not like either of us gets up to anything," Mid added. "At least, I know I don't. What about you, Kanta?"

"Nope. Nothing I can think of."

"Are you sure?" Tai broke in. "I wonder if last night was the first time this year you've come back wearing the same clothes as you wore the day before. Maybe it happened at camp all the time."

He'd always gotten back before the next morning, so technically she was wrong. "Nothing happened. The guys and I were out late, so I stayed at Freid's. There. An explanation, even though I'm not the one who owes an explanation here."

"I don't owe you anything. But—since you think you deserve one—it was the same thing. We were out late with the others, so I told Mao he could stay here."

"Oh, yeah. That's just the same. My staying at Freid's—two straight guys—versus your inviting your male friend here. Where did he sleep, exactly?

Or do you not owe me that either?"

"In one of the guest rooms! Where else?"

Mid started to say something but Kanta spoke over his sister. "Why didn't you invite Silsa back, then? Or why didn't he stay with another guy? I assume there were other guys. Or was it just the two of you? At the tavern, I mean, not in your bedroom."

Tai shoved back her chair and got to her feet. "Save the rest of your interrogation. I'm not dealing with your shit anymore."

"Where are you going?" Kanta demanded, as she pulled Mao to his feet.

"I'll be back later. Maybe."

"You can't just leave!" Kanta called, getting to his feet as Tai and Mao headed for the hall. "We're not done! And my clothes—"

Mao stopped, turning back to him. "Yes. The clothes. Thank you for letting me borrow them. I'll send some money back with Tai. Renting fees. Nice to meet you all." And Mao disappeared into the hall.

Tai was startled by his input. She shot one final glare at Kanta, and followed Mao. Moments later, the front door slammed.

Kite was still scribbling on his papers. He pulled back, having finally finished his equation, and said to Kanta, "You handled that remarkably well."

Mid burst out laughing. Kanta stormed out of the dining room and up the stairs. Mid's laughter followed him.

Chapter XXVI

Gods, I'm sorry about Kanta. He can be such a … such a …" Tai struggled for a word to describe his insufferable, superior, haughty, impossible attitude but ended up sighing.

She and Mao walked down the street, which was busy at this time of day, heading away from the market. They should take the opposite direction if they wanted to reach Mao's home, but neither commented or changed their course.

"Are you two together?" Mao asked.

"No. Gods, no."

"Has anything ever happened between you?"

"Why?"

"It would explain why he was acting so possessive."

Tai pulled her coat tighter around her. She'd grabbed it from the hall, a long one that would cover more of her sweatpants. "Nothing's happened. Not really. It could have, maybe, but that was back when … when my brother left. Romance was the last thing on my mind. Kanta was really good about it, too. He helped me look for my brother, like I told you, and since then we've gotten closer but … not in that way. Maybe he feels like, after all this time, if I did decide I wanted anything like that, it should be with him."

"That's disgusting."

"I don't mean it to sound that way. He can be an ass sometimes, but he's been really good to my family and me over the years."

"So he thinks he should get first right of refusal over you?"

"I didn't say that."

"You did, more or less. Do you agree with him?"

"He doesn't think of me that way. I'm sorry if that's how I made it sound, but Kanta isn't that ... shallow. I mean, he *is* shallow, but not in that way. He doesn't think he has any kind of claim on me."

"It didn't seem that way," Mao said quietly. Then in his normal tone, "You didn't answer my question."

"There's no point in answering it since he doesn't think of me that way."

"I wasn't asking what he thinks; I was asking what you think. Do you feel so much indebted to him that you would let that control your feelings?"

"No, it's not like that."

"Then you genuinely care about him."

"Of course I do, but not like that."

Mao was quiet a moment, then he shook his head. "Sorry. I shouldn't have said any of that. It's not my place to pry."

Tai hadn't expected him to say that. "It's okay."

"It's not. I hate it when uninvolved parties pry into my business. It happens all the time. I shouldn't do that to you."

He viewed himself as an uninvolved party, then. Tai was startled by the fact she picked up on this. "In that case, I'm sorry too."

"For what?"

"Prying. Last night."

Seeming to recall their conversation about his past, Mao looked away, muttering. "That was different."

"Why?"

"You told me about what happened to you. It was

kind of … an exchange, I guess. We're even now."

Even. Tai hadn't thought of it that way. For her it had been more about opening up, not balancing things out. But Mao viewed it that way. The way she would have viewed it, in the past, not wanting to be indebted to anyone, even if it was the debt of her own life story. She'd want to even it out, not have fanciful ideas of being comfortable enough to open up. When had she gotten so soft?

Suddenly, Tai was angry. She'd told Mao her story—things she hadn't told anyone, not even Kanta— and he was saying he'd done the same because he didn't want to owe her anything. Hadn't he accused her of being the same, in her feelings toward Kanta?

Tai stopped walking. Mao did too, turning back to her. "What?"

"I'm going back now. Good luck with field training."

"What are you talking about? That's it? Good luck with training?"

"What more is there to say?"

Mao caught her arm. "I don't understand. Why are you being like this?"

"Like what? You said it yourself: we're even now. That's why you told me about what happened to you, because you owed me that. You've paid your debt, and I've paid mine for interfering last night, by letting you stay at the manor. We're even, so what's the point in talking? We might owe each other something else. Might as well stop now."

"Are you serious?" Mao demanded. When she didn't reply, he said in an exasperated tone. "Gods, did you think that's what I meant when I said we were even? I worded it badly, okay? No, not even that. I lied. I didn't tell you my story because I felt obliged to; I told you what I did because ..." Mao's hand tightened around her arm in frustration. Then, seeming to realize what he'd done, he released her.

"I wanted to tell you," he said finally. "I thought maybe you'd understand what it was like, after I heard your story. What it's like to be so helpless when it comes to your own life—to be so miserable. I just wanted someone to understand for once. Not to pity, but to understand. I know our stories are different, but when you were telling me about losing your family and your home and your brother, and the stress of looking after your younger siblings and your curse, I couldn't relate to what had happened to you, but the way you described it was so familiar. It was how I feel about my mother's being gone, and all the stress my father puts on me to be the perfect hunter, like he thinks if I succeed exactly how he wants me to that will somehow make up for how much I ruined his life. But he's ruining mine, just like those villagers ruined yours. Just like your brother ruined yours by choosing to leave. That's why I told you. Not because I wanted to make everything even and part ways. That's the last thing I want."

Tai felt like she'd been holding her breath the entire time, and now that he was finished she still didn't know when to let it go. Mao's face was slightly red when he added, "I didn't want you to think less of me. That's why I didn't tell you all of that in the first place."

Tai didn't think any less of him. If anything, she thought less of herself, for reacting so badly and so quickly to what he'd originally said. Looking back, she couldn't even come up with a good excuse for acting that way.

"Can you say something?" Mao asked.

"I haven't told anyone," Tai said. "What I told

you, I haven't told anyone else before. Only Paige knows everything, because she was there too. The little twins—my youngest siblings—they don't even know about the curse. They don't remember our father at all, so they don't remember his insanity and don't ask about it. Aside from Paige, no one knows about the curse, and Paige doesn't even know how ... how terrified I am about it. Terrified that one day I'll start going crazy, start seeing or hearing things that aren't there, and I won't know the difference. She doesn't understand how horrible it is not only to lose our brother and wonder if he's safe but to know that my own safety counts on his. It's like ... it's like that man last night pressing his gun to my head. He could have shot me at any moment, and I wouldn't have seen it coming or been able to prevent it or prepare. It would just happen. Brighton's like that for me: he's like a gun pointed at my head these past two years. And I'm holding a gun to his head too, and neither of us knows who's going to shoot first. That's what I feel like all the time." Tai stared at her hands, imagining a gun in one of them. They were shaking badly, but she couldn't get them to stop. "Paige doesn't know I feel like this. Kanta doesn't know either. He doesn't even know about the curse. You're the only one I've told everything to, and I don't even know why. I don't tell people these things. I don't talk about them. But I'm talking to you and I don't know how to stop and I don't know if I want to."

Tai really hadn't intended to say the last part, and caught her breath in a gasp as the words came out. That was the first time, internally or externally, that she'd admitted to wanting to share her problems with someone. Until then, she'd never entertained the idea, instead chastising herself for divulging any personal information to someone else, revealing any weakness. But it was true, she realized, she *did* want to talk. She wanted to talk to Mao, even if talking didn't help very much. She was still cursed. She and Brighton were still pointing guns at each others' heads.

"Do you remember Gareth's talking about ghost gods in the mess hall a few weeks ago?" Mao asked. "You said you didn't believe in them. Is that true, when you believe in your curse?"

"I ... I don't believe they're gods, but I believe they exist. At least, I believe Phantasma exists. This curse is real, so the ghost who created it has to be, and since the curse still exists, Phantasma must as well. Somewhere."

"Somewhere," Mao echoed. "What if you could find that somewhere? What if you could find Phantasma and give her back her guns and her fire?"

"What are you saying?"

Mao met her eyes, his own impossibly pale. "What if you could break the curse?"

Chapter XXVII

After the entertainment that was lunch, Mid decided to go for a walk through the City. Since getting home, she'd particularly indulged in Henna's expert baking. Mid didn't want to fall out of shape over winter—or, as she aptly called it, the lazy months—so she tried to maintain some form of exercise. Such as strolling through the City and stopping at sweet stalls. That involved exercise. Mid wasn't about to let Bear become a couch rock either, so she dragged him along.

Mid had just finished filling Bear in on the drama of the morning. Bear, by his reaction, found it absolutely scandalous.

"Kanta was furious!" Mid related gleefully. "The Fire Demon was pretty mad too, by the end of it. I've gotta say, though, Bear, I was surprised. I thought she and Kanta would eventually hook up, and then she'd find out the hard way what a player he is. I didn't think she'd turn out to be the same way. Oh, but you should have been there, Bear! It was marvellous! Kanta definitely deserved it!"

Bear, agreeing, urged her to buy more candy when they passed another sweet stall. Yes, Bear was definitely urging her to do that. The look in his eyes said it all.

"Fine," Mid said, "since you're forcing my hand."

After buying another bag of sweets—hard candies, Mid's favourite, second only to caramels—Mid decided to go visiting. They went all the way to the east end of town and, like always, Bear cleaved a path through the busy roads for them. Finishing her last candy just as she got to the door, Mid tossed the paper bag in some bushes below the living room window, then knocked.

Mist opened the door.

"Heya Mist. Silsa in?"

Mist leaned back into the house and shouted for her niece, then turned again to Mid. "Enjoying your break, kid?"

"Tons. You?"

"I prefer a mattress to rocks. No offence, big guy," Mist added, to Bear.

"None taken," Mid said.

"Auntie Mist, you wanted—" Silsa, appearing from the hall, trailed off when she saw who was at the door. "Mid!"

"I'll leave you to it." Mist went back inside just as Silsa dashed past her. She jumped into Mid's waiting arms. The two hugged, and laughed as they pulled apart.

"Mid, I've missed you so much!"

"I know! That's why I've decided to give you the honour of my company this afternoon!"

Silsa was delighted. She called out to her aunt that she'd be home later, then snatched her trainee jacket from a nearby hook and went outside, closing the door behind her. When she and Mid were on the street, Mid linked their arms together.

"So? How's trainee life? I noticed you only wrote me 12 times this year."

"Sorry. It's been really busy. I was anxious for the field test this whole year, so I worked even harder than usual. I went in on weekends for extra practice."

"I admire your dedication. I don't admire your craziness. Who trains on a weekend?"

Silsa laughed. "That's easy for you to say! You've been training for years now, actually in the field. I've been training just to be allowed in the field."

"I suppose you're right. I am special."

"That's not what I meant."

"So you're saying I'm not special?"

"Don't be silly." Silsa lightly swatted her arm. "Mid, you're spectacular!"

This was why Mid and Silsa got along so well.

"Oh!" Silsa exclaimed, as if remembering something. She gripped Mid's arm tightly. "You have to tell me about your first boss! You wrote me about it, but tell me in person! I want to hear everything! And then I'll tell you about my boss!"

Right. Mid had forgotten Silsa had also killed a boss. That somehow made her hesitant to tell her story—what if Silsa's boss battle was more impressive?—but Mid wasn't one to keep back her accomplishments. She told Silsa the story.

It had happened shortly after last winter, when they'd returned to hunting. Mid was officially a field trainee, and would be for two years, even if she'd been training in the field prior to that. Thalus still wanted to keep to protocol as best he could, and most field trainees didn't take their hunting test and earn their licence until they'd completed two years of successful training.

Mid was the youngest field trainee in the unit. Despite this, she was more determined to kill a boss than all her fellow trainees combined. Kanta had killed his first boss just before he turned 14, so Mid was already behind. She was determined not to let the gap widen.

She'd orchestrated it—a fact she left out from her retelling of the story—by going to the ghost town they'd been clearing during the day. She'd gotten the scoop on the building she, and some of the other trainees, had been assigned to clean that night. During the day, when they weren't active, most ghosts in a haunted building were said to drift around the general area of the boss. Mid had assessed the building thoroughly before making her prediction on which half the boss was resting in.

That night she, Bear, and two other trainees—Gladis and Arch—went to the building, a former school. It was much smaller than the schools she and Kanta had cleared in other cities. It had only 10 classrooms, a measly excuse for a cafeteria, and no gymnasium to speak of. It was also only one story high. The town had been small, so such an inadequate school hadn't been surprising. Still, Mid missed the bigger, flashier haunted buildings.

As soon as they'd arrived and shot the ghosts in the front hall, Mid had said, "Bear and I will take the left side of the school. You guys cover the right."

"We aren't supposed to split up," Gladis had protested. She was a stickler for protocol, not to mention a suck-up. Mid didn't like her much.

"Let's put it to a vote. Who votes we don't split up because hunting's much more fun with our friends?" Gladis meekly raised her hand. "And who votes we split up and kick some ghost ass like real hunters?" Mid waved her hand and Bear raised his arm.

"I abstain," Arch said, gun ready if any ghosts attacked while they were talking.

"Great." Mid put her hand down. "Looks like team kick-ass wins. Have fun in your half."

"But we're breaking the rules—" Gladis whined, but Mid was already gone. As expected, her half had been more highly populated. Still, she managed to finish before Gladis and Arch, whom she called periodically to check if they were done. She'd always mouth *amateurs* at Bear when they said no.

Finally, they finished. Gladis called Mid, "Let's meet in the front hall for the boss fight."

"Let's not." Mid hung up. Gladis called her back a few times, but Mid didn't answer. Calls were still coming in when the Hallow Hour signal sounded from her WT. After it had finished its 12 beeps, Mid turned off the communication device to keep from hearing more of Gladis's nagging.

Mid felt the boss awaken in one of the classrooms. Hurrying to the appropriate one, she reached the door just as it came barrelling through. Mid shot a stream of plasma at it, catching its attention. The boss shrieked and dived at her, claws extended.

She sidestepped and the boss flew through Bear's extended plasma knuckles, then through the rest of Bear. Bear was unaffected by ghost contact, but the boss hadn't been as lucky with Bear's knuckles. The blow left it disoriented, and it spun drunkenly through the air. Mid aimed and shot, nearly getting it in the third eye. She cursed when the plasma fell short. If the boss stayed high up, she wouldn't be able to reach it.

"Hey!" Mid yelled. "Scissor Hands! I've seen hellkittens with bigger claws than you!"

The boss spun its head, its focus completely on Mid. She shot at it again to keep its attention and then dashed into the classroom. Sure enough, there were still desks standing. One had a chair. Mid jumped on the chair and then the desk. She whirled around just in time to see the boss materialize through the wall. It dove at her and Mid ducked, hearing a faint hiss as its claws just missed her head. Mid snapped back up, pistols aimed at the boss. It was too high up, but only by a little.

"Wanna play rock, paper, scissors?" The boss whirled back around with a screech and dove at her.

"I'll give you a hint," Mid yelled as she took aim at the ghost barrelling toward her. "I always choose Bear!"

Her plasma caught the boss right in the middle eye, seconds before impact. It shrieked as it dissolved into bluish white mist, which flew around Mid as she shoved her pistols into their holsters. "Shoulda picked paper, dummy."

Chapter XXVIII

Kanta didn't talk to Tai when she got home later that day. He was still mad and, evidently, so was she. They didn't speak on Sunday either, looking away whenever they passed in the halls. By Monday, they'd had no communication since the incident, and Kanta was regretting how he'd acted. What if it really had been a misunderstanding? Still, he couldn't just go up to Tai and apologize. He just couldn't.

Freid stopped by that afternoon. They'd made plans Friday night to go for lunch on Monday, since Kanta had assumed he and Tai would spend Saturday and Sunday together. Instead, both days had ended up being boring and frustrating.

"How was your weekend?" Freid asked, as they walked to the diner.

"Don't ask."

"Why? What happened?"

"You just asked me twice. I said, don't ask."

"When someone says not to ask, they generally want to be asked. Is something wrong?"

"Sort of …"

"Is it Tai?"

"How did you know?"

"What else would it be? So? Did she find out you've been fooling around with a platoon of girls for the past year?"

"Why would you use the word *platoon*? It sounds so weird."

"It's just another way of saying group."

"Yeah, a weird and pointless way."

"Kanta, answer the question."

"No, she didn't find out. But it's not like I'm hiding it. Nothing serious happened with any of those girls."

"So you'd be fine if she found out?" When Kanta didn't reply, Freid rolled his eyes. "Of course you wouldn't. What is it, then?"

"When I went home Saturday morning, it turned out she'd had someone stay over."

"And that's a problem because ...?"

"It was a guy."

Freid opened his mouth but then closed it. "Oh."

"That's right. *Oh.* See the problem now?"

"So she and this guy, they're an item?"

"Maybe. Probably."

"Did you ask her?"

"In a manner of speaking."

"And what did she say?"

"That he was a friend from training, and she'd let him stay over because they'd been out late at the tavern."

"So basically exactly what happened with us on Friday?"

"No! No, it's not at all like that! Unless we're in a secret relationship. Tell me, are we dating, Freid? I'd have forgotten, since it's you."

"I'll answer after I'm done throwing up."

They reached the diner. The server led them to a table and gave them one rough menu. Kanta took it before Freid could and scanned the short selection of food and long selection of drinks.

"You're having problems with Tai because she was hospitable to her friend?"

"I'm having problems because I think she was more

than hospitable." Kanta turned the menu over, but the other side was blank. "They call this a lunch menu?"

"So what?"

"So what? Don't you care that we only have two types of soups and three types of sandwiches to choose from?"

"That's not what I mean, Kanta. So what if Tai and that guy are together? So what if she's had guys over before?"

"Are you serious?"

"I wouldn't say it if I wasn't."

Kanta flicked the menu at him, but it didn't go far, landing instead on the table. "You're supposed to be my friend. We're supposed to bitch about bitches together, not bitch at each other."

"Can you be a bigger hypocrite? Kanta, what right do you have to complain about Tai's love life? You've never tried anything with her, and you're always making it clear you guys are only friends when someone mentions otherwise. Maybe if there was something between you two, and you didn't fool around with a *platoon* of other girls, it would be justified."

Kanta was struck by how much sense his words made, struck by the fact Freid—*Freid*—was giving him thought-provoking relationship advice. He had a good point. Even if Kanta felt like there was something between him and Tai, what right did he have to be mad at Tai for getting together with someone else, when *he*'d never tried to further their relationship?

Kanta merely replied to Freid, "I really can't take you seriously when you use the word *platoon*."

Freid tossed the menu back at him. "Pick your gods-damned soup."

Chapter XXIX

It was Tuesday afternoon, and Tai was getting ready to meet Mao. They'd intended to meet sooner than this, but they'd had to postpone, due to Mao's father. He hadn't elaborated on what was going on with his father, exactly, beyond "hunter" and "family" stuff. Tai knew that if she'd pressed he would have given her a detailed reason, but Mao didn't seem to want to talk more about it, so she'd let it rest.

Tai was putting on her coat in the foyer, when Kanta walked down the hall. She busied herself doing up her coat buttons. She waited for Kanta to go away, as he'd been doing when they crossed paths since their argument. Instead, he walked right up to her.

"Where are you going?" Kanta asked.

"Why? Do you need to approve it?"

"Okay, I deserved that."

He sounded normal. Looked normal. All signs of hostility toward her were gone.

"Could we ... do you think we could maybe talk for a minute?" Kanta asked.

"I have to go," Tai said. "I'm meeting someone."

"That boy?" Kanta asked, an edge of the hostility returning.

"Yes."

Kanta fought with himself for a minute, and then asked in a tight voice, "Are you guys ... are you together now?"

"No. And we never were. I told you that."

"I know." Kanta met her eyes. "I'm sorry I didn't believe you."

"Do you believe me now?"

"Yes."

Tai searched his gaze a moment. He seemed genuine. "Are you going to apologize for how you acted?"

"Yeah. I'm sorry for that too. Really sorry. I was a jerk, and if I ever see your friend again, I'll apologize to him in person."

"You will?"

"Promise. You should go, if you really have to meet him."

"Yeah, I should ..."

"Can we just try to go back to normal? Or, at least, can you forgive me for being such an asshole? I promise I'll be on my best behaviour until you do."

"Maybe I'll never forgive you, then."

Kanta smiled, relieved. "Are we okay now? Okay-ish?"

"Okay-ish. Maybe okay."

"Good. I'll see you later then. Don't make any plans for Thursday, all right?"

"Why not?"

"Dance practice," Kanta reminded her. "For the New Year's Ball. Whether or not you'll still be my date, we all need a refresher on the dance steps, as we all have to go."

Tai hated the dances at the Ball. "Right. That."

Kanta hesitated a moment. "Your friend's probably going too, since he's a trainee like you. If he wants to practice with us ..."

"Thanks." Mao would likely refuse, but it meant a lot to her that Kanta was willing to extend the invitation.

Maybe even more than his apology.

"I'll see you later, then," Kanta said, slightly awkward.

"Yeah." Tai opened the door. "Bye."

It took Tai almost 10 minutes to reach the spot where they'd agreed to meet, at a fountain in the market. Mao was already there, sitting on one of the benches encircling the fountain, hands stuffed in his dark brown jacket, eyes tracing the lines in the cobblestones. He looked small and separate from the rest of the bustling market, as if he was part of an entirely different world. A darker, lonelier world. A world more like the one to which Tai belonged.

"Hey," Tai greeted him. Mao moved over, making room for her.

"Is it okay to talk here?" Tai asked quietly, sitting close to him, to keep the conversation as private as possible.

"Everyone's busy with their own lives. No one will notice us."

Tai still didn't feel completely comfortable. Even if it was unlikely anyone would hear them, let alone someone Tai knew, she didn't want to take any risks. She scooted closer to Mao.

Slightly amused, Mao leaned in and whispered in her ear, "Would you feel better if we talked like this?"

Tai pulled back, startled. Mao chuckled softly. It was a surprisingly boyish sound. At first Tai liked it, but then it made her remember Mid's comments about their age gap, small as it was. Then she remembered Mid's comments in general.

Trying to discreetly put some distance between them on the bench, Tai asked, "Will you tell me your idea now?"

After Mao had spoken to her about breaking the curse, he admitted it had been on his mind for a while after hearing Tai's story. He'd mentioned he had an idea, but he wanted to think about it a little longer.

"I'm not sure you'll like it. It involves witches."

"Tell me."

"I was thinking more about what Gareth was saying, about cults for the ghost gods. I know it's true. There was a Phantasma cult in the town my mother and I used to live in. They didn't stay there all year, but they visited for one of their festivals and set up just outside the town. If there's any hope of breaking the curse, the only way to find out more about it and Phantasma would be through the witches that worship her. Even if they might be dangerous, they know more than anyone about the ghost gods."

"How could I find them? Where would they be now?"

"On the road. In a week, they'll likely be by my old town. They stay for two weeks before moving camp again. I don't know where they go after that."

"How far away is your town?"

"Not that far. When I came to Hunters City from there, I was in a large group. It took us a little over a week. If the group was small and travelled light, it would probably take half that time."

About four days to get there and four to get back, on top of a few days to question the witches. The trip would take under two weeks, in theory. But she'd have to act soon, while the witches were still at Mao's old town. And how could she do that now, in the middle of New Year's celebrations, with no excuse for leaving for such a long period of time? How *would* she do it? She didn't know the way to

Mao's town, didn't know who to talk to about renting a caravan, didn't know what the roads would be like.

"It's impossible. Even if I could come up with an excuse for my absence, I'd never be able to figure out the trip on my own."

"What if I went with you? I was going to suggest it anyway. I know the way there and I know what the town's like. Between us, we could make the trip."

"I couldn't ask you to do that. What about …"

"My father? He wouldn't worry, not for me, anyway. And you'll believe me when I say I'd be happy to get away from him for two weeks. There's no doubt he'll request me for his unit when I start field training, and after that I'll be stuck with him indefinitely. Going with you would be a final break. Besides, I want to help you."

"Are you sure? Even if it's not a long trip, travelling anywhere these days is dangerous."

"It would be more dangerous if you go on your own. So, yes, I'm sure."

Usually, when someone helped her, Tai felt gratitude, but also indebted, as if she carried a burden until she paid off that person's good will. This time, surprisingly, all she felt at the thought of Mao's coming with her was relief.

"Let's plan."

Chapter XXX

It was Thursday and everyone in the manor had assembled in the living room. Henna had laid out biscuits, sweets, and tea on the coffee table before going home. She would spend New Year's with her family and wouldn't return until Monday. Wendy, who had come over to practice, was picking at the snacks while he chatted to Paige, asking her about life in Hunters City. Mid sat on the arm of the couch next to Wendy, who seemed oblivious that Mid wasn't just playing with his hair, but composing it into a series of little braids at the back of his head. Grippa sat next to Paige, kneeling up so that she could access her sister's hair. She was copying Mid's braiding style, bending over to peek at the older girl's work every few seconds. Her twin sat with Kite at the piano in the corner of the room. Alton watched as Kite's fingers ghosted over the keys, playing a silent tune.

Kanta, slumped in an armchair, observed everyone. He'd just pushed back all the furniture, so they had a fairly open space in the middle of the room. They'd need it.

Every year they went over the steps to the various dances that took place at the New Year's Ball. As annoying as it was, it was the only time such proper etiquette was required of the hunters—the ball was the only big event of its kind in the City, a way to mark their surviving another year—so they tried to do the dances properly. Still, after a year without performing the steps, it helped to take some time to practice them.

When Tai came in, her hair in a loose ponytail, wearing a plain green sweater and grey pants, Kanta sat up in his chair. Tai had picked up the dance quickly their first time attending the Ball, even if she hadn't liked it, so last year she and Kanta had demonstrated to the others when they practiced. They'd agreed yesterday to do the same again.

Since his apology, things had almost gone back to normal between Tai and Kanta. He still felt he was treading on thin ice around her, but he didn't know how to change that. Maybe with time he'd feel totally at ease again.

Getting up, Kanta offered her his hand, gesturing with his other at Kite to start playing. Kite was the only one who could play the piano—a skill Regailia had taught him at a young age—and therefore played during their practice. Kite never danced at the ball anyway, not since he'd turned 10, managing to slip out every time.

Tai took Kanta's hand and they walked to the middle of the cleared room. Kite started with a fast song. It echoed through the room, the quick steps of the dance accompanying the quick tempo. Wendy and Paige fell silent as they watched them dance, and Grippa gave up her braiding. Mid continued.

The first and second dances were fast, designed for pairs. The third, although also fast, involved a switch in partners.

"Wendy, you're up," Kanta announced. "Paige? Mid? Who wants to be Wendy's partner?"

"That's sexist," Mid said. "It doesn't have to be boy/girl pairings for the dance. Last year Mist's date was a woman."

"Okay, so you want to be Paige's partner?"

"Don't be stupid. I'm merely pointing out another of your unattractive traits, nothing else."

"Thanks." Kanta turned to Paige. "Up for it?"

Paige nodded, and got to her feet. She remembered the steps better than any of them. Despite being slightly clumsy in everyday life, Paige was a rather good dancer, at least when it came to following the correct steps. They switched twice during the dance, so everyone was back with their original partners.

"My turn." Mid shot up from the couch. "C'mon, Kite. You're my partner."

"I can't. I have to play—"

"Not anymore." Mid gestured to Alton, who'd stayed seated with Kite the whole time. "I caught you two yesterday at your lessons. You've taught him how to play."

"You did?" Tai was startled.

"He asked me to teach him."

"You didn't tell me Altie learned how to play," Tai said to Paige.

"I didn't know." Paige was more surprised than Tai. "When did you teach him?"

"Mostly during the week after school, on the days you went to the market."

"I wanted it to be a surprise!" Alton shot Mid a dirty look. "I wanted to wait until I got really good so I could surprise you guys!"

"You're really good now." Kite switched the sheet of music in front of him before sliding off the bench, clapping Alton on the shoulder. "You can play that, can't you?"

Alton scanned the music a moment, and gave a determined nod. Kite walked over to Mid, who looped her arm through his and dragged him to the centre of the room, pushing the others out of the way. "Move it, losers."

Kanta scowled at his sister, but got out of the way. He sat on the couch, Tai beside him, and Paige next to her. Wendy sank into the cosiest armchair, exhausted by the dancing he'd done.

After a moment of silence, Alton started playing—shaky at first but steadier the more he played. Mid and Kite started dancing. It wasn't one of the faster ones, but it wasn't a slow song either. It involved detailed footwork, and Kite stumbled more than once, still adjusting to his longer limbs. Mid laughed at him and gave him a light shove, causing him to almost trip, which made her laugh even more. Alton's playing was much better than Kite's dancing.

At some point during the song, Kanta looked at Tai. She was watching Alton, her eyes shining with pride and something else.

Kanta leaned in and whispered, "He's really good."

Tai nodded. "I want his future to be like this. His and Grippa's. I want them to be happy."

"They *are* happy. Why would that change?"

"It won't. I'm not going to let it. I'm going to do whatever I can to preserve their happiness."

Figuring this talk stemmed from her sisterly pride at Alton's accomplishment, Kanta squeezed her knee. "I know you will. You're the best big sister ever."

Tai smiled at him, and although she'd looked so happy for Alton before, something in her expression was now sad.

"I hope so. I really hope so, Kanta."

After they finished practice, Mid offered to walk Wendy home. Kite had gone back to his apprentice work, Paige was busy making supper, and Kanta and Tai had taken the little twins outside to play, so she was the only one there to make the offer. She would have anyway, of course, since she was just that good a person. Besides, it was nice to have some Old World catch-up time.

"Alton's playing was rather marvellous, I must say." Wendy rubbed his mitt-covered hands together as they walked.

"And I must say, Wendell, over-excessive much? Do you really need mittens, a knit hat, a knee-length winter coat, and two scarves?"

"It's just the one scarf, but I can see how you would make that mistake. The inside is a different colour and pattern, and it's awfully thick."

"My comment remains."

"You know how sensitive I am to the cold, Mid. Besides, I've been feeling under the weather lately. Best to bundle up, just in case."

"Still, two scarves?"

"It's one scarf! See!"

"Whatever. Bear, you think Wendy's ridiculous, right? It's not cold."

Bear walked behind Mid.

"Bear agrees. He says this is practically summer weather."

"Bear is a rock giant, Midgard. He isn't as affected by the temperature as we soft, vulnerable humans are."

"Bear's plenty soft! He's a big old teddy in comparison to most rock giants! You know, in an emotional way."

"I'm well aware of Bear's tender temperament, but we're discussing the weath—" Wendy broke off in a sudden, spluttering cough.

"Whoa, you okay, Wends?"

"As I said, I've been feeling under the weather." Wendy dug a handkerchief from his coat pocket. "Do you believe my attire quite justifiable now, Mid?"

"I s'pose. You won't come dressed like that to the Ball though, will you? 'Cause if you aren't spiffy and proper, you're not being my date."

"Bear is always your date!"

"Ah, right you are. Then if you dress like that, I won't dance with you."

"You never dance with me either!"

"Hm … true enough. Then I'm not pigging out at the buffet with you."

"That … Well, that is true—a pity. The food is always awfully enjoyable."

"Yeah, and it goes quickly. You need my ninja reflexes there to secure the best tasties for you."

"Also true. Very well, I'll dress my best. But for now, allow me my warmth." Wendy coughed again and blew his nose.

"Yeah, whatever. Just go get some cold medicine or something, okay, Wend? I don't want you making me sick for the Ball."

"Aren't you worried *I*'ll be sick for the Ball?"

"Like you said," Mid grinned at Bear, "the handsome one's always my date."

Chapter XXXI

It was finally Friday, New Year's Eve. In about an hour Tai, Kanta, and the others were due to arrive at the Hunter Association Headquarters. Tai, who'd showered earlier, was picking moodily through her closet.

"I can't believe you left it until the last minute to decide what to wear," Mid said, from her cross-legged position at the centre of Tai's bed.

"I can't believe you're here giving your opinion."

"I don't like being here anymore than you like having me here."

"Then why *are* you here?"

"It's mandatory for girls to get together before something like this and help each other with our hair and compliment each other's outfits. Or in this case, *critique*." Mid pointed to the dress Tai held. "That's not your colour. Or your style. Is it even a dress?"

Tai glared at her, but put the dress back. She didn't have much clothes except her training gear, and only a few dresses, which she'd worn to several summer festivals her siblings had begged her to attend with them.

Paige and Grippa came into her room through the bathroom. Grippa wore a powder blue dress that went perfectly with her eyes. Paige had found it in the market a month ago. Grippa loved its long flared skirt that reached to her ankles. She'd thought it perfect for spinning, and said so her sisters.

Grippa spun her dress to show off. Paige had put Grippa's hair in a neat braid, which whipped against her back as she turned.

Mid clapped. "Encore! Encore!"

Grippa beamed and spun again. When she finished, she was dizzy. Wobbling to the bed, Grippa climbed up and leaned against Mid, who didn't seem to mind. Paige hurried to fix Grippa's skirt so that she wouldn't crinkle it.

Watching Grippa lean on Mid, Tai felt a twinge in her gut. She couldn't remember the last time her little sister had wanted even that much support from her. Not since the Brighton incident.

Tai turned back to her closet. Paige, who was wearing a simple blouse tucked into a calf-length violet skirt, with a pair of white tights underneath, came up beside her. It wasn't as formal as Paige had gone last year, but the look suited her, Tai thought.

"There's something I want to t-t-tell you …" Paige mumbled, so low that Mid and Grippa, who were swapping school and ghost horror stories, couldn't hear.

"Go on."

"You know how the rest of the City has its own celebration in the m-m-markets?"

"Yes?"

"H-H-Harven asked me to g-g-go with him and I'd like t-t-to."

It took Tai a minute to realize her sister was asking permission to skip the Ball. "You're springing this now? An hour before we have to go?"

"I k-k-kept looking for the right t-t-time to ask, but it n-n-never c-c-came."

"Basically any time other than today would have

been better. Fine. But make sure he has you back home before midnight."

"B-B-But it's N-N-New Year's …"

"Before one, then." Tai wasn't Harven's biggest fan, not only because she'd only met him a few times but because he was just a few months younger than she was, and Paige was still two months away from her 17th birthday. The age gap might not be that big, but Tai didn't like the thought of her little sister going out with an older man. Still, Paige seemed to like Harven, and he was apparently good with the little twins, and always got Paige home at a reasonable time. Those were the only reasons that Tai was letting her go. That, and it wasn't really her place to stop her sister. Paige *was* almost 17.

"Wear this one." Paige took out a dress—the one Tai had worn the year before to the Ball. It had spaghetti straps, a V-neck, and a skirt more flared than Grippa's and stopped just above her knees. It was red—the reason for Tai's immediate attraction to it.

Now, Tai was beginning to think she'd developed an aversion to the colour.

"You looked beautiful in it last year," Paige assured her.

"Wear that one," Mid called from the bed. "This is taking forever and I'm bored!"

Tai rolled her eyes, took the dress, and changed in the bathroom. She put on sheer black tights; the year before she'd worn thicker black leggings, but they'd been too warm. Even if she'd be cold on the way there and back, she'd be more comfortable overall.

When Tai returned, Mid leaped to her feet. "Finally! Time to go!"

Mid was, as usual, the most eccentrically dressed:

a long purple tunic over black and green striped leggings, a cropped leather jacket, and her plasma goggles on her head. When she showed up dressed like that, Tai asked about the goggles. Mid informed her that they were also for fashion as well as hunting, adding that Tai wouldn't understand.

The guys, already dressed, were waiting downstairs. Kite was seated at the piano, and he and Alton—who was wearing a pale blue tie to match Grippa's dress—were going over a new song. Now that Alton's secret hobby had been outed, there was no point in the two being selective in their practice time.

Kanta was sitting in his favourite armchair, idly playing with his black tie. Spotting the others, his attention immediately went to Tai, gaze travelling over her, and again more slowly. Tai was both irritated and flustered by his attention. She went straight to Alton, who had slid off the piano bench while Kite put away their sheets of music.

Tai kneeled down in front of her brother, about to fix his tie, but whoever had helped him with it had done a perfect job. At a loss for what to do, Tai straightened her brother's collar.

"Do I look handsome?"

"You look like a gentleman, Altie."

Alton beamed and Tai got up, smoothing down his hair. Mid had pounced on Kite, whose tie was already a mess. She only worsened the article's state, which thoroughly annoyed Kite, who had been trying to push her away.

"I hate ties." Mid gave up. "They're impossible."

"It was fine before," Kite insisted.

"It looked like a six-year-old had put it on."

"Now it looks like a three-year-old did."

Mid turned to her brother. "Kanta, fix his tie. I'm not going to the Ball with this guy degrading our group. It's bad enough Paige is wearing her peasant clothes."

"I'm not g-g-going with you g-g-guys."

"You're not?" Kanta asked.

"N-N-No. I'm going to the festival in the m-m-market."

"We'll miss you, then."

"Can I go too?" Grippa asked. "I want to go to the market instead. I can still wear my dress, right?"

"No, Grippa," Tai said firmly. "You're coming with us."

"Why does Paige get to go and I don't? That's not fair!"

"Paige is older."

"But I could go with her!"

"No, you can't. Paige is going on a date."

Tai hadn't wanted to announce it so bluntly in front of everyone, knowing it would embarrass her sister—which, judging by Paige's red face, it had—but she didn't know how else to handle Grippa. Her youngest sister hadn't always been so problematic.

Grippa pouted, but didn't complain further. Everyone went into the hall to put on coats and help the little twins into theirs without rumpling their clothes. Tai put on a longer coat to cover her shoulders and more of her legs, but she knew the wind would still bite. It would be worth it once they got to the Ball.

Outside, they met up with Bear, and said goodbye to Paige.

"Good luck." Tai heard Kanta whisper to Paige, who blushed again. As much as Tai wanted to see her sister being supported, she wasn't sure if she was thankful to Kanta for supporting her in this in particular detail.

Mid waved at Paige. "See you next year!"

Mid led their group, chattering to Bear and showing him her outfit, which he apparently was showering with compliments. Kite walked in the middle, monitoring the little twins, looking unhappier than usual. This left Kanta and Tai at the back.

"You look stunning," Kanta whispered.

"I'm wearing the exact same thing I wore last year."

"Not exactly. Last year your tights were solid." He flashed The Grin. "I like your choice better this year."

The regular Kanta was completely back. He'd recovered from their fight. Tai wasn't sure if she was relieved or disappointed.

"There's something I should tell you." Tai figured since they were basically alone, now was as good a time as any. She didn't want to put it off until the last minute, like Paige had with her news.

"Like what? I look incredibly dashing this evening? I already know."

"I'm going on a trip after New Year's."

"A trip?"

"It won't take long, maybe two weeks. Some of the trainees planned it, and I'm going too. We're heading out next week, so we'll be back way before the break finishes."

"Oh … um, so where are you guys going?"

"To someone's village. It's not that far away."

Kanta fell silent again. Tai waited, hoping he wouldn't ask any more questions, like why she'd want to go on something like that, or who exactly the trainees were. Luckily, he didn't, but he didn't speak for the rest of the walk.

By the time they reached the Hunter Association Headquarters, Kanta was almost back to his pleasant mood. They were admitted by the guards at the entrance and, after dropping off their jackets at the coat check in the hall, went into the ballroom.

The Headquarters was where the Council met and the various sections of the Association had their offices and labs. Each area of the Association had its own wing, and at the centre of the building was the massive main hall that served as the ballroom for New Year's. There were two sets of stairs on either side of the room, leading up to the second level and the wraparound balcony. Glancing up, Tai could see guests already congregating there, leaning against the railing while they socialized. The main floor was just as, if not more, crowded than the second. Row upon row of tables offering drinks and food lined the walls, and at the back of the room on a dais was the band that always played for the Ball. They'd already started—a simple, calming tune that carried through the massive room. It was something to listen to before the dancing started.

Mid and Bear immediately broke off from the group. Bear wasn't the only rock giant. Tai spotted two others, from other units lucky enough to acquire such a member. Bear was, however, the only rock giant with a too-short tie looped around his neck.

Grippa and Alton dove for the closest buffet. Kanta took one look at what this particular table offered in beverages, clapped Tai on the shoulder, and said, "I'll get us something to drink."

"There's punch here," Kite pointed out.

"Not the kind I want" was all Kanta said before he disappeared.

Kite shook his head and turned to get a glass of punch. "So Harven asked Paige to the festival."

"Yes."

Kite didn't say anything else. Something in the crowd had caught his attention. He gestured for Tai's benefit. "There."

In the midst of the crowd were Thalus and Regailia. Even though they were a couple, and had a son, Tai still wasn't used to seeing them together. Thalus wore a crisp black suit and white dress shirt, but no tie; Regailia, a dark blue dress with long sleeves and a long skirt. Next to Thalus, she looked very small, but no less elegant. The two were talking to another couple, who had their arms linked and were very animated in whatever they were discussing. In contrast, Regailia and Thalus weren't touching at all, and both wore closed expressions. Seeing the two of them, aloof and distant in their demeanour, it was easy to tell that they were Kite's parents.

"I should go greet them," Kite said. "Mother will expect it."

Tai had always found it strange that Kite, although he always referred to Thalus by his name or title of Commander, only ever called Regailia *Mother*.

Kite headed toward them. Unlike last year, Tai didn't lose sight of him in the crowd; his head stuck up above most of the hunters now. He'd likely have a tough time escaping the dances this year, Tai thought, and was surprised that the notion amused her.

Kanta still hadn't returned when she heard someone call out to her. "Tai!"

Turning, Tai was surprised to see Gareth and Korel.

Both wore their trainee jackets, as was the custom of trainees attending the Ball. Gareth wore a dark green dress shirt under his, which didn't match well with the jacket's bright green stripes but suited him otherwise. Korel wore a gold dress that shimmered in the light.

"Why aren't you wearing your jacket?" Korel gave Tai's outfit a once-over. Tai wasn't sure if the frown indicated Korel's envy or disapproval.

"I couldn't find it."

"Too bad. Nice dress."

"You too."

"Are these your siblings?" Gareth asked, spotting the blonde heads behind Tai.

Tai waved the kids over. Grippa brought her plate of food with her, and Alton had a piece of garlic bread stuck in his mouth. "Grippa, Alton, meet Gareth and Korel."

Alton didn't say anything, suddenly shy. Grippa on the other hand, didn't hesitate. "Are you guys hunters like my sister?"

"Indeed we are!" Gareth gave a mock bow. "A pleasure to make your acquaintance, milady."

Grippa giggled, but Korel pinched his arm. "Don't scare them with your idiocy."

"My idiocy scares no one. In fact, most delight in it."

"I love your dress!" Grippa exclaimed, silencing whatever Korel had been about to say to Gareth. "It's so pretty and sparkly!"

"Thank you." Korel was taken aback by the compliment.

"Have you seen Mao?" Gareth asked Tai. "I haven't seen him since last Friday."

"Mao?" Grippa asked, then to Tai. "Wasn't that the guy at our house?"

Tai tried to quiet Grippa, but it was too late.

"When was this?" Korel asked.

Grippa replied, "It was Saturday. He stayed over, and Kanta got mad."

Normally, Gareth would have perked up at the mention of Kanta, but he was too stunned to react. Korel's mouth hung open. She grabbed Tai's arm and tugged her away, calling over her shoulder. "Gareth, watch the kids a sec."

When they were far enough away, Korel let go of Tai. "Why was Mao at your house? What happened with you guys? Did you—"

"No!" Tai had had this conversation with Kanta a dozen times. She didn't want to have it again with Korel, of all people. "I found him on my way home and said he could come back with me if he wanted, okay?"

"No, that is not okay. Tai, why would you do that? You know who his father is, don't you? He'd be beyond pissed if he found out Mao had stayed with you! That could jeopardize your hunting career! Not just that, it could also cause problems for Regailia and Commander Thalus! They're already on bad terms with Mao's father!"

"They are?"

"Yes! Didn't you know? Never mind. Look, it was okay when we were all in a group together, but you're better off keeping away from Mao. He's a troubled kid, and his father's a hothead. It would only cause problems for you."

"You stood up for him before, that night at the tavern when Damian was saying those things. Why are you against him now?"

"I'm not against him, and what Damian was saying was horrible, but it wasn't entirely wrong. I feel bad for Mao but, Tai, you have to understand, there's nothing we can do about his problems. We'd only cause more trouble for ourselves if we tried."

"Have you said all this to Gareth?"

"No. I can't, can I? His situation's the opposite. He *has* to associate with Mao. If he didn't, Mao's father really would make problems for him and his brother. He doesn't have a choice. It wouldn't help him if he knew my opinion."

"So you faked concern that night, when you went with Gareth to look for him?"

"No. I was concerned, but not for Mao. Do you know how pissed his father was when he didn't return home? He blamed Gareth."

"That's why you're saying this to me, isn't it? It isn't because you're worried about me. It's because you're worried I'm going to get Gareth into trouble again."

Korel's expression cracked, revealing anger underneath. "Can you blame me? It's your fault Gareth got into trouble! If you hadn't invited Mao back to your place, to do whatever the hell you two did, he would have gone home and everything would have been fine! Gareth's been keeping tabs on Mao for three years now! He only has two months left before field training starts and Mao isn't his responsibility anymore! But after last Friday, Mao's father threatened Gareth—*threatened* him—saying if anything else like that happened, he might have to reconsider Gareth's position in his unit. He even insinuated that he might need to have a word with Gareth's instructors to see if he was actually ready for field training. This could ruin his entire career as a hunter! Do you think I'm going to let that happen just because you've decided the quiet guy in the group is more interesting than the hot one that's been hitting on you since you arrived?"

It took Tai a moment to realize Korel meant Damian. She remembered what Mao had told her, how Korel was only giving Gareth her attention because Damian had rejected her.

"You were jealous." Tai was incredulous as realization struck. "You were jealous of Damian's interest in me. Gods, Korel. How can you stand here going on about your concern for Gareth when you're only using him to get over Damian?"

Korel gaped at her a moment, then she was furious. "It's not like that at all! I *do* care about Gareth— we've been friends for a long time, and he's been great to me ever since … ever since … Maybe I *was* jealous. You just showed up from out of nowhere, pretty and clueless and older, and Damian decided he liked you more than me, and you never even spoke to him! Maybe I was jealous. But I'm not anymore. Damian can go to hell for all I care. Gareth is the one I'm concerned about, and, believe it or not, I'm concerned for you too. If you screw over Gareth by pissing off Mao's father, you'll be screwing yourself over too. And trust me, it won't be worth it."

Before Tai could say anything else, Korel whirled around and stalked back to Gareth. Trying to calm herself so that the little twins wouldn't suspect anything, Tai followed. She had to ignore Korel, who probably exaggerated anyway. Tai knew Korel tended toward the dramatic, so there was no point in dwelling on what she'd said. No point in letting it get to her—although that was difficult at the moment.

When Tai reached her siblings, she was surprised to find Korel had yet to pull Gareth away. Kanta had returned with their drinks, and Gareth was frozen to the spot, staring at Kanta with a star-struck expression.

"Tai," Kanta said, relieved. "This is one of your friends, I take it?"

Tai accepted her drink from Kanta. "Kanta, this is Gareth. Gareth, this—"

"Is Kanta, from Unit Q17, age 19, youngest hunter to ever kill a boss, at nearly 14 years of age. Youngest ever to earn a hunting licence, at 16. Uses a katana, altered to take plasma by Kite, son of—"

"Gareth, you're losing it," Korel reminded him.

Gareth shook himself, as if he'd just awakened. He gave Kanta a sheepish look. "I'm, uh, kinda a fan. Do you think maybe I could get your auto—"

Korel elbowed Gareth in the side before he could finish. "Sorry about him."

"It's fine. You guys trained with Tai?"

"Yes, she's very skilled!" Gareth offered. "One of the first of us to take out a boss, and she also took out the final boss we went up against in training!"

"I didn't take out that one," Tai reminded him. She'd just picked the right room.

"Then who …? Oh, right, Mao." Gareth's eyes darted to Tai as he said the name, obviously recalling what he'd just learned. Did he blame her like Korel did, Tai wondered?

Kanta took Tai's free hand. "I saw Ike and his kids a few minutes ago. Why don't we see if the little twins want to play with them?"

"Okay."

"Nice to meet you two," Kanta said to Gareth and

Korel as he pulled Tai away. "Good luck with your field training."

Before she disappeared into the crowd behind Kanta, Tai locked eyes with Korel. For a split second Tai thought maybe she was actually genuine in what she'd said, actually worried for Tai and everyone involved. But then Tai thought of Mao, and everything he'd said about his father, about his miserable life, and she didn't care what Korel had said. Mao's father couldn't have so much sway that it would put Gareth's career on hold, and what would be so bad about his joining a different unit? No, her mind was made up. She was going with Mao to his old town next week, and she was going to find a way to break the curse. That was all that mattered.

Chapter XXXII

Paige met with Harven in front of his family's shop. When he saw her, he broke into a wide smile. "You look beautiful."

Paige couldn't help blushing. Harven took her hand and they walked to the market. They didn't speak, and the entire time Paige's mind raced to find a conversation topic, but kept turning out blanks. Paige wondered if Harven disliked the silence, but then he gave her hand a squeeze. Paige relaxed.

They reached the market, which was decorated for the festival. Musicians were set up throughout the square, and food stalls had stayed open for the event. Game stalls offered small trinkets and sweets as prizes. Children ran past, carrying balloons, the current year painted with stars on their cheeks. The little twins would have loved it, Paige thought, running around, getting their faces painted, and playing games. But she was glad Tai hadn't let Grippa accompany them. She wanted to be alone with Harven.

They lined up at one of the food stalls. Paige pulled her purse from her skirt pocket, but Harven lightly touched her hand, stopping her. "My treat."

Paige was about to tell him he didn't have to do that, but Harven added, "I was the one who invited you, remember? It's my responsibility to treat. I'd be insulted if you didn't let me."

Paige put her purse away.

They were almost at the front of the line when

someone called out to them. Turning, Paige was surprised and delighted to see Basil.

"What are you doing here?" Paige asked. "I thought you'd be home by now."

"And miss such a wonderful sales opportunity?"

"Your stall's open tonight?"

"Yes, in the usual spot. Check it out. Is this young man your beau?"

Paige blushed. She didn't know what to say, and Harven wasn't helping. If anything, he was waiting for Paige's answer.

"Are you two enjoying the festival?"

"We've only just arrived." Harven seemed disappointed at not hearing Paige's response.

"Won't your wife miss you tonight?" Paige asked Basil. "It *is* New Year's."

"To be honest, we don't really celebrate New Year's." Basil didn't correct Paige's use of the word *wife*. "I miss her, though. I miss her whenever we aren't together."

"That's so sweet."

"Yes, well, I'd like her to think so." An odd expression crossed Basil's face before his usual smile returned. "I'll leave you two now. I don't want to impose. Remember to drop by my stall if you get a chance."

Paige promised, and waved to Basil as he left.

"That man looked vaguely familiar," Harven acknowledged.

"You've met him before?"

"No, I don't think so, but he looks so familiar …"

"Maybe you've seen him around the market? He visits often."

Harven was unsure. "That must be it."

It was their turn to order. Paige focused on the menu.

Chapter XXXIII

Kanta had thought that after dropping the little twins off with Ike's kids, he and Tai could have time alone. Unfortunately, when they'd found Ike in the crowd, Yano was also there. Although they didn't have to worry about Grippa and Alton anymore, Yano stuck with them, chattering non-stop for half an hour.

Yano paused mid-sentence, spotting someone. A sly grin spread across his face. Kanta wasn't surprised to see Rudy. She was talking to Mist and Mist's date, Jara, a brunette a few years younger, who'd been Mist's date for the past five years.

"See ya," Yano said. "If you don't mind, I have to go inform that lucky lady I've chosen her as my dance partner."

"You mean convince that older woman to spare you one dance," Kanta said, but Yano just waved him off as he wove through the crowd.

"He's interesting," Tai said, bored. She'd finished her drink and was entertaining herself by swishing the rim of liquid left at the bottom back and forth.

"Want another?" Kanta realized they were finally alone.

Tai shrugged.

Taking her arm, Kanta led her through the crowd to one of the tables and refilled their glasses. They sipped their drinks, surveying the people around them. Kanta tried to stay calm, but he couldn't help fidgeting at the thought of his plan. How would he ever hope to execute it? This wasn't like him at all, getting so nervous.

Before Kanta could think of a reason to pull Tai aside, Thalus came up to them. He wasn't with Regailia or Kite, as he had been earlier, but with another commander, a fairly short man, with a broad, muscular build and shaved head.

"Kanta, Tai. May I introduce Commander Jules of Unit K12. Kanta, the two of you have met before, I believe."

They had, but briefly, at one of the Balls when Kanta was younger. He remembered it now. Commander Jules had gone through training at the same time as Thalus and had risen to the rank of commander shortly after Kanta's uncle. Though not as renowned as Thalus, Jules was reputed to be a great commander. Kanta knew the two commanders weren't on the best of terms, although he didn't know why. Whenever they were together in a setting such as this, Thalus would do his best to seem cordial with the other commander, but always ended up sounding stiffer than usual.

After the introduction, Jules focused on Tai. "So this is the recruit you brought back, Thalus. I've heard good things about her. Planning to take her for your own unit?"

"That remains to be seen," Thalus said—in his stiffer-than-normal voice.

"I'm sure it does." Jules's smile was in no way kind. "I believe you were in the same field testing group as my son, Mao."

Kanta felt Tai stiffen. He was just as surprised. Mao was Jules's son? But that would make him the kid involved in that scandal a few years back.

"Nice seeing you again, Commander," Kanta

said, when he realized Tai wasn't able to reply. "If you'll excuse us, we were just about to dance."

"By all means, don't let me stop you," Jules responded. "We'll talk later."

Kanta pulled Tai toward the band, where some couples had gone to dance. Instead of stopping there, however, Kanta led Tai down a corridor at the back of the room. Kanta wasn't familiar with this part of the building, but he thought it might lead to the commanders' offices.

"Where are we going?" Tai started to ask, when Kanta stopped. They were away from the party now, completely out of sight of the ballroom.

"Kanta, why are we here?"

"Why did you react like that, when you heard that guy's name?"

"What do you mean?"

"Mao. His name comes up all the time lately, and, when it does, you get this *look* on your face. Why?"

"I thought you were over this."

"I guess I'm not." He took her arms when she started to turn away. "Tai, I'm going to ask you this again. Please be honest. Is there anything between you two?"

Tai was quiet a moment. "No, Kanta. There isn't."

There isn't … she hesitated.

Maybe it was true. Maybe there wasn't anything between them. Maybe there would be. Kanta had been thinking about it for a while, more seriously than before. Even if it wasn't with Mao, eventually a guy was going to come along that Tai would be interested in and he would make a move, or maybe Tai would. Either way, Kanta wouldn't have a right to get mad, like Freid had said. Unless he made a move first.

Still holding on to her to keep her in place, Kanta leaned in and kissed Tai. She was startled, and for a moment there was nothing. Then, slowly, she kissed him back.

Kanta wanted to deepen the kiss. More than anything that's what he wanted to do—what he felt was right—but he didn't want to overstep his bounds even more than he might have already. Gently, Kanta pulled back. Tai stared at him, wide-eyed and stunned, her cheeks tinged with pink.

Kanta offered The Grin and let her go.

Shakily, Tai reached up and touched her lips. "Kanta ..."

"Don't say anything right now. Just ... think about that, okay? Think about that and then we can talk. I'll come find you when the dances start." With that, Kanta left. He glanced back, but Tai didn't turn to watch him leave. She stood there touching her lips.

Smiling softly to himself, Kanta returned to the party, his heart doing backflips at the thought of what would happen when the first dance started.

"Tai."

Tai whirled around, thinking Kanta had come back to ... say something? Kiss her again?

Gods-That-Remain. Kanta had kissed her.

She'd kissed him.

It was Mao.

He was wearing a black dress shirt over black pants, which made his pale eyes stand out even more than usual. His expression was closed.

"What?" Tai croaked. Had he seen that? No, he couldn't have. She and Kanta had been alone. He couldn't have.

Mao watched her for a moment and then walked toward her, slowly. He stopped farther away than she expected, keeping that isolating distance he did with others. She was thankful for it, though, even if it puzzled her. If he came any closer, she was afraid he'd hear her heart hammering in her chest.

"My father found out that I was planning to leave. If you still want to do this, we'll have to go tonight. He's too preoccupied with the party to notice my leaving, but after tonight he won't let me out of his sight until field training. If you want my help, we have to go now."

Tai *did* want his help—she didn't know how she'd do it without him—but what about ... what about Kanta? What would he think if she disappeared? Would he be worried and try to find her, or would he be angry, thinking she'd run off early with her trainee friends? And after that, what he'd just done, how could she leave? She'd even been considering telling him the truth—about the curse and her plans—though she hadn't yet decided one way or another. What if he didn't believe in the curse and thought it was foolish of her to run around trying to break something imaginary? What if he believed her and became even more supportive, and she fell even more in his debt?

What if he kissed her again?

"It's now or not at all. My father will notice I'm gone from the party soon. What do you want to do?"

"Go. We should ... go."

Mao didn't wait for her to follow. For a moment, despite her words, Tai wasn't sure if she would. She could still change her mind. She could still stay and work things out with Kanta and maybe get his help. Or she could leave, now, quickly, and risk hurting

Kanta and ruining everything. But if she left, she might also find out how to break the curse, and if she stayed she might lose that chance.

Every second she wavered that loaded gun stayed pressed to her head. The luxury of time was something she'd never had.

Tai wiped the back of her hand across her mouth and followed Mao.

Chapter XXXIV

It was nearly time for the first dance. Kanta couldn't find Tai anywhere. He resorted to asking some of the trainees, those he'd run into earlier, where she was. The last anyone had seen of Tai, though, was when she was with Kanta.

"Sorry, haven't seen her," Browen said, when Kanta asked him and Silsa.

"We could help you look," Silsa offered.

Kanta was about to take her up on her offer when someone in the group next to them said, "Don't bother."

Kanta didn't recognize the guy wearing a trainee jacket. He'd been talking with some other trainees, but stopped to speak to Kanta.

"What are you talking about, Damian?" Silsa asked, startled.

"I saw her leave an hour ago—maybe more than that. She was with that little bastard. Surprise, surprise."

"You shouldn't call him that," Silsa said, but Kanta spoke over her. "Is that true? Did she really leave?"

"Yeah, though I'd say sneaked is more accurate. They had that look about them."

Rage boiled in Kanta. It had to have been Mao she'd left with. Who else would it be? So she'd been lying when she said nothing was going on. Or maybe she hadn't lied. Maybe nothing had been going on before, but she'd decided she preferred him over Kanta after the kiss. And she hadn't even stuck around to tell him.

But that wasn't like Tai. It wasn't like her at all. She'd face him, even if it was for a rejection. And he wasn't so sure she would have rejected him, not with the way she'd looked after that kiss.

Either way, Kanta had to find Tai. He strode away without a word to anyone. He'd go get his jacket, check at home for her, and if she wasn't there … He'd find out where Jules lived, and he'd go to his house. If that failed, he'd keep looking. He'd find her eventually, even if it was the next morning when he got home after searching all night, only to discover she'd returned before him. Because no matter what had happened between them, she'd still go home. Her siblings were there, and she'd never make them worry, not for something this trivial.

Kanta reached the hall and handed in his coat number, anxious to get his jacket and leave. Then the loudest sound he'd ever heard exploded in his ears— louder than the wail of a hundred dying ghosts.

Chapter XXXV

Mid hadn't seen Summer, or the red-haired girl, and not for lack of looking. She hoped they'd managed to get in with her ID. If they'd been denied access, Mid figured she would have been pulled aside and questioned about the ID, so she assumed that hadn't happened. But if they hadn't been held up there, then where were they? Hiding somewhere until the ideal time to address the Association? Had they given up?

Trying to quell her anxiety, Mid focused on talking to Wendy. They were near one of the buffet tables, which Wendy continued to pick at while telling her about the Old World comic his parents had surprised him with for New Year's. Normally Kanta would get Mid a New Year's gift, but she didn't think they'd be exchanging presents this year, so she hoped Kite had gotten her something as cool as Wendy's gift. Cooler.

The little twins and Yano's siblings were playing on the stairs by the table, peeking through the bars at each other. Grippa was in the process of climbing over the railing onto Bear's back, as he was standing right next to it. She'd ripped her dress, but didn't seem that bothered. Finally, she sat back on the stairs.

Then Bear's head shot up and he looked at the band's dais. Normally Mid would have thought it was the music that had caught his attention, but the band had taken a break to get something to eat. Maybe it was Summer? Turning away from Wendy, Mid stood on tiptoes to better see the dais but found her gaze blocked by rock.

"Bear, what are you—"

Pure noise shattered Mid's eardrums as light exploded around Bear. The floor shook under Mid and her feet gave way under her. On her knees, Mid pressed a hand to her ringing ear, using the other to steady herself. She blinked the stars from her eyes and tried to look around. Those who hadn't fallen were disoriented and clutched their ears and eyes.

Slowly, the ringing faded and Mid registered other sounds. Shouts. Screams.

Mid staggered to her feet, immediately attuned to a new danger. She reached instinctively for her pistols, but of course they weren't there. Using Bear for support, Mid peeked around him to find the cause of all this. Mid didn't understand the debris floating through the air around the hole where the dais had been. Then it clicked.

A bomb.

Mid saw something sail through the air. It looked like a regular tin can, but as it clanked against the floor it released massive plumes of smoke. Another fell somewhere in the room. Then another. Mid snapped on her goggles to see through the smoke, covering her mouth as it wafted toward her. Looking up, Mid spotted the people on the second floor dropping the cans. All wore trainee jackets.

Mid turned, and dragged Wendy to his feet. Bear had blocked Wendy as well as Mid, but the tech was still disoriented.

"Wendy!" Mid slapped him to snap him out of it. "Get the kids outside!"

Wendy nodded, dazed. Mid dashed past the terrified children up the stairs. "Mid! Where are you going?"

Mid ignored him and pounded up the steps, Bear behind her.

Mid grabbed her pocket knife from her jacket as she reached the second floor. She never left home without it, like any good hunter, even if they were in Hunters City. Doing a quick scan of the floor, Mid saw it was empty except for those wearing trainee jackets. Everyone else had gone downstairs earlier to prepare for the first dance.

Mid, spotting a flicker ahead, was horrified to realize that the attackers were going to drop torches into the crowd.

"Hey!" Mid screeched as loud as she could, so startling the closest person he dropped his unlit torch and lighter. He whirled toward her, unsheathing a dagger. When he spotted Bear, his eyes widened. That was all Mid could see of him: his eyes. His hood was up and a mask covered his nose and mouth.

Yanking out something that looked like a WT, the guy spoke rapidly into it. Mid ran at him with her knife, knowing it would do little against his dagger, but also knowing Bear would take care of what she couldn't.

Instead of standing his ground, the guy ducked around Bear, and fled. Mid wanted to give chase, but the others still upstairs were already dropping torches. Mid tried to reach them, but she was too late, and when she got to the spot one of them had been in, they'd already run away.

One person stood at the back of the second floor in front of a large painting of the Hunter Association's founder. Not much was known about him. His only lasting legacy was the Association and the good it had done for the world. No one knew his name.

"Bear, go block their exit." Mid twirled her knife. "I'll get the last one."

Bear pounded off, back down the stairs.

Mid slowly approached the person standing in front of her. It was a girl, Mid realized, older than herself. The girl pulled back her hood, revealing dark brown hair in a tight bun at the back of her head. She yanked down her mask then and smiled at Mid, hazel eyes shining. "Yo, what's up?"

Mid was confused by the familiar voice and tone. Then realization dawned. This was the red-haired girl from the other night, the girl who'd been sitting with Summer.

"I wanted to get a look at him." She nodded at the Association's founder. "See the guy who set the groundwork for this whole mess."

Mid was shaking all over. "Where is she?"

"Hmm?"

"Where is she?" Mid screeched.

"You wanna see Summer? Funny. She said she wants to see you too."

Pain exploded in the back of Mid's head, and suddenly she was falling face-first toward the floor. She blacked out for a moment, but then her spotty vision registered two figures above her. The blonde man—Summer's cousin was holding something like a club. Next to him, the girl. She crouched in front of Mid, holding something: Mid's ID.

"Thanks for the help." The girl winked. "Not 100 per cent necessary but made things smoother. Two IDs get more people in than one, after all."

As Mid's vision faded, she dropped Mid's ID, revealing another behind it.

The last thing Mid saw before losing consciousness was her brother's ID.

Chapter XXXVI

Kanta gripped the coat check desk as the floor rocked under him. When the shaking stopped, he let go and steadied himself. The guy working at the coat check picked himself off the floor. He'd fallen while coming back with Kanta's jacket. They looked at each other. "That came from the ballroom."

Kanta didn't say anything but rushed for the ballroom doors. Just as he reached them, they burst open and people piled out. Among them were several trainees, hoods thrown over their heads.

Pushing through the crowd, Kanta found the ballroom in a state of destruction and confusion: smoke everywhere, and people appearing from the haze, dragging themselves toward the doors. Some were injured.

Kanta ran through the ballroom, calling out for Mid, helping people up when he found them on the floor. He supported an older woman all the way to the door, where someone else took her from him. Pressing back into the smoke, Kanta covered his arm and continued to shout for Mid.

"Kanta!"

Turning, Kanta saw Freid coming toward him through the smoke.

"What's going on?"

"I don't know." Freid coughed. "I think it was a bomb."

"A bomb?"

"Yeah. All this smoke came from somewhere."

"Have you seen Mid?"

"No, but I'll help you look for her."

They parted ways, both calling for Kanta's sister. Kanta also called out for Kite and the little twins, heart hammering when he realized they'd all still been in the ballroom. If anything had happened to any of them, or Regailia or Thalus …

"Kanta!"

Relief flooded Kanta to see Wendy in one piece, and that relief tripled when he saw Grippa, Alton, and Yano's siblings behind him.

"Thank the gods …" Kanta reached over to give Wendy a quick hug before pulling back. "Mid! Have you seen her?"

"She was with us. She's fine, and Bear's with her but, Kanta, she went running upstairs for some reason! I would have followed her, but I need to get the kids out."

"I know. It's okay. You do that. I'll go find Mid."

"Kanta, I'm scared!" Grippa grabbed his sleeve. Alton looked just as terrified.

Kanta kneeled down in front of them and squeezed their shoulders. "It's going to be okay. You guys are safe. Wendy will take care of you until I come back."

"What about Tai?" Alton asked. "Where is she?"

"She's safe. She left before this happened. You'll see her soon. Just go with Wendy for now, okay?"

Getting to his feet, Kanta nodded at Wendy, who herded the kids away. Kanta plunged back into the smoke.

He'd gotten halfway up the stairs when something on the second floor caught his eye. It took a moment to realize what the flickering was. *Fire.*

Kanta rushed up the stairs, shouting for Mid as he went. He ran toward the source of the fire, shocked to see it was the Hunter Association founder's portrait. Almost nothing remained, the image blackened to ash below the flames. Kanta felt a squeezing sensation in his gut when he realized nothing else around the portrait had caught fire. This, like everything else, had been deliberate. It was an attack against the Hunter Association, and the Hunter Association alone.

Kanta could do nothing about the picture. Soon enough the flames would burn out, unable to climb beyond the metal frame. Kanta scanned the second floor, deflated when he realized it was completely empty. He hurried back downstairs, hoping Mid had done the smart thing and retreated outside to safety with the others. At the very least, he hoped to find her in the middle of the smoke-filled ballroom, foolishly helping others to safety despite the danger. Scanning the ballroom, Kanta was horrified that there was fire down there as well.

Reaching the main floor, he dove into the smoke, almost knocking into other hunters who were dragging more people to safety. Kanta wove around all of them, until he came across a pair of his friends supporting each other.

"Kanta …" Freid gasped, his arm looped around Yano's neck. "I'm sorry I couldn't find Mid …"

"What happened to you?" There was a gash in Freid's stomach, oozing blood from around his fingers.

"One of the trainees …" Freid tried to explain, but he couldn't continue. He had a dazed look about him, as if he'd knocked his head, or lost a lot of blood. The latter, Kanta thought, was *very* likely.

"The terrorists are dressed like trainees," Yano explained. "One of them attacked Freid with his dagger. A crazy redhead. He ran away when he saw me coming."

"He laughed …" Freid wheezed. "He kept laughing when he stabbed me."

Kanta was horrified, but didn't have long to react because Yano gripped his arm with his free hand, getting his attention. "Can you take Freid? I know you need to find your sister, but she's 15 and Jun and Kyo are only kids. I have to find them."

"Wendy took them outside. They aren't hurt."

"Are you serious?"

When Kanta nodded, Yano's eyes shone with gratitude. "Thank you. Look, just let me get Freid out and I'll help you find Mid."

"Thanks." Kanta dove back into the haze, hoping Mid hadn't encountered the same crazy guy Freid had, or any of the other terrorists.

Kanta hadn't been searching long when he came upon someone wearing a trainee jacket out cold on the ground. For a moment Kanta was on guard, but then he recognized her as the red-headed girl from Tai's trainee group. The guy with the glasses was next to her, also knocked out. He tried to wake them up.

"Damn it." Kanta still needed to find Mid and Kite, but he couldn't just leave these two. Hooking his arm around the girl's shoulders, Kanta pulled her up.

Chapter XXXVII

Paige felt as if her heart had stopped when the explosion echoed through the square. In no time, word spread that it had come from the Hunter Association Headquarters. She'd left the market immediately, terrified at the idea that any or all of her family had been hurt or worse. She'd apologized quickly to Harven, but he'd understood and had come with her.

Now, she waited in the crowd outside the main building of the Headquarters. Paige wanted to go inside and search for her family, as others were doing, but Harven told her to wait where it was safe. He went inside, leaving Paige alone and trembling with fear. She could see the smoke pressing against the two-story windows in the ballroom, but nothing else, which made her even more worried.

"Paige!"

Paige whipped around to see Wendy pushing through the crowd. Her younger siblings ran straight to her. Paige gasped, catching them in a hug when they reached her. She didn't let them go for a long time, tears pricking her eyes.

When Paige could bring herself to look up at Wendy, she asked, "T-T-Tai …?"

"Kanta said she's fine. He said she left before the attack."

Paige felt a tear slip down her cheek and she wiped it away. "G-G-Gods be thanked. Is everyone else okay?"

"Kanta's fine. He's gone back in to look for Mid.

My parents are okay. I was just with them when I saw you, but I don't know about anyone else. I haven't seen Thalus or Regailia or Kite or anyone else from the unit, and I don't know where Mid went …"

Paige hugged her siblings tighter. Wendy's words made her concerned all over again. She'd lived with Regailia and Kite for two years and, even though she spoke little to Regailia, and felt small when she spoke with Kite, she couldn't imagine anything happening to either of them.

"I shouldn't have gone to the festival. I should have come here with everyone. At least then I would have been … I could have …"

"It's better that you weren't here, Paige. If you were, something might have happened to you, and everyone would have been even more worried. The fact that we all knew you were safe was a blessing."

Paige knew Wendy was right, but she couldn't help wishing she'd been with her family when it happened. She felt that she'd let them down.

Harven came out, supporting someone. Paige ran over to them, the little ones and Wendy close behind.

"Let me go!" Kite yelled, pushing Harven, who was keeping a firm hold around his shoulder. Kite coughed but kept speaking. "Damn it, let me go! My—"

Kite stopped in surprise when Paige hugged him. He hadn't seen her come up. She didn't even know she was going to hug him until she did. He tensed against her. But she was so *relieved*.

Kite gasped in pain, and Paige pulled back. Then she saw the bleeding gash along his chest. One of his pant legs was ripped below the knee, revealing cuts and scratches between the strips of material.

Paige was horrified. "What happened to you?"

"My leg got stuck under a chunk of the dais." Kite's voice was breathy. Harven had stopped supporting him and he had to lean some of his weight on Paige. "I had to pull it out but the wood splintered and cut me."

"What about—" Paige realized how bad the wound was. "Lie down."

"Wha—"

"Lie down," Paige ordered, the years of watching her mother work with injured people flooding back. She helped Kite onto the cobbles. Other people were lying down, either injured or unconscious. Paige pulled off her coat and wadded it up as best she could, pressing it to Kite's wound.

"Wendy," Paige called over her shoulder. "Go to the manor. Take Grippa. Grip, you know where my bag is in my room—the one with the jars of funny coloured cream?"

Grippa nodded enthusiastically.

"Good. I want you to bring that back. Wendy, there's gauze in the bathroom in my room. Bring that back too. As much as you can. It looks like many people are hurt."

While Wendy hurried off with Grippa, Alton pressed closer to Paige, kneeling with her beside Kite. "Is he going to be okay?"

"Yes, don't worry, Altie." She then asked Kite, "Did you get this in the explosion too?"

Knowing she meant the chest wound, Kite shook his head, which didn't surprise her. It was too precise, too clean. "One of the terrorists tried to attack my mother— she was with me, but she fell when the explosion happened and hit her head. She was unconscious. I got in between them and ..." Kite gestured to his chest, wincing as Paige pressed harder to stop the blood. "Someone needs to ... and make sure she's okay. Make sure none of the others got her ..."

"I understand. Just rest for now." Paige turned her attention to Harven, who'd been watching quietly the whole time. "Thank you so much for getting him out. I hate to ask this, but ..."

"I'll find her. You just help these people."

Harven went back into the building.

Kite let out a dry, scratchy laugh. "If he gets my mother out, I guess I'll have to like him."

"Don't talk. Just focus on breathing. Wendy will be back soon, and Harven will get your mother. Everything will be fine."

As Kite closed his eyes, Paige could see that a fever had broken out on his forehead. She anxiously bit her lower lip. She hoped she'd been right—that Wendy would return soon with her medical supplies, and that Harven would stumble out with an unconscious but otherwise unharmed Regailia.

She hoped everything would be fine.

Chapter XXXVIII

Mid awoke with a serious headache. She was being carried over someone's shoulder, arms tied and mouth gagged.

"Oi, Mina, she's coming to. What do I—"

High-pitched laughter pierced Mid's brain. "You should see your face, Charney. She's just a kid. At most she'll probably bite you or insult your manhood."

"That's not reassuring."

"Why? Not confident in your manliness?"

"I meant the biting!"

The girl laughed again.

Mid, more or less conscious, writhed in her captor's hold. She'd hoped to surprise him, which, judging by his yelp, she had, but not enough for him to drop her. Mid kicked at his back and he grunted.

"She doesn't even have to say anything to insult your manhood, does she?" Mina asked. "It insults itself. You're such a wimp."

"She's kicking me!"

"Yeah. Toughen up."

"Let's just hurry. The others are probably at the boat already."

Boat? Mid struggled and kicked as hard as she could.

"Gods-That-Remain! I'm gonna get a bruise, brat!"

"Now, now. She's no brat." Mina grinned at Mid. "She's our cute accomplice!"

Mid froze at the word.

"Much cuter and more accommodating than our other accomplice." Mina flipped through the two IDs in her hand. "It took me forever and three slow songs to swipe his ID. Dancing that close to that guy—yuck. Even thinking about it grosses me out."

"You volunteered."

"'Cause your acting skills are more or less shit. All of you. Naturally the job of info and ID acquisition fell to me. Though I gotta admit, with this recent show, Summer's proved to be a pretty solid actor. You've got an amazing cousin, you know."

"I get the feeling you never say that to Summer."

"I tell her she's amazing all the time!"

"I mean that she has an amazing cousin."

"But she doesn't. Her brother's awfully cute though—such a sweetie!"

"Glad to know my contribution to the group is appreciated."

"Don't go fishing for compliments, Charney. It's unmanly."

"Next time, how about you and Sum—"

"Shit!"

Charney frowned at Mina, who was gaping over her shoulder. "What?"

Mina took off at a run. Charney followed, managing to hold Mid even in his hurry. Still, Mid squirmed as much as possible.

"Her bloody freakin' rock giant!" Mina yelled as they reached the docks. Instead of taking the few steps down the harbour she hopped off the ledge, landing hard on the planks below. "He's coming after us!"

Charney swerved around, which enabled Mid to see behind them. Sure enough, Bear was pounding down the road toward them. Mid screamed into her gag, but all that came out were muffled noises.

"Shit!"

"Yeah! I know! Hurry up, Charn!"

Charney took the steps in quick succession and followed Mina to a boat, whose sails had been released for departure. People were gathered on deck, all of them around the same age as Charney and Mina.

They ran up the plank of wood leading to the boat. Charney handed Mid to a man with long black hair, who wasn't as broad as Charney but just as tall. This guy had no trouble holding Mid, despite her continued thrashing.

"Just watch her until we're out of port, okay, Kam?" Mina clapped the guy on the shoulder. "I'm gonna go report in with Summer. Hold the fort and all that."

Mina disappeared into the captain's quarters. Charney scrambled up to the wheel, shouting orders at the people on deck, readying the boat to depart. Bear had yet to reach the docks. At this rate, the boat would be gone before he reached them.

Kam carried Mid below deck and propped her up against a support and went to retrieve a pile of rope thrown against a crate. Mid could see the barrel of a shotgun poking out of the top of the crate.

"I hear we've got a guest onboard." A guy Mid didn't recognize descended the steps. Spotting Mid, he grinned. "This is the loose end, I take it?"

Kam continued uncoiling the rope.

"I don't get Summer's keeping this kid around. She's obviously never going to get it. If Summer had to lie in the first place to make her help us, wouldn't it be better if we just cut her loose?" He slid a dagger from his coat.

Kam, still with his back to them, didn't notice the

guy approaching Mid with his dagger. Mid screeched into her gag and struggled more.

"Oh? I think she wants to say something! Already she's more talkative than you, Kam." The guy used his free hand to pull out Mid's gag. "You wanted to say hello?"

Something like that. Mid snapped her teeth around the guy's fingers before he could pull his hand back. She bit down as hard as she could, and he screamed. Fury flashed in his eyes and he raised the dagger, but Mid released him and rolled out of the way. The guy cursed at her and lunged. Kam was just in time to block the guy—who dropped his dagger— and the two wrestled, the redhead's eyes wild as he screamed at Kam.

While they were distracted with each other, Mid inched toward the dagger. Picking it up between her bound hands, Mid deftly sawed through the ropes. She ran around the fighting pair for the stairs. If she could reach Bear, she'd be safe. She had to get to Bear.

"She's getting away!" the redhead shrieked.

On deck, Mid found herself face to face with the barrel of a revolver. Holding it was a calm, impassive Summer.

Mid seethed. "You!"

"Now isn't the time to talk. You won't believe me anyway."

"Unlike the last time you pointed a gun at me, huh?"

"Summer!" It was Charney, leaning over the rail above them. "We've got to go! Her rock giant—"

The pound of familiar footsteps echoed nearby. Mid's gaze shot to the port. Bear had nearly reached the boat. Hope flared as he ran toward them, his steps so heavy they left dents in the dock.

Staring at the dents, Mid screamed, "No! Bear, stop! Go get help! Don't—"

Bear didn't stop. He ran right onto the gangplank. To her surprise, and extreme relief, it held.

When he reached the middle of the gangplank, Bear's foot snapped the board. A loud splash resounded throughout the dock, followed by silence.

Mid was more horrified than she'd been in all her life. She opened her mouth to scream for Bear, but nothing came out but a gaspy, choked sound. She ran to the rail, prepared to throw herself off, to drag Bear up, to save him before—

Summer caught her around the waist and hauled her back onto the deck. She said something to Mid, something that sounded almost soothing, but Mid couldn't understand her. Everything was muffled, everything but the sound of her own sobs.

Mid crumpled to the deck as the boat left the harbour.

Chapter XXXIX

Kanta felt hollow as he stumbled out for the last time. Finally all the flames had been put out and everyone evacuated. Smoke still clouded the building, but it was thinning rapidly. There was nothing more to do now but care for the injured.

He walked dejectedly through the crowd on the street. Those who'd been hurt were being tended while they waited to be moved to the Association's clinic.

Kanta spotted Paige, going from patient to patient. Grippa and Alton shadowed her, carrying a bag of supplies and gauze. Paige was in her element, Kanta realized with some surprise. He'd never seen her so focused, so determined.

His surprise quickly faded. He didn't have the energy or the emotion to feel surprised anymore. He hadn't found Mid.

Kanta stopped when he came to Thalus, face ashen under his scratches as he stood next to the inert bodies of his wife and son. Kanta stared at them for a long time, unable to tell if either was breathing.

"They're alive." Thalus didn't look at him. "They've had cursory treatment until they can be moved to the clinic."

"Why haven't they been moved yet?"

"They aren't the most critical."

"So what? Aunt Regailia's part of the Council, and Kite's your son. They should be treated before anyone."

"You know it doesn't work that way, Kanta. When it comes to life and death, rank doesn't matter."

Thalus was right. Kanta *did* know that. But he was so tired and frustrated and angry and all of that came second to the emptiness closing in on him.

"Where's Midgard?" Thalus asked.

"I ... I don't know. I couldn't find her. I went back in again and again and I helped so many people but I couldn't find *her*! I couldn't find my sister!"

Thalus stepped over to Kanta and wrapped an arm around his shoulder, pulling him close. It was the most affection Thalus had ever shown him. "You did your best."

"No!" Kanta pushed away from him. "No, you don't understand. I didn't find her. I didn't do my best because she's still not here. She's still gone!"

"Kanta, try to calm down. I spoke with Wendell, and he claims Midgard was fine when he last saw her. She could very well be at the manor right now."

Kanta didn't say anything. Mid wasn't at the manor. He was sure of it. She wouldn't just leave like that. Despite the fight they'd had, she'd look for him. She'd make sure he was safe, and everyone else. Barring that, she'd at least want to be around the action. She'd want to help find people and bring them to safety and put out the fire. She'd want to fight the terrorists.

No, Mid wasn't back at the house. The only place she could possibly be was where he himself was at that moment. But she wasn't. Something had happened to her.

Kanta just didn't know what.

"Will you stay with them?" Thalus asked Kanta, meaning Kite and Regailia. "I've been asked to join in an emergency meeting with the Council, but I don't want to leave them alone."

"Yeah. Yeah, okay."

Thalus squeezed Kanta's shoulder, the same way Kanta had done to reassure the little twins. "We'll find Midgard, Kanta. I promise."

Kanta wanted to take comfort in Thalus's words, but he was too exhausted. Nothing penetrated but his aching concern for Mid and the seed of panic it instilled, waiting to bloom into full-blown hysteria again.

Kneeling next to Kite, Kanta watched the rise and fall of his cousin's chest. It was faint and uneven, but at least its being there meant that Kite still was too. Regailia seemed barely able to breathe at all, and Kanta still couldn't believe Thalus hadn't insisted they be taken right away, even if it went against protocol.

But maybe Thalus had insisted. Maybe he'd tried before he remembered his place. Kanta hoped so.

As he watched two of his few family members sleep, Kanta thought back to the last thing he'd seen in the ballroom. His ghost eyes permitted him to see through the haze, offering him slightly better vision than the average human's. Someone had sprayed something above the dais, post-explosion by the looks of it. Kanta had navigated the hole in the floor and surrounding debris to get a closer look: a sentence, spray-painted in a bright scarlet smear, covering the white stone wall. Kanta still didn't know what it meant, or why the terrorists would write it there, but the words haunted him.

The ghosts aren't the killers.

Chapter XL

The caravan Mao had rented for their journey was small and required only one horse. Mao was driving, as he had since they had left the City an hour ago. Tai stayed up front next to him, sipping from the flask he'd given her. It was tea, and although Tai wasn't sure she liked its bitter taste, she did enjoy its warmth. The night had gotten even colder.

Tai offered the drink to Mao, but he shook his head. Wrapping both hands back around it, Tai gazed at the road ahead. After leaving the Hunter Association Headquarters, Tai had gone back to the manor. Mao had retrieved his bags and met her there. He'd changed into travelling gear, as had Tai. She wore the thick black leggings that many hunters wore in colder weather—warm but good for moving. Over that she'd thrown on a T-shirt, a sweater, and a coat. Mao had bundled up much the same way. Winter was coming quickly. Neither wanted to freeze while they were on the road.

Tai covered a yawn. Though leaving in such a hurry had given her an adrenaline rush, she'd since calmed down and even grown tired. Mao glanced at her. It wasn't the first time she'd yawned.

"I'm fine here on my own if you want to lie down in back."

"I'm fine." Tai betrayed herself with another yawn.

"I'll wake you up when it's your turn to drive."

Tai finally conceded. There was just enough room for her to roll out her sleeping bag, which she burrowed into for warmth. Tai thought it would take her awhile to get to sleep, because of the constant bumping of the caravan and the wind howling outside, but she soon drifted off.

Even the distant bang didn't disturb her. Before she fell completely into the tempting darkness, Tai fleetingly thought that the City must be putting off its New Year's fireworks. More time had passed than she'd thought if it was already Hallow Hour.

Tai woke up with an ache in her neck. Groaning, she lifted her head, shocked to realize she was sitting up, leaning against the caravan wall. How had she managed to get into that kind of position?

Tai moved her hand to rub her eyes, except her hand wouldn't move. Neither would her arms. Tai struggled a moment, wondering what was going on, then she realized something held her wrists. Searching, her fingers brushed rope.

Someone had tied her hands behind her.

Tai was instantly alert. Pushing herself up as much as she could, she blinked and looked around the caravan. She wasn't in the caravan. She was in a tent, and her hands were tied to one of the back supports.

What was going on? Had they been attacked? Kidnapped? What had happened to Mao? If he wasn't here with her …

For a few minutes, a panicked Tai fought her bonds. She didn't want to call out. Whoever owned this tent was clearly hostile, and she didn't want to alert them to the fact that she was awake. Tai couldn't free her hands despite her efforts. If only she could get to the dagger in her boot! In just a few minutes she'd be free.

Tai was still struggling with the ropes when a shadow fell across the tent entrance. The flap was pulled back, revealing a woman with long, wavy black hair and an even blacker gaze. Taking in Tai, her full red lips curled into a smile.

"Lovely." The woman's voice was deep and rich. "I thought we were going to have to wake you."

Glaring at the woman, Tai refused to say anything. Her age was impossible to guess. She wore a white blouse with puffy sleeves, and several layers of brown and yellow skirts. Over this ensemble she wore a long shawl tied at her neck. It was gold, covered in darker gold moons and symbols that Tai didn't recognize. Below the knot of the shawl rested a large opaque pendant. She walked up to Tai, studying her.

"Perfect," she whispered, turning her attention to the tent entrance. "The elders will be pleased. You've done an excellent job."

Mao stepped inside. "Thank you, Mother."

The woman's smile broadened. She walked up to Mao, brushing back his hair, hand lingering on his cheek. "You'll no doubt be welcomed back to the coven, after this. For now, my son, look after the immune one. She has much work ahead of her."

Mao inclined his head, saying nothing as the woman swept from the tent. Tai didn't even look at her as she left. She could only stare at Mao.

"What's going on?" Tai tried to demand, but her throat felt dry and her voice came out scratchy. "What the hell's happening?"

Mao walked over to her and kneeled down, pulling something from his belt. Tai was horrified to see a gag. She tried to jerk away from him but she couldn't with her arms bound, keeping her in place. Mao tied the cloth tightly around her head, making sure she couldn't shake it off, then returned to her level, his face inches away.

"What's happening?" His smile was fleeting. "Hallow Hour's happening. Happy New Year, Tai."

Acknowledgements

I would like to thank the following for their support: the Newfoundland and Labrador Arts Council, the City of St. John's Arts Grants, Moya Greene, and Marshall and Glenda Godwin.

I would also like to thank editor Stephanie Porter, copyeditor Iona Bulgin, and graphic designer Mona Atari for her beautiful book designs.

To my friends Jeanie and John Staple, thank you for all the support and encouragement.

To Donna Morrissey, thank you for the excellent coaching and showing me how reading in front of a crowd is really done.

To all the students to whom I've read, thank you for the enthusiasm and feedback.

And, finally, to my amazing Mom, Sharon Smith, for everything she's done for me and the support that has made writing this series possible.

Photo by: Doug Allen

About the author

Caighlan Smith is a student at Memorial University of Newfoundland, working toward a BA in English Literature. Her debut novel, *Hallow Hour*, which she wrote at the age of 17, was released in 2013. Caighlan lives in St. John's. Visit her at www.caighlansmith.com.

2677